Vera Bianchi

Prologue:

I0677221

"Most people are other people. Their thoughts are someone else's opinions. Their lives a mimicry. Their passions a quotation."

-Oscar Wilde

As I read 'De Profundis' sitting on my California king bed in beautiful France, I knew my life was anything but ordinary, or like anyone else's. And yet I found happiness evaded me and I knew why.

My chateau in France was over 10,000 square feet, our gardens of flowers and rare plants were over 2 acres. The ecstasy of the interiors amazed me every day even though it was my home for six months out of the year for as long as I can remember. My villa in Italy matching our chateau in both size and beauty was my living quarters for the other six months. I am an incredibly loved individual, while my sister, Baye, must love me most; Papa couldn't have been far behind. On the surface, my life seemed like a fairytale… But I had a secret… And the pain of it was only beginning to bud. I'm 17 years old, my name is Vera Bianchi, and this is my story.

Chapter One: Perfect Childhood No More

It was a hot June day in Paris France. After I read that passage from Oscar Wilde, I decided I needed to get out to think. I left my bedroom picking up my bodyguard on the way out. I found myself strolling the gardens thinking and contemplating on the meaning of happiness, and if happiness was something that was genuinely attainable. If so, shouldn't one's pursuit in life be joy? Happiness means entirely different things to everyone, so what would be the price one would pay for the ultimate gift? While my meditation of late seemed to paint on my face the picture of pain, only one seemed to notice, Stefan, my bodyguard. He wasn't much older than I in age; however, his temperament is that of an old, old soul. He never left my side of course, which was something of a nuisance sometimes. Most of the time it was great, he was witty and funny, serious and passionate. No one knew these parts of him but me. I knew him best, and he knew me best. This is why I don't want him around right now! I was going to make a decision that would alter the course of my life; I wanted privacy.

"Vera, is something wrong?" He asked in his French accent.

"I know I can't hide anything from you Stefan," I said with a deep sigh "so all I'm going to say is that I have a lot on my mind. I would appreciate some space." Even though he was good at doing what he was told by my Papa, toward me, he was pushy and a little nosy. But we had an understanding because we were around each other all the time, if either of us wanted some personal privacy, it would be granted them-- no matter what. He nodded in recognition to what I said, and I continued mauling over my plight. I wanted to try out a 'normal' life. Though I knew it mattered not your status and monetary wealth, I figured I wanted to go somewhere that was populated by people who lived simpler lives. Perhaps they were happier than my pretentious and ostentatious friends and surroundings. I made up my mind then and there that I was going to go to a public school in a foreign country; it had to be foreign or else I would not honestly be free.

"I'm sorry to disrupt you Vera, but I think you need to start getting ready for the gala." Stefan wasn't looking at me, and his tone sounded as though he'd broken some kind of promise by speaking to me.

"Yeah," I pursed my lips, "I guess you're right." We walked back to the chateau; everyone was hustling and bustling to prepare for the evening. It was simply magnificent seeing how different it all looked. Tonight was a unique white and black occasion; the schedule tonight involved dinner, ballroom dancing, and a show put on by a local ballet studio. I usually knew every detail of the parties Papa put on, but not this time, and not for the last three months or so. There was a shift in the wind because I started realizing the life I lived was a miserable one only the selfish and greedy would trade everything for. Everyone else wouldn't touch it to save their lives.

It all started when Baye and I walked through the streets of Paris; we were shopping as usual. I felt adventurous that day and insisted we try a new bakery for lunch. I wanted to go to the impoverished part of town because I heard the bakeries there were better. Something about putting your heart and soul into your work when you lived scantily and needed customers was I all I could think the reason could be for such a possible fact. After all, they couldn't afford the best ingredients.

I wasn't scared because we had a platoon of bodyguards. After begging Baye, she finally agreed. Walking through the streets I was mortified, it stunk, and the people were stick skinny from starvation. One picture, in particular, stuck out in my mind of a little boy 6 or 7; he had a crutch handmade of wood. He lied on the gross and dirty streets with no one around; he was ready for death to take him, I could tell. I ran out to him and Stefan, of course, followed the closest. My face was twisted in concern.

"Hey! Please, let me get you some food! Wait right here, don't move!"

"J'ai besoin de nourriture." I need food.

"Okay don't....Move."

I looked up at Stefan and went back to Baye and the army of bodyguards. I quickened our pace to the closest bakery. As we entered the man at the counter gasped lightly, I let it slide and greeted him kindly.

"Hello, can I please get 12 of the best things you make? Also, there is a little boy on the street with a wooden crutch. I don't know his name but please give him at least one meal a day for the next year and deliver it to him. I'll pay for it in advance."

"Ah, oui! Hold on one moment, madam." The kind baker said happily.

Another man walked out from the back about my age. I supposed the gentleman at the counter was his Father. After the young man gawked for a minute, he gained his composure and looked at his Father ready to take orders. This pleasing attention was not something new to Baye or me. We waited patiently for the food. The young man and the Father came out with a lot of food, as we dug in the father spoke softly.

"Pardon me, are you the Bianchi sisters?"

My sister couldn't have been bothered by the gentleman because of his class in society; this was something I disliked very much about her. So I was the one who answered him.

"Yes, does my Papa, have the pleasure of knowing you?"

"No, but your family is well known on the streets. And the beauty of the daughters is also spoken of, although no one knows what you actually look like."

I knew what he was saying; he was saying it very politely. He was talking about my Papa's iffy dealings that were a significant source of income to this part of town. Papa didn't amass his vast wealth just by transactions that were entirely legal. Baye smirked at his comment about 'the beautiful daughters.' She basked in the attention she received on that topic. I, on the other hand, was already ready to change the subject.

He spoke again, "Please forgive my bluntness. What is your name miss?"

"Vera, and yours?"

"Ah, a beautiful name for a beautiful young woman. Enzo, Madam. You seem very kind; I do pity you."

"I'm sorry?"

"I would never throw my family to the wolves like your Father, madam, er Vera."

"You are quite bold Enzo." He suddenly realized exactly what he said, and he saw the fury in Stefan's face then became afraid. My eyebrows rose, and my face became playful "I like you!" Stefan threw me a look because he knew I loved it when people were daringly themselves, and honesty was something I valued. I also figured he was coming from a good place; he seemed so genuine and kind. I further asked, "How do you know my family so well?"

"Your Father often hires people from around here for his maidservants and manservants. Usually, those that come from this background expect little and work very hard. When they come home, they always have the most elaborate stories to share." Enzo took a liking to me, and he also sensed my tendency to like people like him. I flattered him, and he was about to peel into a deep conversation of right from wrong with all his knowledge, and opinion on the matter when Stefan interrupted.

"It's getting late; I think it is time for us to leave," He eyed the baker unkindly.

I was disappointed, but I knew he was right. "Another time my friend, I will visit you, and we can discuss a plethora of philosophical theory." Enzo was quite pleased both about me and about the smarts he suddenly felt he had. You could see the confidence gleaming from his face. I got up to settle the account when we left.

On the way out of the bakery, I saw the little boy scarfing down the food he was given. I walked up to him and gave him the rest of the lunch I didn't eat.

"I have bought a meal a day from that bakery for you for a year. I don't think they'd be dishonest and keep the food from you, but I like to help keep honest people honest. Please be sure to eat there every day."

The little boy began to cry. "Oh thank you miss!" I left feeling on top of the world. It wasn't until later that Enzo's words started to sink in. What could he mean by Papa throwing us to the wolves? Undoubtedly Enzo was wrong, what could he know about my family? But the seed was planted, and I couldn't help but think about it, I always needed to explore truth. When the occasion arose, I would speak to Anna, my maid about the matter.

After we got home that day, Papa announced another party and presented Baye and me with gifts. Papa's love language was most definitely giving gifts. They were dresses that were of the most exceptional quality and color, the gifts he bought us often coincided with some plan of his for fun. As we prepared for the party at that time, I seized the opportunity to talk to Anna; my bedroom was the only room Stefan didn't join me in. He was always outside my door ready to follow me when I left.

"Anna?" she was busy making my bed. We talked all the time, so that part didn't startle her, what did alert her was my morose and severe tone.

"Yes?" She asked cautiously.

"What is your opinion of my family dynamic and culture?"

 She tried to brush off the topic, and I could see the panic in her eyes. "That is a vague question Vera, shall I fetch you some water?"

"Please, Anna! I know you know what I'm asking. I can feel something is wrong, like something bad is going to happen- lurking in the shadows if you will."

Her eyes pleaded with me to let the subject go. But, once a moment passed and she saw that my desperation was thicker than hers, she revoked her silence. She hid her face that was blushing and even had tears in her eyes. She came at me with a high pace and stopped just short of a foot from me and grabbed both my arms. Her face was intent and determined as though this was something she had rehearsed in her mind a lot.

"Vera, I have been here for a long time now. And I have seen many things take place in this household. Please do not be angry with me!"

"Anna, I will only be angry if you do not tell me everything."

She was relieved and passionate. "Your Mother, may she rest in peace, treated you and your older sister like show dogs.

7

She dragged you to dance classes, rhetoric classes, voice lessons, and classes on how to hold yourself, even how to walk. She molded you to be supermodels at 9! 9 Vera… You were supposed to be playing with dolls!"

As she spoke, I realized how right she was. And it hurt, up to this point I had never thought of my perfect life to be anything but, well, perfect.

Anna continued, "But at least she had a limit. Your Papa does not. He flaunts you and Baye to his business friends. And his gifts are often something to make you more appealing to the eye. Just look at how provocative this dress is Vera!"

I looked, and I saw what she was saying. I had never noticed! But then I thought back on the gifts I received from him, and they all seemed to serve some purpose or another. For some reason it always felt like it might have even been just to gain my affections. Could it be true that his love is selfish? If so, why- what was his gain?

"Why would he do this?"

"Vera, you do not know this, but he offers a night with Baye as part of his business dealings to persuade the buyer or seller to whatever it is he wants. It's only a matter of time until you are next. He's been grooming you for years. Think about it Vera…. What does your gut tell you right now?!"

I started thinking…I somehow recalled one morning when I left my room and saw a man named Alan Pierce leaving Baye's room. Funny thing is that I know for a fact that he had just bought something from Papa.

I remembered another time in a party a little while back where Papa introduced Baye to another man. He shot her a wink and bit his lip in a creepy way. He too had bought something valuable… It wasn't conclusive evidence, but something told me that this was correct. "You-you're right" I stammered. "Anna, what do I do?"

"Runaway, Vera! Sooner or later you're going to be more than just eye candy to your Papa's business partners. And you'll be the bargaining chip for him to get something he wants. He's created an illusion of you to others as being a piece of fine art, or a rare jewel. You must RUN!"

"How…Where…. I-…"

"You are smart Vera; I know you can figure it out. Whatever you do you have to get far enough away to be outside of your Papa's influence!"

I nodded, and I was stunned. Could it be so? Could my foundation of unconditional love and support be a mirage? This was my core, what I based my beliefs and decisions off of. I was contemplative as I continued getting ready for the party. I couldn't believe she was right! But now what do I do?! I paid attention that night; eyes watched me like vultures on their prey. Of course, my dress didn't help with that.

I eavesdropped on other conversations when I was usually making my own. Baye bragged about the little boy we fed, and how heroically philanthropic she was. Papa talked business in code and also bragged about how amazingly deep his daughters were for feeding a starving boy. This would have been normal for a parent to say, and it eased my fears. I began speaking to myself how foolish I was to think MY PAPA could be anything but honorable with his love for me. How stupid could I be to believe anything else?

He didn't know I was there standing close to him when he said, "Whoever gets her will be one lucky bastard! If you know what I mean." Then gave some kind of knowing look. I flushed and paled at the same time. The room was spinning, and I pretended I wasn't listening- after all I could have been far enough not to hear him. I tried to ignore the eight eyes now glued to me in a vulture-like manner like everyone else at the party. I was nauseated and panged with sadness that pierced my soul. In a moment everything I had built was crumbling. The walls appeared to be closing in on me. I wished it was happening to someone else. But the guilt of that feeling made me relent the thought, 'no, no, I can handle this… I can't wish this even on my worst enemy'.

I felt dirty, and my insides were like a tumultuous sea that swirled with numbness and desolation. I wasn't loved the way I always thought I was; Papa had plans for my virtue- that much was clear. I faked being ill to Stefan –and I looked sick too- so I could leave the party. Stefan seemed very concerned and took me to my room.

For the next month, I sorted through my feelings and reality. I kept my eyes open for the new theory to be confirmed; time and again I saw and felt the truth of it. I was finally ready to run, but I had to be smart! I had to run in such a way that didn't provoke alarm, or else I'd never be able to get out. But how could I leave Baye?! She'd be all alone to fend for herself. I had to try to convince her to come with me! I had begun hinting at my feeling adventurous and how I was going to go away for some time. Preparing for the gala was the perfect opportunity to speak with Baye. We were in her bathroom which was larger than most peoples' homes. We were doing our hair as she was gossiping about who all would be there and judged each of them harshly for their smallest imperfections.

"Baye?" I interrupted.

"Hmm?"

"I'm going to a foreign school this next year, and I'd love it if you would come with me."

"Are you crazy Ver? Why would you want to give this up, even just for a year?"

I wasn't sure if I could trust her not to give up my real intentions to Papa. I gave her a nonchalant answer shrugging my shoulders. "I want a break from all this hustle and bustle. Plus I think Mr. Petrov is getting a little too interested."

"Ha! Ver, relax! I mean what's the worst that can happen? You two have sex? Oh…" She pulled a face like she was mock dying. "Ha-ha, it's no big deal."

"Baye! Have you…. Made love to any of Papa's business partners?!" I had to confirm everything Anna had told me.

"Oh, sure! How else do you think the Meriton merger went off without a hitch?"

"Baye! Don't you think that's wrong?!"

"No, he was all over me." She celebrated, "I have him wrapped around my little pinky finger! I love it."

I was perplexed and disgusted! But then a wave of guilt hit me like a dump truck; I felt like it was my fault for not getting to her sooner. She had been so primed to be this way, how could I have not seen this sooner?! I should be able to save her! But her choices were her own; I knew that. So what now? Leave her to protect myself? Would that expose her to more questionable business closings?

 She broke my train of thought, "So what, are you trying to tell me you're a virgin?" She asked indignantly.

"Well, no. But I agree with Charlie Chaplin who said 'your naked body should only belong to those who fall in love with your naked soul.' I've only made love to those who have met that criterion."

"Whooo, Stefan?" She dragged out Stefan's name teasingly. "Hey I don't blame you, the man is like freaking 6'5" and built like a freaking ox! Plus mmhmm deliciously handsome!"

I was so embarrassed! My cheeks were so red they were practically purple. "Oh, Baye!"

She laughed, while we got ready. She continued to go on and on about who was coming to the gala. I slipped into my white dress which had a stark contrast to my olive skin tone. My dress was all lace and form fitting to my 5'7" figure that was often compared to Candice Swanepoel's. My dress was sleeveless and had a white see-through mesh for its backing. I finished my makeup relining my eye's which were a golden green color. I took on many features from my French mother; I had large eyes, an oval face shape, a feminine nose, high cheekbones, and large full lips. From my Italian Papa, I inherited my olive skin tone, long eyelashes, and my brunette hair. I had my hair down with curls that framed my feminine face.

Baye and I always arrived late to the parties properly descending from the staircase with our bodyguards behind us. This set the precedence of prominence, which of course Baye loved. The night began with the dance, and I saw Mr. Petrov making his way to me which made my stomach drop. I was saved by a man around my age named Peter; Peter was a different individual. He and his small family were always a mystery to me.

"May I have this dance?" he bowed.

"It would be an honor." I dipped my head smiling.

We stepped out on the floor, and he began leading our waltz. Peter and his family all looked alike. They were pale and perfect… Eerily perfect. They all had Green eyes and darkish under eyes. I couldn't believe it was their real eye color! Peter was very cold to the touch, and it always sent chills up my spine and goosebumps down my arms. He always laughed at that. Though their beauty was indescribable, I didn't like them. They all acted above everyone else, why Peter always asked me to dance at these events was beyond me. He clearly didn't want me. They were like everyone else here in a way, too high to be bothered…ugh, pretentious people. But they differed because they acted like they were the elite of the elitists. Like death itself couldn't touch them.

I always started talking small with him, mostly just shooting the breeze. He usually loved it when I tried talking to him, but acted above it. I hated that I couldn't stop too, there was something conquerable there, and I wanted him to crack and tell me what was going on in that big head of his. I tried all the topics I could think of: literature, politics, philosophy, gossip, world events, local events, I even stooped to the weather! I finally sighed in defeat.

"Peter, what are you thinking about? What goes on in that little brain of yours?"

He laughed heartily and said, "I don't think you want to know, Vera." He then gave me a mischievous look that was extremely attractive. Peter was a flirt with everyone but you knew everything he said was sarcastic and demearing. I hated that the challenge made me more attracted to him because I loathe that personality type.

"Let's say you give me a straight answer for once, yes?" I said firmly. He looked at me amused and curious. I continued; "Why do you ask me to dance all the time when you won't even talk to me?" He loved my question.

"Maybe I love you, Vera." He said half whispering, staring intently into my eyes and pulling me close with the arm around my waist till there wasn't a single centimeter separating our bodies. Then he winked playfully and sarcastically.

I rolled my eyes, "Ugh, please! I said straight." I pushed him gently, so the space between us was enough to start dancing again.

"Perhaps you entertain me. And I love how Petrov never stops staring at us, and for that matter neither does Stefan, or any other man in this room. The others are just more discrete about it."

"So it's a game to you then is it?" I asked as I tried to hide the fear when he mentioned Petrov.

"Isn't that what life is all about, having fun? Especially if you can make the fun from bothering other people."

"I suppose to you, it is. See I have a theory that happiness is what life's all about, and to you, playing people and their emotions is what makes you happy. Even though you know it's psychopathic, you indulge yourself anyway." I said this entirely coolly, and I even matched his sarcasm.

He loved it and laughed so hard it drew attention to us. The dance ended and he kissed my hand locking eyes with mine, and then looked up at Petrov and snickered. I walked away amused as well; it was hard not to be drawn to him. He was so graceful when he moved.

To my luck the rest of the night was fun, I'm an extrovert to the extreme. Petrov didn't make any more attempts to be near me. I even made time during the ballet show to create a scheme that would convince Papa to let me go to a foreign school.

That night as I washed my face and showered I made up the best plan to get what I needed. I was excited, and I wanted to execute the idea right away. I called it Plan R.A.F.F. which stood for run away for freedom; I knew I was being a little childish in my imaginations.

I didn't want to sleep that night, but sleep quickly came because I always woke up at 5:00 am for my daily workout, shower, and get ready routine.

After I was ready for the day, I walked to breakfast eagerly. Stefan was pleasantly surprised by my buoyant behavior; I had been so down lately.

"What has you so happy?" He asked while grinning.

"I have a favor to ask Papa that I'm really excited about!"

"What is it?"

"Shh, it's a secret!" I said as I touched his arm lightly, this didn't go unnoticed. He blushed a little and moved closer to me. I pretended not to notice and hopped, skipped, and jumped to the dining hall. Papa was there, as usua , reading the morning paper.

"Papa?"

"Vera! What brings you to breakfast at this hour?" He smiled delightfully as though I was his favorite person in the world.

I was so scared because I knew this conversation could mean the beginning of a new future for myself. I exhaled loudly, I tried to seem confident, but I was a lousy liar. He looked at me critically all of a sudden.

"Vera, darling, you know you can ask anything of me, right?" He took off his glasses and put the paper down all the way.

"Yes Papa, but it's not anything like what I usually want." My face looked a little more desperate than I wanted.

"Ha-ha well don't keep me on the edge of my seat, Vera."

I gulped, "I want to go to a foreign public school alone for my senior year of high school." I was looking down, and I couldn't bring myself to face him for some reason. Perhaps it was because I didn't want him to read any ulterior motives than just pure adventure and curiosity?

"Why?"

"I'd like to try something new, and live differently for a while."

"Where do you want to go?"

"I don't know; I thought I'd ask first."

"Okay, well, will you come home for visits?"

My heart leaped, and I knew I was close to freedom, I could practically taste it. I looked up at Papa and smiled, "Yes, I'd want to see you, Baye, and Stefan of course!"

"Okay then." He said in a higher pitch then continued, "I think you have made up your mind about this, as long as you come for visits I don't see why not." He picked up his spectacles and continued reading.

I was utterly shocked because it was easier than I expected, it was almost suspiciously too easy. It made me frightened, but I told myself I was being paranoid. I ran and kissed him on his forehead. "Thanks, Papa!"

When I turned around, I saw a face of horror. Stefan. I didn't acknowledge him and walked past him. I went up to my room to begin researching places for me to live. Russia seemed cold, China seemed dull, and I wasn't interested in being under any communist rule after this. 'America…. Yes, the land of the free! That's where I'll go,' I thought to myself. A knock on my door startled me. I looked up quickly as the person let herself in, but I was looking at the wrong door. My room had two entrances and exits, one to the main hallway, and one that was nearly invisible- it was the servants' door.

"Anna! You'll never believe what's going on!" I said this excitedly but whispering because I didn't want there to be any chance of Stefan hearing.

She looked grave like someone had killed her closest family member. I jumped from my desk, "What's wrong, are you ill?"

"No," she walked to the bed to start making it, "Your Papa is making plans to plant spies wherever you go to ensure your safety and to stay apprised of your every move."

I wasn't surprised. I started laughing, "Sneaky… Well if that's how he wants to play it." My eyes were dancing at the thought of beating someone at their own game. "It'll be a last minute decision; I might even leave it up to chance, a roll of the dice."

Anna was finishing up my bed; she was putting the decorative pillows in place when she looked at me. "Vera, you need to address your Papa, set a clear boundary, and maybe still make a last minute decision. Pick three places to live and set up living arrangements, then decide without telling a soul."

I suddenly felt the weight of what was happening, what I had discovered, and what I was about to do. I started feeling dizzy, and I sat down without thinking through the motion first. I began tearing up, and then I realized I hadn't cried for a long time. My emotions were guarded, they had been guarded for a long time--years perhaps. I think my subconscious had always been warning me of the danger I was in being around Papa, and his greedy tenancies. But I couldn't bring myself to cry, I wanted the sweet release, but it wouldn't come. I was too stubborn and too tough for that. I stood up abruptly and looked at Anna, who had paused her work to look at me; this was something she rarely did.

"You're right. Where's Papa now?" Though Papa worked from home we never crossed paths, we lead different lives, and this was becoming all too clear to me.

"I don't know Ver; you'll have to ask around." She looked relieved I had listened so well.

"I have some boundaries to set, I'll see you tonight." I left immediately. I was on a mission, and I had no intention of stopping. I had no idea what to say, but I'd be damned if I had to live under his crushing wing the rest of my life. As I descended the stairs, I paused to ask Stefan where Papa was.

"I think he might be in the study." He was down, and his eyes pleaded with me silently not to go away.

I didn't say anything or do anything; I didn't know what to do. Stefan loved me, and there was a part of me that loved him too. But I knew that his ultimate loyalty lied with Papa. Loyalty was his biggest weakness and strength; he was blindly loyal. As I approached the study, I did indeed see Papa there. I knocked even though the door was cracked open; luckily it was only him and Big Al, his bodyguard.

"Two surprise visits in one day, Vera?" He was completely collected. Papa could've been a politician.

"Papa, I've heard some distressing news. Are you planning on putting tails on me the entire time I'm away?!" I was bold; I said this without looking away from his eyes. I may have been abnormally shy this morning, but I was channeling the part of me that was more like my Papa, and I was determined to get my way.

"Yes."

"Papa, I can't allow it. I want my privacy, I'll. Be. Just. Fine."

"You can't know that."

"Normal people don't have bodyguards and spies, and they make it out just fine!"

"Normal people are not you. You are coming from a background with top secret dealings. I will not allow my daughter to have any chance of getting into trouble from my business. Not to mention your exotic beauty, no doubt some men will try to take advantage of you."

I was fuming, and it took all of me not to start screaming at him 'You're in that category.' "This is my life, and it is my choice. You cannot dispute that!"

"You're right that I'm encroaching upon your agency. But I don't care. I'm your Papa, and that is final."

"Papa, you get out of this life what you tolerate. You have taught me this; I'm refusing your lifestyle. I want to be free from the cares of dangers from your occupation. What you do is your choice, and what my life becomes will be mine. I want freedom. I want to be myself without worry of people always hearing what I'm saying, or watching what I do."

He started yelling, "I doubt you could ever be normal!"

I was un-phased, I was usually exceptional under pressure. The fact Papa was yelling meant he was on his emotional brink. Either I was close to winning, or losing sorely. "Papa, 'our doubts are traitors, and make us lose the good we oft might win by fearing to attempt.' What better good can you give your daughter than the gift of freedom?" Shakespeare was Papa's favorite; therefore, I had read a lot of him growing up, and in my private school that was incredibly advanced scholastically.

He sighed, "Oh Vera, you are truly my favorite person to be around. How can I refute that?"

"Let me set my boundaries, Papa," I pressed.

He looked at me a long while, he was trying to conjure up some argument we could debate on the matter, but ultimately knew he was beaten. He shook his head, "When did you grow up?" I didn't say anything because I refused to deviate from my course. He sensed this. "I cannot disagree with you, Vera. Just do me one favor, please stay as long as you can before school starts. Don't be too eager to leave me."

I was skeptical of his request; did he have something in mind for me?

"Vera, I want you to have all the comforts of home I hope you'll continue to use my accounts?"

Was he trying to buy my time? Buy my affection? This is the problem with selfish love; it's hard to decipher what was real, and what was selfish. Ultimately I knew I needed to let him win something. "Okay, I'll leave a week before school starts."

"Three days," he countered.

"Deal," I went up to kiss him on the forehead and gve him a hug.

When I turned around Stefan looked relieved. I had no idea what he was thinking about, but I didn't want to ask. I went

19

straight up to my room to continue my search for a new home. I didn't want to consider any big cities, but rather small towns. I stumbled across a little town in California called Arcata, it seemed homey, and there was something that pulled me to it. I had no idea why.

Who could I live with? I wasn't old enough to be on my own in America, so I needed to find someone to take me in. I figured whoever it would be I'd pay well for my rent. It should be someone the people trusted, the mayor perhaps, law enforcement officials…? I ruled out politicians, so I looked up the man in charge of law enforcement. 'Hmm, Mathew Charter, Sheriff. Okay I'll reach out, the worst he could say is no.' I started my letter:

Dear Mathew Charter,

My name is Vera Bianchi. I'm a 17-year-old high school student from France. I'm going to the United States this Fall for school, and your cute town caught my eye. I'm not in a program to help me find housing, while this is a large stretch- I was hoping you might be open to opening your home to me. I'd be willing to pay $2,000 a month for my stay. It may seem like I picked a home at random, but I have some logic in this request. I figure that if the people trusted you with their safety, then I could too. If this is something you're not interested in, perhaps you may know someone who would be. But, if you are interested, please give me a call.

Vera Bianchi

I left my number with the letter. I didn't want to take any chances of Mathew writing back to me and having my letter confiscated.

I knew politicians could be bought, so to increase my chances of getting into a public school I made a donation of USD 100,000 to the school system along with a letter to the Mayor. I asked what I needed to provide so I could be admitted to Arcata high school. I started getting my visa processing to go to the United States right away. Anna did a lot of my dirty work so it could stay a secret. I'd picked out two other places as Anna suggested, but my heart longed for Arcata. My visa processed faster than average because money speaks in this world, I could be a permanent resident if I wanted to be.

A couple of weeks passed before I received a call from Mathew 'Matt' Charter. He and his wife had agreed to house me as long as I needed. He was a quiet sort of guy, he wasn't very outgoing, but he seemed pleasant and kind. Just the sort of person I'd imagine living in such a small town. Plus, something told me my ruse worked with the mayor, and he put Matt under duress to accept me into his home. I didn't want him to take me in if he didn't want to, but I decided it was ultimately Matt's choice. I was so excited I could barely contain it.

The next few months of parties went smoothly; Stefan took me to picnics like we used to do to try to convince me to stay. But it didn't work. No amount of nostalgia could deter me from what I knew was right, though if I was honest with myself, it almost got to me. This was something he sensed, and it gave him hope which was painful for me to see.

It was two weeks before my departure date when Stefan's mood shifted. I was in my bathroom getting ready for bed, as I religiously, did when I heard a knock on my door. I wasn't expecting anyone, so I was a little frazzled. I was in my pajamas which were silky and provocative like all my other clothes. They were black, short bootie shorts with lace on the bottom and a deep V spaghetti top.

"Just a minute," I said as I threw my robe on. My robe was also silky, black, lacy on the bottom, and came halfway down my thighs. My hair was still curly because I shower in the evening with a shower cap. I had just finished taking my makeup off, and brushing my teeth. I was surprised to see only Stefan at my door.

He took me in for a minute. "Wow, I forgot how beautiful you are without makeup." He stared at my face for another minute.

I looked down and smiled at his sincere compliment. "Thank you, Stefan."

"Can I come in? I need to talk to you."

'Oh crap here it comes, the whole don't leave me speech.' "Can this wait till morning?"

"No."

"Okay, come on in." I gestured for him to come in. "Stefan, I don't want to hear about what a terrible decision I'm making moving away. Nothing you say will-"

"Shhh," he interrupted while putting his finger up to my lips. He took two large steps into the doorway. He grabbed my shoulders which I was not expecting. He stared into my eyes and said, "Vera…. I love you! I don't want you to leave for me, not because I think you're making a bad choice."

I was stunned; I didn't know what to say. "Stefan- I-"I couldn't tell him the truth of why I was leaving though I wished now more than ever that I could.

Before I could respond, he tugged me close and wrapped his arm around my waist, and he laid his other hand beside my face pushing my curls back, intertwining his fingers in my hair. He pulled me in to kiss me gently. I didn't resist; if there was anything I was good at, it was knowing what I wanted. I enjoyed exploring what exactly it was that brought me happiness. I kissed him back and crushed my body to his even tighter. The feeling was euphoric; there had been so much sexual tension built up to this point between him and I that it was not a moot point to try to pretend I didn't want this too.

He picked me up to his waist, and I wrapped my long legs around his torso. One of his hands explored the length and softness of my leg while the other supported my body weight. He pushed my body against the wall and kissed my neck. This gave me a minute to breathe, but not to think. He pulled me off the wall and onto the bed; this is where I knew I needed to draw the line.

"Stefan, Stefan, Stefan."

"Hmm?" He asked as he continued kissing my neck.

"We can't... Do this."

"Why not?" He wasn't angry or stopping.

"Because I'm leaving, and I don't want to give you any hope that I'm staying, or that I love you in the same way you love me." I was lying; I loved Stefan just as much as he loved me.

He stopped; finally, his eyes pleaded with mine. "Vera, please love me." What he said was simple and from the deepest part of his soul.

"You could never love me more than you love my Papa, and what he wants. That's why we didn't stay together after the first time. I have to leave for myself, Stefan."

"I can't let you go!" He said this as he pushed my body onto the bed the rest of the way. He ripped off the covers and pulled us both under them. He wasn't trying to be intimate; he was almost child-like like he needed comforting from me and the sheets.

"You're going to have to Stefan, I'm sorry." I was facing him, I had one hand on his giant chest, our faces were inches apart.

He groaned in pain, "I'm never giving up on you Ver." He grabbed my waist again to emphasize his point.

"Shh," I said as I stroked his hair and temple, I could tell he was exhausted like he hadn't been sleeping in days. "Just go to sleep, it'll be better in the morning."

He couldn't resist the fatigue, his Mother used to stroke his hair before bed, so I knew this was something that would instantly calm him. When he was deeply asleep, I told him the truth, "Stefan I love you too. In the way you mean it, but I'm not safe here. I'm about to become a glorified prostitute. And I don't want that."

The servants' door opened, Anna came with a glass of warm milk. She eyed the situation then said quietly, "The poor man has never taken on any other lover his whole life because of you."

"Really?" I asked, but I already knew that was true.

"Yes, humph, 20 and single, for a man like that it should be a sin." She set the milk on the nightstand.

"Thanks, Anna, but I already brushed my teeth; will you switch it out for a cup of water instead?"

"Absolutely miss. I hope he isn't changing your mind." She looked at me with her maternal look.

"No, no. Though, I will miss him a lot!" I said this looking into his beautiful face which was now resting peacefully.

"Good, you have 13 more days to survive, and then you're as free as a bird!" She said this with hope and enthusiasm; she loved me like my own Mother. Anna virtually became my surrogate after Mother passed away when I was 12. I would miss Anna too. "Good night miss."

"Goodnight, Anna."

I closed my eyes and tried to relax, but having Stefan in my bed with me made it really hard to concentrate on going to sleep. Even though I knew I loved him, I couldn't justify that love with a ball and chain from Papa for the rest of my life. I drifted off to sleep with these thoughts.

5:00 am came early, and Stefan pulled me back when I turned off the alarm. "You're not going anywhere," he said half dazed.

"Ugh, why are you so tempting?!"

"Because I'm sexy," he said matter of factly but jokingly.

"Yes you are," I said under my breath, he heard it and smiled. He leaned over and kissed me. It was like the walls had come down between us, he was going to give this his all.

I stayed in bed since I had no choice, his grip was like an anaconda, I wouldn't be able to escape if I tried. We were both back to sleep in seconds.

It was 8:00 am when I finally woke up. He was already awake and staring at me, like this picture and moment was something he was engraining into his brain so he'd never forget.

"Morning, beautiful," he said smiling. "I don't care what you're going to say. We're staying in bed all day. We'll watch movies or something."

"Stefan-" I started saying a protest, but I knew he wouldn't hear it.

"I'm picking the first movie." He got up from the bed still in his black designer suit. He stretched and started taking it off, beginning with his dress shoes. "Ugh, my feet are so sore!" He was down to his boxers when he reached my TV that was hidden in a beautiful armoire. I don't think he even paid attention to what he selected, just whatever he saw first and popped it into the DVD player.

"I'll call up some breakfast," I said. I knew this was a losing battle, so I might as well make the most of it. Besides, a day in with Stefan wasn't the worst torture in the world.

"That's the spirit!" He said with so much happiness that I couldn't help but smile ear to ear.

"You do realize that I have to take bathroom breaks and I will get up to brush my teeth no matter what you say, right?" I was enjoying myself a little too much.

He laughed, "I guess you'll have to twist my arm." He walked up to the bed holding out his arm. He was so serious when he said this that I wasn't sure it was a jest.

"You're joking right?"

He simply looked at his arm. I started getting up to test him. He swooped me back into bed in a single movement. I looked at him playfully, he knew me too well, I was always up for a challenge. I was way too competitive, I knew I'd never win, but I couldn't help myself. I grabbed his arm and tried twisting with all my might, I stopped after a minute and looked determined. I took off my robe and tried again grunting with the force I was trying to use on him. He chuckled and spun me around on my back and pinned my body against his body and the bed. His face gloated the victory.

"Stefan!"

"Don't be a sore loser," he said laughing, "You get points for trying."

"Oh good, because I really do need to go to the bathroom- and you're squishing my bladder."

"I didn't say I was letting you go right this very second. I have you where I want you." His eyes danced sprightly. I hadn't seen this side of him in a long time, and he started kissing my neck again. It felt so good to lose. He got up and gestured for me to get up and go to the bathroom in peace. When I got up, I heard a wolf whistle in the background.

"And I'm changing my clothes," I said without looking at him heading straight to the bathroom.

He laughed.

I'd never had a more perfect day in my life. We slept together again that night; while I was extremely attracted to him, I couldn't bring myself to let my guard down. I knew what was best, even though it was the hardest thing I'd ever done in my whole life.

The next 12 days went by slower than molasses. I was near breaking point the night before I was due to go, how could I leave Stefan?! Luckily Anna came to my rescue. She brought a cup of warm milk, and when she saw my distress, she started instantly.

"Now Vera, you know as well as I do what's on the line here. Please be strong and don't back down."

"I know, I know, I know." I knew she was right. I tucked my head into my folded legs.

"Once you're gone it'll be much easier. I—" Anna looked down and shuffled her feet, "I love you, little miss. And I can't let anything bad happen to you, as it has with Baye." She had tears in her eyes; you could tell she held a great weight of guilt on her shoulders.

"It's not your fault, Anna. I tried to get her to leave with me, but she has made her own choices."

"I know you speak truth. Baye doesn't understand what les consequences are." Whenever Anna was emotional, her English tended to get choppier.

"Yeah," I was put back in the right mind. I was ready to leave, ready at last.

Vera Bianchi

Chapter Two: A New Life

That day was a day of goodbyes and was both sad and happy. I insisted Stefan be the one who took me to my destination. I 'last minute' picked Arcata. In a jiffy, Stefan and I were on the plane headed to Eureka. I laid my head on his shoulder, and he put his arm around me. Now that we were out of Papa's sight, we were free to be ourselves. We got lucky and didn't have to wait for our rental car.

I felt so alive! I knew this was the right thing for me to do, colors were more vibrant, texture was more pronounced, and a cobweb seemed to come off my brain physically. I was safe. Leaving was hard, but it was a smokescreen, and once I passed through it I was in a whole other world!

While in the car I was going on and on about how lushly green it was, and how much wildlife we could spot just from the road. Stefan couldn't help but be happy with me; my enthusiasm was overflowing and contagious. We reached Matt s house in 20 minutes. I got out quickly and raced around to help Stefan with my luggage… I had a lot of baggage. I could feel the energy in my every movement. I loved the quaint dark blue house with beautifully groomed shrubs that was to be my home for the next school year.

After grabbing the all the luggage, we went up to the door. I had called Matt at the airport, so he was expecting us today. I was wearing a short red travel dress that was cap sleeved; it showed off my body's curvatures. My hair was in an elegant up-do. We walked up to the door, and I gave the doorbell a ring. When Matt came to the door he stared for a second wide-eyed, perhaps it was the size of my luggage, or maybe Stefan's stature, but most likely it's that I didn't look anything like he imagined... At all. I reached my hand out to shake his.

"Hello, you must be Matt! I'm Vera, and this is Stefan. He's helping me with my bags." I looked more than happy to see Matt. He was a handsome guy, brown hair, clean shaven, mid-forties, and a slightly protruding stomach; a handsome man. His wife, Sarah, met us at the door with outstretched arms, she was clearly more outgoing than Matt. She had strawberry blond hair, blue eyes, and she was quite round. I loved her maternal look and feel.

After her warm embrace, Matt wasn't so nervous looking. "Oh er, yes, I'm, uh, Matt." He reached his hand out to greet mine. "Uh, won't you come in?"

"Thank you." The doorway creaked underneath us as we stepped in. It was a small, homey place. Matt led the way to my new bedroom, Stefan and I filed behind him and dropped the bags. I could hear Sarah in the living room watching something on T.V.

"I guess I'll just leave you to unpack then," Matt said, eyeing Stefan on his way out.

"Thanks, Stefan, I've got it from here."

Stefan looked at me for a long minute, grabbed my face gently and kissed me one last time. "Come home soon to visit, okay?" He stared straight into my eyes as he said this. He was no longer sad, but happy for me, and hopeful to see me soon.

"I'll try," I smiled. He took one more long look at me, then clenched his jaw. He sidestepped my luggage and left. I could overhear Stefan paying Matt the amount of rent for a full year in advance. No doubt my Papa already had the check prepared.

I finally took a real look around. There was a dark hardwood floor, queen bed with a white quilt, a small desk in one corner, and my dresser in the other. I had previously decided I wouldn't change anything about the place I was moving into, but, I wasn't entirely confident I could do that. I had my own bathroom which I was thankful for. It was small, but I wasn't complaining. After I put my clothes into the dresser and put away all my toiletries, I walked downstairs to get acquainted with Matt and Sarah. They were sitting in their living room watching the sports channel. The living room had three chairs and a love seat. It seemed like an odd configuration. Matt heard me coming down, and he got up, wiping his hands on his jeans.

"Oh uh, do you like sports?" His eyes crinkled in a cute way when he said this, almost like a little boy who hoped his Mom would approve of whatever he was doing. I could already tell that he was a very kind and generous man.

"I do, I played futbol, ran long distances, and danced back home. Besides I want to see what it's like here in the U.S. You know, to be a part of your culture."

Sarah piped in with a, "Oh dear me child, you need more balance in your life." She was someone who seemed to enjoy a more relaxed lifestyle.

Talking with Matt and Sarah, I never realized I had a slight French accent. I thought I had my American accent down pat.

Matt smiled and said, "Well this is Football, not to be confused with futbol mind you. This sport is way better." He sat himself down in the chair and chuckled to himself.

"I think I'll be the judge of that," I teased as I plopped myself down on their couch. I crossed my legs and sat perfectly straight; this was something I'd never thought about anymore. My Mama put Baye and me into many classes to make us proper.

"Dinner is almost ready," Sarah said as Matt leaned in close to the T.V. apparently something important was happening in the game.

"What is it, I smell bacon?"

"Fried eggs, bacon, and toast," Sarah announced as Matt leaned back again in disappointment about something that happened in the game. They got up and went to the kitchen; I followed them in to see the fattiest food I'd ever seen.

"Do you eat this every day?" My eyebrows furrowed as I looked at Matt's slight gut.

Sarah answered with an apologetic tone, "Yes ma'am, it's all I really know how to cook."

"I wasn't a cook in France either, but I think it might be a fair bet to say that I probably know how to cook more dishes than you. Mind if I take charge of the kitchen?" I was wishful she'd say yes because I was afraid if I ate like this all the time that my belly would grow to be Matt's size in no time. I wasn't meaning to be rude by any means.

"Oh yes, you can!" She was fervent about that. Perhaps she too was sick of her cooking. We moved back into the living room even though there was a table in the kitchen. They resumed watching the game. I was okay with the silence, though it wasn't something I was used to.

"I saw the pictures of your daughter on the wall by the door. Do you mind if I ask what happened to her?" I asked taking a bite of toast.

"Not at all, we were in a car accident, she passed away," Matt said this like it still pained him, though I could tell this happened a long time ago.

"How long ago did she die?"

"15 years ago," Matt said more distracted. He kept eating while we talked and somehow managed to watch the game at the same time. I think it's a bunch of baloney when men claim they can't multi-task. I didn't care though. I grasped the culture of this household very quickly, it was very laissez-faire, and Matt wasn't one to get into the business that wasn't his. And Sarah was quieter than I thought she'd be upon meeting her.

"So there are two days till school starts, can you show me how to get to the school sometime? And if you know anyone who wants to sell their vehicle, I'm in the market." I grabbed Both their dishes as I said this. I walked into the kitchen and quickly put the dishes in the dishwasher.

Sarah was pleased by my kind manners, "Oh my, I feel like a queen, thank you!"

Matt said, "Of course I can, I'd be happy to. And I think I might know someone you can buy an old car from if that's okay with you?" He yelled so I could hear.

I walked through the doorway "Oh yes, of course. Old cars are pretty small town, and that's what I'm all about this year."

He chuckled and looked at me. "Well it's an olllld car, but those are the kind that lasts."

"The older, the better," I said smiling. I was leaning on the doorway with my arms folded and my legs lightly crossed.

"Vera, do you mind if I ask you a personal question?" Matt said looking a little uncomfortable.

"Haha, the first of many, of course, you can Matt." I smiled too at his awkwardness; it was adorable.

"Are you really 17?" His face was scrunched like he'd just said a bad word.

"Hahaha, I can't tell you how many times I get asked that kind of question. Yes, I am 17 though I know I don't look like it." Matt amused me, so I continued, "Don't let my height fool you… Or my womanly… Parts."

"Gah, ugh, I didn't need to hear that Vera," he cover his ears. I laughed so hard; I hadn't laughed harder in what felt like years. Making Matt uncomfortable was as easy as saying body parts like butt. This was going to be a fun joking point with him.

Sarah also laughed at her husband's naivety.

I sat back down on the couch.

He looked over at me briefly, "Why are you sitting so straight?"

"Who, Me? Uhh, I never noticed." I tried to slouch, but it was a poor attempt. This made Matt laugh.

"I'm just teasing kiddo."

"Matt, I think we're going to be great friends."

He smiled and lightly chuckled. After the game I was pretty wiped out, I got ready for bed and fell asleep relatively quickly.

Even though there's a nine-hour time difference between Paris and Arcata, the time was eaten up by staying up late and sleeping longer than I usually do.

5:00 am wakeup call was new to Matt. After my alarm went off, I jumped out of bed and threw on my workout clothes. I walked out of my room to see Matt half asleep running out of his room in his sweats with a gun in his hands. Since he was a police officer, he had a few of them stashed around the house for safety purposes.

"Huh-wha- who's there?!"

"Matt it's just me, I get up at this hour every day." I was holding my hands up, and I crouched down a little.

"Oh, ya itz juz you." He sauntered off to his bedroom slouched over like it would take no time for him to be in sleepy land again.

I always started my workouts stretching and listening to music. Today was Saturday, so it was Pilates, 7-mile run, and then stretching again to end the workout. It usually took an hour and a half. I went outside which was freezing cold even though it was August; this weather was something I was going to have to get used to.

The surroundings were gorgeous, Matt and Sarah lived in the community forest part of this college town. It was foggy and green, and the sun wasn't up just yet so it was somewhat spooky being right next to the forest. The trees were large and thick, it was a part of the national redwood forest. I had no idea what kind of animals could be in there, so after I did Pilates on the wet lawn, I ran on the road. No one was awake from what I could tell, but I knew I had to be careful because visibility was low and it was dark. I made a mental note to buy a reflector. After my runners watch alerted me I had gone 3.5 miles, I turned back and stretched when I finished. It was around 6:30, I rummaged through the kitchen trying to find something with nutritional value 'I'm buying the food from now on' I thought to myself. I grabbed the eggs and cooked up some hard-boiled eggs.

"Morning," came a groggy voice behind me.

"Well good morning sunshine, sorry I scared you this morning."

"No, no it's all good. Do you exercise every day?"

"Mm-hmm."

"I think you're going to be a bad influence on me," he teased. "I don't mind my beautiful gut thank you very much."

I laughed and snapped my fingers. "And here I came to change the world," I sighed, "You shouldn't dash my dreams my second day here." I gave him a plate of dry toast and hard-boiled eggs. He looked a little disappointed.

"No butter, where's the jelly?" He picked up the toast with his index finger and thumb like he was picking up something toxic.

"Haha, in the fridge."

"No wonder you're so skinny, I think you need to eat a cheeseburger or something."

I shook my head, "You're going to be a bad influence on me; I don't mind my washboard abs thank you very much."

We both laughed together.

"Where's Sarah?"

"Oh she's at work already, she works for the university as a biology professor, so in truth, you'll rarely see her. She stays at the university most nights grading homework or teaching evening classes."

"Oh, I see, well that's okay!" I went upstairs to take a shower and get ready for the day. That routine usually took 45 minutes to an hour. It was 8:00 am when I finished, and I decided I'd kick my wake up schedule back 15-30 minutes to make sure I'd get to school on time. After I was ready, I went back downstairs.

"Hey kiddo, I have to go into work today. I usually work most Saturdays; I hope you don't mind."

"No problem." If there was anything I was used to it was an overworking Papa figure.

"But first my friend Kit Multnomah will be here to have his son help you find a car. Remember the dealership I was talking about yesterday with the old car?"

"Oh that is great," I clapped my hands together once, "This place needs more vegetables. I'll grocery shop today." I winked.

He laughed. "They'll be here soon I think." Matt turned on some rerun of a game, and I decided I'd make myself a to-do list. I wanted to buy groceries, a reflector, meal prep for the week, and if I had time; explore the town a little. I wasn't too worried about getting it all done before school because I also had Sunday to do everything. It didn't take any time at all before we heard a loud rumble from a truck. I was almost finished with my grocery list when Matt jumped up and walked out; I thought it was a little odd he didn't wait for them to come to the door. It only took a few more minutes to finish my list.

When I walked out, I saw an old beater truck, and I smiled at just how perfectly simple it was.

"I'd beat you in an arm wrestle any day." I heard from a man's voice I didn't recognize. I then saw a man who must've been Matt's friend, and a boy in his early 20's. I was astounded at their exotic look. They were Native Americans, they had big brown eyes, black hair, and both had very handsome faces.

"Hey, kiddo!" Kit and his son looked up from their teasing. They both stared at me, practically with jaws to the floor.

"Oh excuse my poor manners," Matt said jokingly, "This is Kit, and his son Owen Multnomah." Owen nodded, and Kit tilted his black cowboy hat. Owen was 6'5" and very bulky.

"I'm very pleased to meet you guys." I walked up and shook both their hands.

"Kit here has been my good friend since, well, before I can remember."

"We sure have! We're still on for the game tonight right?" Kit asked looking at Matt.

"Of course, I should get off right around five. We'll make it a welcome Vera party slash game night." Matt looked at me happily from his friend being here. "Tonight it's a sport called basketball, ever heard of it?"

"Ha, well I certainly hope it's better than your football. Or at least maybe you can explain the rules to me this time, so it makes sense."

"I've got you covered there," Owen said enthusiastically.

"Thank goodness," I said.

Matt and Kit gave a knowing look at each other as though they were so hoping they could accomplish our matrimony. I was a little shocked Matt was so… Dad-like.

Kit and Matt went inside to watch more T.V. before Matt had to leave for work and Owen took me in his truck to the dealership.

The owner was a kind, old looking man. "Hello, valued customers! What are you in the market for?"

"A car," I said matching his tone. Looking around the lot the only kinds of cars I saw were old, I had to chuckle at Matt's vagueness.

"Well let me show you what I've got, do you know how to drive a stick shift?"

"I do." I wasn't about to tell him I learned on a Lamborghini. Owen and I jumped in, and I revved the loud engine.

On the drive, which was gorgeous, I was surprised by how smooth the car drove given its noise.

"I can tell Matt really enjoys you and your Papa- er Dad. He's a lot happier when you two are around."

"Nah, it's just my Dad. They've known each other since the dark ages, maybe even sooner than that." Owen smiled at his own joke; he had perfectly white teeth that were perfectly straight. I laughed too.

"Hah, well Matt snores loud enough to be a dinosaur." We both laughed. I continued, "I like this car, it has quite a vintage feel."

"Well, it seems like you'll have to drive it gently like a vintage."

"That's okay, I'm planning on getting a motorcycle too." I kept my eyes on the road most of the time.

Owen looked shocked, "You ride?!"

"Yes I take it you do as well?" I looked at him hopefully.

"Heck yeah!"

"Good, I could use a riding partner; I have no idea where the all good spots are around here."

"Haha, we'll make a great team then." Owen was pleasant and so easy to converse with. He was smoother than I anticipated he'd be. His poised behavior took me off guard because it was mixed perfectly with energy and vibrancy. Another thing I liked about Owen is that he was so unapologetically himself.

We pulled back into the dealership, and the owner asked if it was a good fit for me.

"I'll take it. What do you want for your work of art?" I rubbed the dash like the car and I were meant to be.

"I was hoping for $2,500, but I'm sure you could talk me down a little."

"I think $2,500 is fair." I was surprised it was so cheap. While we walked into his little store, I pulled the cash from my wallet ahead of time.

The dealership owner was very delighted, "It runs great for its condition and price, I think you'll enjoy owning this vehicle." He smiled.

"Mr. Seedall, I think you're in the right line of work," I said thinking about what a happy passion he had for vehicles.

He was pleased by my compliment and put his hands on his suspenders while chortled, "yah, I reckon you're right."

'Wow I really am in the Wild West' I thought to myself. I smiled as he put together the paperwork. I paid the gentleman, and Owen and I left to go home.

I was confused to see Matt still home when we got there. I went upstairs to put away the thousands of dollars I thought I'd need to buy a car. I ran back downstairs to see all three of them watching a game. I walked up to the back of the couch to behold Owen sprawled on the couch with his feet dangling off the arm.

"So what now, do I need to change the license plates on it?"

"I'll help you with all the logistics, don't worry about it now though because most everything's closed on weekends," Owen said as he moved his feet to sit up straight so I could have a place to sit.

"That reminds me, Vera," Matt started, "Do you have a Washington driver's license?"

"No, I do have one in New York though, does that not count?" I was confused, wasn't the U.S., the U.S.? Why should each state have to have different license requirements?

"Fraid not kiddo."

"Hmm. Well, I'd better get started on that right away then."

"It's Saturday," Owen reminded. "I'll take you where you need to go though." He was all too pleased with my current state of unlicensed driving.

 "Before you leave, you might want to put more clothes on too, Vera," Matt said boldly.

I was wearing bootie shorts and a sleeveless shirt perfectly cut to my hourglass torso. "Matt I don't have warmer clothes, you see in France and Italy, when it's summer, it's actually warm." All my clothes were classy and designer, I stood out like a sore thumb here.

"No worries I'm sure I have a jacket at my house we can pick up for you to use, Vera," Owen said pretending to eye my outfit, though really he was looking at me. "Besides we'll have to take Dad home before I drive you wherever you need to go," he said cheerfully.

"Are you sure you want to do that? I have a lot to do today." I was truly thankful for his help because I wasn't used to being alone, and partially because I didn't know where anything was.

"Of course, it's not a problem at all."

We took Kit home in the Multnomah's truck; it was a little cozy with the three of us in the three seat cab. I leaned closer to Owen than Kit, so Owen's and my arms and legs were touching. I didn't mind, and neither did Owen, but once we were at Owens house and Kit was out, I moved to the window seat. Owen ran out with a jacket as promised. He wasn't surprised to see me in the other chair, though he was hoping I'd have stayed.

I was surprised he lived so close to the Charters and me, it was only a 5-7 minute drive. We went back to town and ran all our errands, including going to a sports store for a reflector. There was a boy my age running the cash register, during the checkout he said:

"You must be the French girl coming for school right?" He wasn't very attractive to me. He had red hair in a pompadour, chubby cheeks, with a scrawny body, I was grateful he was kind though. "I'm Kevin."

"Yes, I am. How did you know?"

"You've been the talk of the town for months. I'm surprised you don't know this."

I was a little embarrassed. "Well I arrived just yesterday so this is the first time I've heard of it."

Kevin looked at Owen, then back at me, "I thought you were staying at Sheriff Charter's?" He was clearly fishing for why I was with Owen, an attractive Native American older than us.

"I am," I looked smug because I wasn't planning on giving anything up in regards to Owen. "Hold on a second; I'm going to grab one of those umbrellas." As I walked away, I could feel both sets of eyes on my backside.

They were so obvious I couldn't believe it. That threw me off guard; I thoughtlessly asked: "So do you two know each other?"

Kevin answered before Owen, "No, I don't believe so. How do you two know each other?" This question was more obvious than subtle.

"Matt and Owen's Dad are great friends. Owen here was kind enough to show me around." I nudged Owen's arm and smiled at him. Owen was thrilled I showed this kind of affection in front of Kevin. Though to me, it was just a friendly nudge and smile because I really was thankful. Owen seemed almost too happy with the situation.

"Oh well, maybe I can show you around the school tomorrow?" Kevin asked.

"Oh, well, I guess if Owen can't? I hinted to Owen for help.

"I'm a freshman in college." Owen looked disappointed but shrugged it off with a joke, "I'm afraid I'm too cool now to be going to high school."

I laughed raising my eyebrows, "Right, cool enough. Is that what you tell yourself to help you sleep at night?" I loved that he was so spunky. "I can't wait to go to college!"

Kevin laughed at that assuming I was making fun of Owen or something. Owen loved my poke fun but couldn't think anything to counter.

"A tour would be nice, thank you, Kevin." I finally said.

"Huh, well awesome then. I'll see you Monday, Vera." He was so excited about showing me around that we didn't decide on a place to meet. Nor did he notice that he gave up the fact that he knew my name without me telling it to him.

Owen was suddenly not so happy and rushed the transaction. On the way back home Owen showed me where the school was for the 'uncool' people.

As a last minute addition to our fantastic day, we saw a motorcycle for sale on the side of the road. We bought that too and put it in Owen's truck.

When we got to Matt's, he helped me bring in all the food, we got home around 3:00. That left a reasonable amount of time for me to make dinner and start on the meal prep. Owen went to pick up Kit again for the 'party'.

I made fish and salad for dinner and made some dessert for the game. It was five before I knew it, and Matt was home and hungry. Owen and Kit joined us for dinner and the game which started at 6.

I was getting pretty tired, my body was still on France time, and we had had a full day. I opted out of dessert as the game started. Kit was in his own designated lay-Z-boy, and Matt was in the seat I was now discovering was his favorite chair, which left Owen and me on the love seat. I was very comfortable with people, so it wasn't a big deal at all.

 Owen was patiently explaining to rules to me, it didn't entirely make sense, but I got the gist of basketball. I soon learned that game night wasn't just one game. I was so tired that I folded my arms into Owen's Jacket and leaned on Owen's shoulder to fall asleep. Owen didn't move an inch; he was almost uncomfortably stiff. That made it take longer for me to fall asleep than normal; I was almost out when I heard Kit's voice.

"She's sure a pretty one, Matt."

"Yeah, I was not expecting that at all. When Vera came to my door, I think I was tongue tied for a minute. Of course, she came with a man the size of a gorilla to 'help her with her luggage,' and that didn't help my shock." Matt bunny eared the 'help her with her luggage' part of his sentence.

Owen moved a little when Matt said that, I could tell he wanted to say something, but he was nervous I'd wake if he started talking.

"Well, it was probably her French boyfriend," Kit teased Owen.

Owen smirked beneath his breath like he couldn't care less. He couldn't help himself and whispered loudly: "But he's all the way in France." I was ready for the conversation to be over, but it would be weird if I just suddenly woke up; so I stayed still and endured it.

"He was quite a looker," Matt teased.

"And yet she's on my shoulder tonight," Owen gloated gesturing to me with his free hand.

'Aw crap' I thought to myself, 'why can't you boys just watch the stupid game?'

"Undeniably true," Kit said happily as though he could hear the wedding bells and grandchildren's laughter already. They were finally quiet and watched the game after that remark. I gave it plenty of time before I pretend stirred and eventually got up. I sat up and rubbed my eyes; it was an outstanding performance if I do say so myself. I took off Owen's jacket and handed it to him.

"Well, I'm going to bed."

Matt interrupted me while I was standing from the couch, "Vera who was with you when you came yesterday?" He asked nonchalantly, I was impressed.

"I can't believe that was just yesterday," I started. "His name is Stefan." I wasn't going to give anything more than that.

"Is he your boyfriend?" Matt asked while trying- but failing- to hide a huge smile.

"Nope." 'Oh please stop asking me questions.'

"Well then who is he to you? I mean France is a really long way for someone to help someone else move."

I thought about lying that he was my brother or something because I didn't want people knowing I had bodyguards. That would only provoke more questions. I sighed, "He's my bodyguard." I looked at Matt when I said this.

"Ha okay Vera, whatever." He smiled really big. "Boyfriend it is, you're such a tease."

"Believe what you want," was all I said, I was so tired that I didn't want to delve into the details. I started leaving the room when Owen said:

"Vera, seriously, you don't expect us to believe he was your bodyguard," he huffed.

I shrugged my shoulders; I couldn't tell what was worse. them knowing I had a bodyguard or thinking I was a liar. "I'm not lying," I said.

Suddenly three faces were looking at me with curicsity. "Good night," I left as quickly as possible. I got ready for bed and was out pretty quickly; I was good at being efficient with my routine.

In the middle of the night I heard the front door close, it must've been Sarah getting home. I looked at the clock on my nightstand which read midnight. I couldn't believe how long she worked.

In the morning Sarah was already gone by the time I finished my workout. It seemed I wasn't going to be able to get to know her very much. I giggled to myself at her balance comment when I arrived. No wonder all she did when she got home was relax.

Sunday blew by fast, I cleaned the house and did the laundry, finished my meal prepping and even got to have some time with a book. I was reading 'Mid Summer's Night Dream' by Shakespeare. I was grateful I caught Sarah leaving late one day because she had taught me how to do the laundry. Monday morning was the normal routine, except on weekdays I only ran 5 miles and alternated yoga, ballet, hip-hop, and weights in place of Pilates.

For school, I was wearing a valentine neckline, sleeveless shirt that was form fitting, white bootie shorts that were lacey on the outside, and designer shoes. My hair was curly with a waterfall braid on both sides which came together in a tucked bun. I grabbed my umbrella on the way out; Matt had to take me to school, so we got there quite early. I waved at Matt when I got outside of his police car.

"Have a good day at school," he waved back.

The school looked old and beautiful. It was all brick with an old facade that looked like parts of the masonry was hand carved.

I saw the first and smallest building which had a light on; I could see through the glass doors a large desk and an adult. I decided I'd get directions there since Kevin and I failed to create a meeting spot. I walked down a little stone path lined with dark hedges.

 Inside, it was brightly lit, and very warm. It smelled like an old building, with short carpet and a big desk. The lady inside looked like a librarian; she was skinny and short with large glasses and a tight bun.

She looked at me in awe after I entered, "Hello Dear, are you lost?"

"I'm Vera Bianchi, I'm a new student here, and I was hoping I could get a map of some sort," I said with my French accent.

"Oh, the French student, yes we have been expecting you." She spoke excitedly as she sifted through some papers. "Here we are. I have your schedule in English and French and a route to your classes."

"Thank you, madam; you are most kind," I said as I looked at the English version of my schedule and map.

When I left the office, I saw a lot of students outside, some were visiting, and others were rushing to get inside. I was the only one with an umbrella, and I was the only tan one there, to top it off I also wore to these people what was practically nothing.

I was stared at like I was a celebrity, I was surprised everyone seemed to notice me, maybe it was also because I was taller than most of the girls there besides some of the athletes.

I tried to look friendly and inviting, but it was hard when I caught everyone's attention. By the time I found my first class, American History, I was only a minute or two early. This was just perfect because now I truly was the center of attention. The old lady teacher was bigger and had white hair; she had a lot of wrinkles that mostly looked mean.

I found an empty seat in the dead center of the classroom- oh the irony- the center of attention indeed. The girl next to me leaned over looking at me like she was my number one fan.

"Hi, you must be Vera." She paused to swallow, "I'm Savanna, how do you do?" She was extremely friendly, and I liked her already because on top of her extreme kindness she was also quirky.

I smiled and popped my hand out, "Very nice to meet you, Savanna." At this point the teacher started, all day, in all my classes most people were either really friendly, shy or hated me already.

Savanna was miraculously in most of my classes and introduced me to everyone she knew. When we got to the cafeteria for lunch, I already developed a fan club of boys and girls alike. I packed all my meals; I usually ate 5-6 small meals a day. Savanna, Kevin, and a boy named Oscar who was in robotics always bought lunch together.

I looked around at my table to see one other girl and three boys, all attractive, but not enough to tempt me. I glanced around at the student body in general. I could pick out the Jock groups and the nerd groups, the loners, emo's and druggies, and the popular table.

There was a boy who spotted me from across the cafeteria, I was pretty sure he was from the jock group.

He walked over confidently; his face looked bedazzled looking at me.

"Well hello, beautiful, I'm Kirby Stout."

"Hi, I'm Vera Bianchi." Something about him was arrogant and annoying. I shouldn't have let it get under my skin, but I could tell this guy was going to give me grief. He was probably the most handsome guy in the school; however, his attitude ranked him as one of the ugliest.

"What's a pretty thing like you doing in a place like this?" He put one hand on the table and leaned on it.

"I'm a transfer student from France." I was pleasant to him, but I kept looking over my shoulder to Savanna, I wished the food line would hurry up.

"Are you a senior?"

"Yes, I am."

"Are you 18?"

"No, I'm 17."

"Haha well, who cares what the legal age is right? A lot of my co-students are going to the Arcata pool on Friday. You should come; I think you'll find yourself having a great time."

"Okay, yeah, maybe. I'll probably bring one of my friends if that's okay with you?"

Kirby grinned, "Well if she looks anything like you, hope you have three or more new friends."

I rolled my eyes and put my fork down.

Savanna, Kevin, and Oscar came back from the food line happily discussing Oscar's upcoming robotics competition. I smiled at my new friends sitting down thankful for their impeccable timing.

Kirby looked at them briefly and continued, "So, Friday then." He stated this excitedly, and almost forcefully, as though no was somehow unacceptable.

"We'll see, thanks for the invite, Kirby."

I tried to play it casual so that the glares coming from Kevin and Oscar would dissipate. "So Savanna, would you go around and point out who's who in the cafeteria?"

"Course," Savanna started moving her torso side to side in a quirky manner. "Over there we have the wrestling team." I couldn't pay any attention to specific names, and I was impatient for some reason, her words ran together until she reached the football team's table.

".… And Kirby, and Ethan. What did Kirby want by the way?"

I swallowed my previous bite. "He invited me to a pool party on Friday. Do you want to come with me, Savanna?"

"YES! Kirby and the football team, all in swim trunks? Count me in. I just hope Kirby is in a speedo or something."

A piece of lettuce from my salad almost went up my nose I snickered so quickly. "He's all yours, my friend!"

 "Yesssssssssss!" Oscar and Kevin relaxed after I backed down from the 'hot football star'.

I was a little disappointed she was as elated as she was. "My next class is in building 2 room 201. Anyone headed my direction?" I said picking up my Tupperware and finishing my apple.

"I am," Kevin said thrilled. "I'll drop you off, I'm going to room 215."

My class was philosophy, and I was excited about the prospect of debating. During the class I realized how basic the material was, I was really disappointed. At the end of my day, I realized my only romantic prospect was Kirby. That was also a depressing thought, but I wasn't going to let it get me down. After all, I didn't come here for love.

Matt came on time to pick me up in his police car. I looked around one last time to behold the new wonderful place I was going to go to for the next year. I inhaled a deep breath of satisfaction and climbed in.

Matt took me to the DMV so I could take the multiple choice test and get my temporary license. We took care of the other necessary legalities for my car. I even had time to drop it off to a mechanic in town so he could tone down the cars noise- which worked like magic.

When we got home I started dinner in the kitchen and Matt helped me dice the chicken.

"Are we having more rabbit food for dinner?"

"Haha, you know it. That and grilled chicken."

"I think I'm going to order a pizza too," he said happily still chopping the meat.

Matt never called a pizza place, he was lingering in the Kitchen for a while trying to help where he could, but it was pretty apparent that wasn't going anywhere. Instead, he turned the T.V. on and waited for dinner to be finished.

I called him in when it was ready.

"So, how did you like school? Have you made any friends?" He asked as he was taking seconds- Matt must not mind the rabbit food as much as he complained.

"Yes, a girl named Savanna, and two boys named Kevin and Oscar. I might go to a pool party on Friday if it's okay with you?"

"Oh sure, you go do your teenage thing. Just be careful, okay?"

"Course. How was work?"

"Nice and slow, as usual. I like it that way."

"Why does Sarah work so much?"

"It's something she started to do after our daughter died, it was kinda what she did to distract herself. You know, I can't tell you how happy she was to hear a teenage girl wanted to live with us…"

I smiled overwhelmed with joy that I was truly wanted here. "Well I'm very grateful you guys were up for the task!"

This was one of those moments where you didn't say anything more, we sat in contented silence for the remainder of dinner.

We finished dinner and Matt went back to his game, I went upstairs to do some homework and to do my nightly bedtime routine.

The next morning was the same as the others, cold, wet, and foggy. I did some advanced yoga in the front yard on a mat and ran 5 miles. I decided I should make a trail in the forest by the house; the visibility on the road was close to nil.

I stretched and got ready for the day, putting on some extra perfume, 'Roja Parfums Amber Aoud Absolue Precieux'. I always put some on in the morning after my shower, and in the evening after my shower.

Matt had to take me to school still because my temporary license was yet to arrive in the mail. It was a beautiful day even though it was overcast. It smelled clean here, and I loved that-- no smog.

When I got to my class, I was glad I was early instead of right on time. I shuffled through my book and notepad to get ready for the lecture. I heard students come in and I tried to ignore all the stares and looks. Savannah finally came, thank goodness. I thought about Friday and whether or not I was going to go. Savanna begged me to go, I figured it wouldn't hurt anything if I did.

During lunch, I tried to dodge Kirby, but I failed instantly. Kirby saw me come in and walked up to me, "Hey beautiful... Are you coming Friday?"

"Yeah I will, and so will my friend." I gestured over to Savanna who was in the food line already. He looked disgusted, I had to smirk, I couldn't help myself. 'serves you right you ding-bat with a stupid high ego and expectations.'

"Oh, good." He finally answered unable to hide his frustrated tone.

I smiled so big I almost laughed out loud. He must've thought I was beaming with interest in him. As soon as his face changed, I knew it was my cue to leave.

All of my classes were easy compared to my private school. I found myself looking forward to the pool party because it was something new.

On Thursday the weather was beautiful! After school I took my motorcycle out to go for a ride, I had invited Owen, but he said he was doing drill. I wasn't quite sure what he meant because he wasn't in the military.

I walked my bike a ways from my house so that Matt wouldn't hear the engine start. I wore booty shorts, a spaghetti shirt, and mid-thigh high black boots. I worried I'd get a funky tan, but I brushed the thoughts aside so I could enjoy my ride.

I zoomed past a colorful splotch of green and pavement. The town was a mixture of large redwood trees and then a port on the opposite end of the city there was a bay that met the cold Pacific ocean. I rode into town unsure where I was going; I looked for the Arcata pool.

I was glancing around not paying attention, and the traffic light had turned red. I pulled on my brakes as hard as I could. I would like to think I looked like a cool superhero sliding sideways to a stop, but who knows. I looked over at the driver of the nice vehicle next to me.

The driver looked at me like I was a lunatic. I was more thankful than ever to have a dark visor and helmet that covered my face.

Looking at him distracted me, he was frankly gorgeous. From my brief glance, I saw he was very muscular, he had green eyes and light brown hair.

He looked at me the whole time as though he could see straight through my visor. Maybe he was looking at my long leg on the side of my bike or something? I didn't have the guts to fully look over again, I was too embarrassed about my irresponsible driving.

I drove off quickly as soon as it was green. I found the pool, parked, and looked around to memorize what my surroundings looked like so I could get here again.

Passing on the main road, I saw that same beautiful car, with the good-looking man stealing another glance at me again.

I rode home wishing I could've seen more of that guy, he was undoubtedly more handsome than any person I had ever met.

I went home and walked my bike back to the house. Matt was watching T.V., so I sat on the couch with him to spend some time together.

The driver never left my thoughts, 'how old was he.' 'who was he,' 'where did he live?'

He continued to occupy my mind the entire next day too. I felt dumb, 'you'll probably never see him again, let it go.' I told myself to no avail.

Savanna was chatting away while she walked me to the parking lot. "Oh, Vera, I forgot to tell you, I can't go to the pool tonight."

"Oh?" I answered, "Why?"

"Ugh, I have lame parents who don't want me around that group of people. They said there might be alcohol at the party."

"Oh, okay. No problem, I'll just have Matt take me. I'm sorry you can't make it, I was really hoping you'd be there."

"I know, me too! I'll probably never get married with how babied I am!" Savanna was a little dramatic. "At least I'd be a forever bachelorette, that's sexy, right?"

I laughed sarcastically, "Yeah, Savy. It's so sexy to be an old maid."

 She laughed along, we were getting really close. I could tell this was going to be a strong friendship.

Matt pulled into the parking lot and waved me into the car.

"Hey Matt," I said closing the door. "Could you give me a ride to the pool party tonight?"

"Sure, but I might take you a little late, I have a game to finish tonight. I doubt we'd be later than a half an hour or so."

"That's fine. I'll call you when I'm ready to be picked up."

Matt looked over at me briefly. "Vera, I know I'm not your real Dad, but I'd appreciate it if you left the party when or if the beer comes out."

I was untroubled entirely by his words. I knew they came from love and I was grateful I had the great fortune of having him as my 'Dad'. "Matt, you're far better than my Papa. Trust me on that. I'll be smart, I promise."

Matt smiled to himself. The look on his face told me I was like the daughter he wished he had. It made me sad to think that he was robbed of his only child. Matt deserved so much more.

After we got home, I fixed up some dinner and got ready for the party. I was wearing a navy blue bikini with a white sundress. I didn't bother to take my makeup off because I wasn't planning on getting my face wet.

When I arrived at the pool, I could hear a lot of rambunctious teenagers yelling and splashing around. I walked in all by myself; the splendor of the energy was terrific. It was a public pool, so there were more people there than just the teenage party.

One of the football players came up to me excitedly. "Vera! I wasn't sure you'd come, follow me, I'll show you where to drop your stuff."

"Great, thanks!" I was happy to receive such a warm welcome.

"Right here," he pointed and smiled.

As soon as I put my bag down, I took my sundress off and put it away. Ethan, my helper, laughed a little and grabbed my hand pulling me toward the party of boys and girls.

"Vera!" Kirby said running up to me giving me a huge hug.

I laughed winded by his aggressive hug, "Hey Kirby."

Kirby looked at Ethan and playfully pushed him. "You trying to steal my girl?"

"Whatever, she isn't your girl."

I scratched my head and tried to leave the now awkward conversation.

Ethan and Kirby sprawled for a minute and then Ethan yelled. "Where do you think you're going?" He ran up to my fleeting body and turned me around. "The party's over here."

Kirby walked up to us and spoke, "Vera, tell this knucklehead you're with me tonight."

I looked annoyed, "Well actually, I'm not with anyone this evening." I pulled away from Ethan's arm around my shoulders and sauntered off to my bag to put a swim suit cover on and walked to a row of lawn chairs on the side of the property.

I laid there for a while until I saw a little trailhead. I grew curious and left to explore. It was well paved and long; I saw deer, birds, and squirrels. I was farther from the pool than I thought, and going back took a long time.

When I finally came all the way back I heard boisterous laughter and yells, everyone had left the vicinity except for those who were in the high school party group. I squinted and crinkled my nose when I smelled the beer.

"She's back!" I heard a slurred voice say, it was Ethan.

"I'VE BEEN WAITING ALL NIGHT FOR YOU, GIRL!" Kirby yelled pointing an empty bottle toward me.

I turned to get my bag to leave which was on the other side of the pool. I tried to hurry, but Kirby and Ethan both caught up to me. They grabbed both of my arms and pulled me to the table with the alcohol.

"Have a drink," Ethan said with his face close to mine, he had stinky breath.

"No, thank you. I think it's time for me to go home, you're all drunk."

"Drunker than a skunk," Kirby said and laughed along with Ethan. "Maybe she wants to go in the hot tub with us, what do you think Ethan?"

"I think so!"

"No, I want to go home! Let me go!" I said sternly.

They both looked at me like they were going to have their way with me.

Kirby shouted, "Maybe she doesn't want to because she has so much cloth—errr... So many clothes on!"

Ethan started laughing and they pulled me every which way until my swimsuit cover was off. They lifted me by my armpits high enough for my feet to leave the ground, and they carried me to the hot tub.

I kicked behind Kirby's knee, and he let me go abruptly yelling out in pain. My leg slid on the side of the hot tub's rough edge, skinning my calf.

Ethan took full advantage of being the only one holding onto me. He grabbed my other arm and brought me close. He started trying to kiss me.

I punched his side, and he yelled angrily, "Ouch. You stupid woman, you shouldn't have done that. I'm known for my temper, you know."

I was pissed off, "Let me go, Ethan!"

I suddenly felt a quick yank forward. Someone had pulled him away from me, knocking me off balance and I fell backward.

I was well on my way to the side of the hot tub, I could see my head was going to hit the edge. My breath was taken from me when something hit my stomach hard.

I was cuddled into a hug, and my rescuer carried me off until we were out of the pool area.

"My bag," I said once we were outside.

"I have it." I heard a sultry, smooth, velvety voice say.

I looked up to see the handsome face from the nice car I saw yesterday. He was looking at me tenderly like he was beholding his precious child.

"...Thank you," I said after a moment of staring into his beautiful green eyes.

"It was my pleasure." His eyes locked mine while he set me down. "Can I take you home?"

I looked around the parking lot as though I'd find Matt. "Uh, yeah I think I'll need one."

He smiled down at me and gently guided me to his car. "I think you might need some first aid."

I looked down at my leg to see runs of blood covering my wound and the lower half of my calf. "Oh, yeah I guess so. Sorry, I'll try to make sure it doesn't get on your car."

He grinned and glanced over at me, "Trust me, it's okay."

He opened my door for me and over-helped me into my seat like I was severally hurt. He closed the door and eyed me on the way to his side of the car.

After he got in, he said, "I'm Nicholas."

"It's very good to meet you, I'm Vera."

"Is that a French accent I detect?"

"Yes, it is. I just moved here last week."

"Oh, what brings you here?"

"I'm going to the high school here; it's just for a change of pace." I lied unconvincingly, but since he didn't know me, it wasn't obvious. I wasn't sure why I felt like I had to explain myself.

He chuckled beneath his breath, "Is that so? You're in high school?" He asked incredulously. Maybe his shock was because it was a college town, and I didn't look like a high school student?

"Yes, I am." I looked out my window wondering if it was such a good idea to have moved away.

He nodded his head silently biting his lower lip to keep from laughing. "Where am I taking you?"

"Oh, I live by the reservation I'll tell you specifics when we get closer."

"I'm a senior myself. I've been homeschooled with my sister and best friends, but I'm considering going to a public school this year. What do you think?"

I laughed lightly, "I think you should!" I raised my eyebrows to emphasize.

He looked over at me mischievously, "And you'll be there?"

"Yep," I tried not to smile as big as I did, but it was impossible. "Take a left at the light. I live at Matt Charter's house."

Nicholas looked over at me while we sat at the light. "They say how you meet someone will determine a lot about the rest of your relationship. What do you think about that?"

I giggled, "Well you'd better hope it's wrong or else you'll be pretty busy playing hero. Thanks, by the way."

Nicholas laughed all the way exposing a perfect smile and perfect teeth like they were veneers or something. "I'd be your hero anytime, anyplace."

Before we knew it, I heard the gravel crinkle beneath the tires, and I felt a light bump-bump from the curb of the driveway. "Thanks for the ride, Nick. I hope to see you around."

"I'm sure you will." His voice sounded smoother than Frank Sinatra's.

Chapter Three: One Indisputable Favor

The coming Monday I walked into my history class excited to tell Savanna all about Nicholas.

As soon as she walked in, I turned to her and opened my mouth to speak.

"Hello," came a sultry voice behind me. I turned around to see Nicholas take a seat next to me.

"Hey Nicholas, I didn't know you could be admitted to school so fast," I said casually but happily.

Nicholas put his book down and slid into his seat. "I know some people. I think you should know ahead of time that I'm in all of your classes," he said unapologetically.

"Oh really?" I was so excited, "And why is that?"

"Yes, the principal thought it best to schedule me to have all of your classes. I know French, so he figured it would be a kind gesture." Everything he spoke was done alarmingly beautifully.

"Wow, I'm sorry. Don't worry, I'll talk to him, there's no need to make you navigate your whole schedule for my sake." I was disappointed he hadn't come on his own volition, and that worse, I might be a burden to him. That's not the way to get someone to like you!

"No, no. I don't mind at all, to be honest, I'm glad my schedule was prearranged. I would get bored in any other class." He smiled at me kindly; I couldn't believe a person like this existed outside of my dreams-- if I could even conjure up a face and body like his.

I laughed, "Well you may still suffer from boredom being in all my classes." My insides were jumping, 'does he want to be here with me?'

"Perhaps, but I doubt I'd get bored in your classes." He looked at me intensely- I wondered if he did it on purpose.

The kind old teacher called the class to attention. It was different having Nicholas take me to all my classes, my other friends joined us along the way, and we all chatted as we ordinarily did. During lunch, I sat with Savanna and the others.

Savanna hurried through the food line and practically ran up to me. "Okay girl, spill! How do you know the man-cub?"

I cocked my head to the side slightly, "Man-cub?"

She rolled her eyes and let out an excited grunt of impatience, "Nicholas King, of course!"

I looked over to his table where I saw four incredibly beautiful people.

There were two girls and two boys, I couldn't help but stare, they were pale, and all looked older than high school students. They had varying shades of brown hair and green eyes. They sat boy girl, boy girl. The boy furthest left was ginormous like Stefan, maybe bigger, the girl next to him was also large like she lifted weights. The next girl was the only slender one in the group and wore designer clothes I recognized. The last was a boy, who especially caught my attention was also large, but not like Stefan. It was Nicholas. They all had straight and excellent features, like an ideal mixture of modern and traditional. There was a sense of classiness in their wake. They seemed to suffer from ennui, not speaking-just eating.

Something subconscious warned me of danger, but my eyes held on to the perfection they were, and my heart desired to know them better. It was a strange phenomenon to feel such a tear of emotions at the same time, both equally powerful, both demanding my attention.

Savanna looked over and smacked her lips slightly. "Okay so, starting on the far left- the big boar is Aiden, next to him is his girlfriend Olivia, then Victoria and the man-cub is Nicholas. Olivia is Nicholas's sister, and Victoria is Aiden's sister. Their families are best friends- they even moved here together about a year ago."

I tried to look at Savanna, but my eyes wouldn't let me.

Savanna continued, "I had no idea they were in high school. The man-cub and Victoria are single, they're just friends. Good luck trying to take a bite out of that. They only keep to themselves- they're stuck up and boring, both."

"How do you know that? Have you tried to get to know them?" I questioned her to see if the report she was giving was genuinely unbiased.

"Well, no...." she paused, "But if you haven't noticed, they are totally to themselves. And they're very intimidatingly perfect." Savanna said this like it was the most obvious thing on the planet.

"Savanna, what a snob you are. You have assumed their characters before getting to know them?" I said this half-jokingly and in good spirit with a bright smile. She understood my humor immediately.

"Oh ha. ha, very funny, Vera," she said to tease back. I stood up from my seat with only my apple left to finish eating.

"Wait, where are you going?" Kevin asked.

I looked at them smugly. "Gotta be kidding me," I heard Oscar say beneath his breath. Savanna giggled at what I was about to do. I had a conversation point; I recognized the similarities they had with Peter and his family. Dark under eyes, abnormally pale, beautiful, graceful; they somehow looked the same- but not. There were too many similarities.

I walked over with my apple in hand, I reached their table and introduced myself.

"Hello, I'm new here, my name is Vera Bianchi." They all looked at me holding the most curious look I'd ever seen. Nicholas wasn't ogling necessarily, but he held a look of total attraction to me. He was excited I came to his table. "This is a bit of a long stretch and a little random. But I live in Italy for six months of the year, and there's a family there who resembles you quite thoroughly, do you know the Marcus Canali family? All their faces showed a quick glance of fear but settled immediately.

"Well yes, we do," Victoria spoke in a smooth, feminine, and enchanting voice. Their smell hit me suddenly like a pheromone; it was sweet and sexy. My brain started doing flips, but I was focused and composed.

"Are you related to them?"

They searched my question as though trying to figure out if there was an alternative meaning behind it. "I suppose you could say that," answered Aiden, "Quite distant though."

They were all stiff wondering how and why I knew them. The Canali family was like my family because they involved themselves in very illegal activities. I sensed the tension and added after a long pause:

"That's too bad. I'm sorry to hear that." I smiled to help ease the tension. I said that in hopes they wouldn't think I was someone who condoned their actions. "They're a little," I bent my nose to the side indicating their crooked ways. They all laughed completely amused, Nicholas grinned and leaned back folding his arms studying me with his eyes flirtatiously.

His table all looked at him with amazement. It wasn't weird, just different. I turned to leave but stopped in my tracks, turning back I looked at Victoria.

"Oh and Victoria, your Gianni Versace looks good on you. Which is quite the compliment given their… Specific cuts. I haven't met anyone who could truly pull it off."

Victoria was elated, "You know fashion?!"

"Yes, I might have to steal you away for a weekend or two to help me buy a new wardrobe for this climate." I took a bite of my apple.

"It would be my pleasure!" She spoke as though she was on cloud 9.

"Great, I have a passport if needs be. Just let me know when you're available."

"I sure will! It was so nice meeting you, Vera!"

I nodded and took another bite of my apple. The students were starting to file out for class. I went back to my table looking at them confidently, they all had to pick their jaws off the floor.

Savannah smiled, "Well, now I know why the Butler-King clan came out of hiding."

I shook my head, "Did I tell you Nicholas rescued me from drunken football players with grabby hands on Saturday?"

She gasped lightly, "No, you didn't!"

"Another story for another time, it's time to get to class."

Savanna grunted, and Kevin tagged along with me as usual.

On my way out of the cafeteria, Kirby stopped me by the garbage can. "Hey Vera," he said more confidently than he should've, given the circumstances and all.

I had a monotone, "Kirby, what do you want?"

Kirby reached for my hand, "Awe come on, don't be like that."

I yanked my hand away and scowled at him, Kevin seemed to be mentally preparing himself for mortal combat.

Kirby continued, "You can't hold us to anything on Saturday." He laughed and flung his arms out, "We were drunk for heaven's sake."

My face told him everything I thought about that statement. "On the contrary, I think you and Ethan showed some true colors. Don't talk to me, Kirby." I was cool and collected, something Papa always told me was: 'don't raise your voice, improve your argument.'

I turned to leave, and Kirby pulled my elbow, "So you wanna play it that way, huh? You're being a stuck up brat."

I huffed, "Who knows what you would've done if Nicholas hadn't stopped you."

He fumed, "You're over exaggerating the situation. I guess that's typical of someone like you. I'll tell the whole school you're a lying brat, and who do you think they'll believe hmm? You, or me?" His face was triumphant and cocky.

"I don't much care what the populous thinks of me, Kirby. I'm more concerned with my character than my reputation. That's something you need to do better at." His face was downturned and splotched red in anger.

I turned again to leave with the upper hand. I thought about how if I were in real danger, Kevin would not be the person I'd choose to stand by. He was fickle.

Kevin talked a good talk, "If he tried anything I would've punched his face in." He put his hands up with only his index fingers pointed out. "Guys like him make me so mad!"

I laughed, "I doubt he would be dumb enough to try anything in school."

Kevin kept perseverating on the subject.

I randomly looked behind me, and I saw Olivia behind us, it was silly, but something told me she was following us.

When I finished my class, Aiden was casually picking through a book in the hall. The feeling hit me again; 'you're being followed'. I shrugged it off and went to my last class; Math.

At the end of my day, I couldn't help but feel like I was being watched. I took another look around, and I saw more than just the school, about 15 guys, and three girls were staring at me in the parking lot. I hoped this would be something that would change with time. I got into Matt's car, and on the way out I saw Victoria watching me inconspicuously behind a tree. My feelings told me this is who my instincts were warning me about. I felt silly and ignored these 'untrue' feelings. Matt took me home, and I made dinner.

"How was school?" Matt asked shoveling my healthy food into his mouth.

"It was good, I made some new friends, Victoria and Nicholas."

"Victoria… King?"

"I don't know her last name, but she's Aiden's sister."

"Oh, she's a Butler, their friend's name is King- Nicholas and Olivia King I think. They're very wealthy people; they own a lot of real estate and businesses around here. The family friends are partners, good people- very nice and considerate."

"I like them, but I have to admit there's something different about them."

"You can say that again! They're loaded, but Mr. Butler still works like a normal person down at the police department occasionally."

"Well, I think that's admirable! I know I wouldn't want to be bored all day."

Matt chuckled like he was living with a crazy person. Retirement just meant more sports and poker for Matt, and the more, the merrier.

...

It was great seeing Nicholas the next morning, "Good morning, Vera."

I walked up to him slowly trying to gain composure, the way he said my name gave me butterflies in my stomach. 'Good morning, Nick. How was your night?"

"One of the best I've had thanks for asking. And yours?"

"Yeah, why is that? Mine was great, kind of boring, but that's okay."

Nicholas smiled to himself, and Olivia passed us in the hallway. She looked at me gratefully and stared at Nicholas taking in all of his happiness. "I'm not going to tell you what I did, but I hope to help you with your disenchanted life soon."

I smiled but in my head, I worried he was with a woman, people don't usually speak like that unless they made it to second base. The worry on my face was apparent, I hated that I was being clingy.

"Nick, are you dating anyone right now?"

"No, but I'd like to be." He left me on that cliffhanger when the teacher started class. I had forgotten all about our little conversation by the time the lecture ended.

Lunch was the same as yesterday. I sat with Savanna and her friends. I saw from the corner of my eye a little freshman; she looked tired and sad. She was just a little thing eating her pb&j. She still looked hungry when she finished eating. Sitting next to her was a boy in overalls, dirty and small as well, he also only ate one PB&J. I was concerned, and pity took over.

I walked across the cafeteria- all eyes on me. I wasn't sure what I was going to do. By a stroke of luck, the little girl dropped her books on the floor when I got there; I stooped down and helped her pick them up.

"Hello, I'm Vera."

She looked at me surprised, and she took her time answering me. "Stephanie." Her voice was higher pitched but quiet and timid.

"Is this your brother?"

"Ya, Jason."

"Well, it's very nice to meet you two." I sat down by Stephanie "You know, I'm new in town, and I'm looking to make new friends. Can I invite you and your family to my house for dinner this week?"

Stephanie looked up at her brother, he had a morose demeanor and looked like he'd seen too much in his short life. Stephanie looked back at me, "Umm sure."

"Well good, I'll see you tomorrow, and I'll let you know which day." I smiled and left, walking myself to my next class.

I was contemplative trying to figure out how to naturally give them free massive lunches for the rest of the school year. Nicholas caught up to me breaking my trance.

"Vera."

I jumped startled, "Ha you scared me." I smiled and grabbed his arm laughing, "You should be careful, I get startled easily."

He looked down at his arm and smiled, "Oh I apologize, I just wanted to ask you what you were talking about with the Reed's."

"The Reed's?" I asked confused.

"Yes, Stephanie and Jason." He added patiently.

"Oh, well we were discussing some dinner plans later this week."

"Do you know them from somewhere?"

"No, but dinner is a perfect way to get to know someone. It allows for conversation."

"Why them?" The way he asked this wasn't rude in any way, it was genuine curiosity.

"They fascinate me," my poor lie showed through.

"Really, Vera, why the Reeds?" He paused his walking making me stop too.

I turned to him and said, "Alright, but you have to promise me you won't tell a soul. You swear?"

"Yes," he said with complete sincerity.

I exhaled, "They look hungry, and I want to help. Maybe you can help me figure out a way to feed them free lunches for the rest of the school year."

His face lit up, and his eyes twinkled, "I'll start scheming and let you know what I come up with."

I smiled, "We'll be partners in crime."

He smiled, "Partners."

In class I could've sworn I saw him smell the sleeve I had touched in the hall, but it could've been something else.

It was exciting sitting next to him, something about him made me want him very badly. It took all my self-control not to look at him for the whole class and the class after that one. We walked to the parking lot together.

"Can I take you home?" He asked pleasantly.

"Oh no thank you, Matt should be coming soon." I smiled but secretly wanted to say yes.

"Well another time then." He walked away and looked over his shoulder with a half grin.

Matt was there soon after and waved at me.

"Matt, can I have the Reed's over for dinner this week?" I asked getting into the car.

"Of course, but why though?" his face scrunched up when he asked this.

"They're nice kids." I couldn't believe how introverted Matt was.

"Okay, well their parents are scary people. He's the town drunk, and she works all day and is cranky the rest of the time. I don't expect we'll have the absolute most fun night."

I smiled at his pessimism, "How does Friday sound?"

"Don't you have some teenage stuff to do Friday night?" He asked hoping to get out of the dinner.

"This is far more important, I'm on a mission."

He laughed and rolled his eyes, "Ohhh, that explains everything. Alright, I'll play along and be the most gracious host you've ever seen."

"Oh good, cuz you have to wear a tux," I said in a smooth, no joking tone.

"WHA- Oh, gosh kid you'll be the death of me someday. I could've swerved off the road in the shock. Or worse, we could've crashed because I had a heart attack. Then we'd both be dead!"

I just laughed.

In an old, frail voice he continued, "Or even worse…you glued 20 years to my 40 years of life…" He smacked his lips like an old man.

I was belly rolling in laughter, he sounded like Dick Van Dyke. "Matt, I'm joking, but if you make that voice again, I might have to make you wear a tux after-all, you could be the God-Father all night."

…

Upon nightfall I got the feeling once again I was being watched I shook it off so I could sleep. Maybe there was some animal next to the house…?

The next day was different, the sun was shining, and there wasn't a cloud in the sky- my mood was turned up on the happy dial. I rushed to get outside and soak up the sun. I took my motorcycle to school since it was so beautifully sunny. When I got to school, I saw Kevin on the lawn. He jumped up and ran to greet me.

"Vera!"

"Hey, Kev, how are you?"

Kevin started taking me to the side of the building where no one else was at this hour. "Good, well, umm…" He played with the outside of his ear and squinted his eyes. "I uh, just wanted to ask you a question. I kinda like you, and I wondered if you liked me back." Kevin asked this quickly as though he would waste any more time wanting to say it.

"Oh," his direct question took me off guard. "I think you're a great friend, but I only like you as a friend."

"Right, I'm… Sorry I brought it up." He looked rejected. I felt awful, I didn't know what to say to make him feel better.

"No worries," I tried to shake off the awkwardness, "So are you going to watch the big game tonight?" I thought to myself 'no, worries' humph I'm already starting to talk like Owen.'

He was still sulking, "Umm yeah, probably."

We walked ourselves to the clearing, and I saw Nicholas laughing, at what I wasn't sure. But he looked at Kevin like it was him he was laughing at. I rolled my eyes and walked myself to class saying an enthusiastic, "see you later" to Kevin.

Nicholas somehow caught up to me and grabbed my arm to turn me around.

"Hey, you."

His hand was cold, I looked at his hand and grabbed it without thinking. "Jeez Nick, your hands are freezing."

He looked at his hand seriously and let me go immediately. His hands were lightly shaking, and he left sooner than he arrived. I was dazed in confusion; he brought his hands to his face from what I could tell as he walked away. Did he smell his hand?

I felt weird and rejected in some strange way. He made it to class right on time and didn't look at me, it seemed like he was keeping his distance or something.

After history, he walked me to my next class. He calmly apologized for earlier and started a new conversation.

"Where did you go to school before this?"

"A private school in France and Italy."

"A private school eh?" Nicholas asked. I regretted admitting that the moment it came out.

"Yes," I answered honestly, instead of pretending to be normal like everyone else. "And yet math still kicks my butt." I smiled trying to make sure my going to a private school wouldn't be made a big deal of.

"You don't like public school," He inferred.

"Oh no, I do. It's much better than private school. People in places like that are pretentious, and generally far too unkind to everyone they feel is below them."

"So you fell below the popular line?"

"No, quite the opposite actually."

"I should've guessed that." He mused.

"So Arcata is not a difficult place for you to live," he asked with slight confusion.

"You have no idea," I smiled.

He looked fascinated by what I said, perhaps he assumed I was stuck up when he first saw me? A lot of people make that mistake. "Why did you come here?"

I was surprised he asked it to me so.... Directly, like he was digging for a truth that wasn't there. "It's... A very long story."

He looked at me intensely, "Please, tell me." His iris's dilated and constricted in the same moment.

I was distracted and asked, "How did you do that with your eyes?"

He was stupefied, "What?" He looked like a mixture of perturbed and petrified.

"Never mind, sorry." I paused for a long moment, and then made the error of spilling my guts. "My Papa is mixed up with shady dealings, and that is not the life I want for myself."

Nicholas recovered himself, "I have to admit I looked into your family after you mentioned the Canali's." He was suddenly sympathetic, "I wondered a little about you. I hope you don't mind?"

"Not at all, just as long as the whole town doesn't find out, I don't care." My voice sounded distant.

"You don't want people knowing where you came from, even if it would give you more prestige?" Nicholas surmised his tone was very kind.

"No, like I said, I want something different from the life my Papa chose. I'm afraid that if people knew me, the real me, I could never be free from it."

"Why now, why did you suddenly choose to leave it now?"

It felt like he was questioning something of my integrity, it made no sense.

"The longer you're in a place like that, the longer you're doomed to it. Besides," I said too quiet for anyone to hear, "It was getting unsafe for me." I looked down at the floor.

His face looked concerned but cleared in an instant, "Do you have family members other than your Papa?" He asked.

"Yes, I have a sister, Baye, she's 18. My Mama passed away when I was 12. But you know how it is, you have surrogate family members." I said this to lighten what I'd just said.

"So is Baye stuck in the life you despise?" He asked.

I looked at him showing the pain my answer brought me; I wished I wasn't so transparent. "Yes. I tried to get her to leave and escape with me, but she enjoys the lifestyle too much. The consequences are unrecognizable to her for now."

He squinted his eyes, "I think I am beginning to understand, but maybe you should continue."

I sighed. I was mad at myself for explaining this to Nicholas. "She doesn't care what happens to her, she enjoys the attention, the money, the status." My voice was glum by the time I finished. You could hear the guilt in my voice.

"Do you blame yourself for her," he continued asking.

"No, well I try not to. I understand it was--is her choice, not mine to make. But even still how responsible is she for the choice she was primed to make?" I challenged.

"That doesn't seem fair." He shrugged, but his eyes were still intense.

I sighed heavier, "No it isn't. But I have to accept the fact that we have all been given our different burdens to bear, I've decided I can't control what happens to me necessarily-or those I love- but I can control what I do with it and what my attitude is."

"Have I ever met you before Vera?" He asked this energetically but composed. His tone didn't seem to flow with the seriousness of the conversation, he was excited.

"Oh, I'm sure I would have remembered your face, though I'm astounded at how easy it is to talk to you. I've spilled my guts to you in our first real discussion. I shouldn't have." I insisted, wondering why he was staring at me the way he was.

His gaze became coquettish. "I know for sure I would have remembered you. You fascinate me, Vera," he said slowly. "You are nothing like you'd seem to be at face value. And I like it; I've never met anyone quite like you before."

I hadn't realized with the intense study his eyes had on me that he had walked me to the edge of the hallway. That is until I bumped into the lockers. The hall was empty, everyone else was in class. We looked at each other knowing what the other wanted. He took my breath away in every sense of the word-the way he smelled overtook me, and it seemed mutual. He put one hand on the locker next to me and leaned in. He exhaled an icy, sweet, intoxicating, breath looking down at me. He lowered his face to my level, just inches away from me.

"Errr-hem." We heard next to us. It was the Janitor, he beamed at his thwart.

I smiled, "Ah Steven, just the man I wanted to see." My heart was still racing, and Nicholas's hands were lightly shaking again. I stepped toward Steven.

"When does the school open in the morning?"

He scratched his head and adjusted his ball cap. "I think about 4:30 or som'in like'yat."

"Can I come here and borrow the gym?" Even though it was a small school, it still had a barre with mirrors and a sound system so I could dance comfortably here.

"I don't see why not." He said shrugging his shoulders and picking his teeth with his fingernail.

"Great, thank you." I turned and nodded for Nicholas to follow me. My day flew by, maybe it was because being around Nicholas was both the most natural thing, and the hardest. I loved it too much.

During lunch, I changed my mind and made the Reed's dinner party land on Thursday, just in case my Friday actually did need to be freed up.

…

The next morning was even colder than the normally Antarctic mornings. I nearly skipped my workout, but then talked myself into it by promising myself a hot shower when I finished. School was something I had always looked forward to, but now it was something I lived for. And I knew why I suddenly had more pip in my step.

I saw Nicholas waiting for me outside history. "Hey Vera." He said peacefully smiling with crinkled eyes.

"Nick, how are you today?" I asked happily.

"Wonderful, I was hoping I could convince you to sit at my table today. Victoria was hoping to talk to you about a shopping trip soon."

"I'd love to," I said this as excitedly as I would have to any other person who asked me to join their group. But inside I was especially delighted to be with them. I really needed more clothes, and I really liked Nicholas.

...

At lunch, as I passed Stephanie's table, we fist bumped, it was our thing, and I loved it because I loved her.

"Hey everyone," I said. They all greeted me back happily, and Olivia looked at Nicholas especially jovial.

"So what are you doing this weekend Vera?" Asked Victoria.

"I don't think I have anything planned."

"Excellent, I will pick you up at your house Saturday morning at 9 o'clock for some shopping. Is that okay with you?" Victoria continued, "We're going to San Francisco. I feel like you're a human pop sickle every time I see you. The sooner we shop, the better!"

I laughed, "I feel like a human pop sickle. That works for me, of course, I'll have to ask Matt first."

"Oh, well of course!" Victoria's vocals sounded like creamy hot chocolate.

"Victoria," I started, "You have a lovely voice, do you sing?"

Aiden laughed, "She tries to."

Victoria laughed along and smacked him in the arm. "At least I don't get smothered by Nicholas in chess- like you do," she teased back.

Aiden made a pained face, "I can't argue that." Olivia laughed at that as though she won something from the brawl.

I had just finished my quinoa blueberry salad when I turned to Nicholas surprised, "you play chess?"

"A little," he started.

"Oh no you don't, you play chess a lot, and you're way too good at it." Poked Aiden.

"If I told the truth the chess club would be breaking down our door," Nicholas said smugly.

I laughed, "Hah how about a game with me?"

The whole table became really excited, I didn't understand why they thought I was going to be that great of an opponent to Nicholas. They had no way of knowing that I had a ton of experience and training. It was one of the only things Papa and I did with each other.

"Someone needs to pop that big head of his," Victoria gleamed.

"What makes you think she'll win?" Nicholas teased looking part of the time at Victoria and the other at me.

"Okay, tomorrow, here during lunch. I'll take you down, King." I pointed at him and said, "I hope you're prepared to beg for mercy."

Nicholas's face was the happiest I'd ever seen a face be. "You're on, it's only interesting if we have a wager though." He bit his lip hoping I'd let us gamble, It seemed like he already had something in mind.

"I couldn't agree with you more," I started, "What's the bet?" My face was cocky, all I knew was that Nicholas was talented, but that I was better; so I wanted the wager to be decent.

"One indisputable favor." He said staring into my eyes.

I loved it, how perfect was this going to be. "It's a bet." I got up from the table and held out my hand for him to shake on it. He reluctantly held out his hand probably worried about how cold it was. I smacked his hand hard and firm in the shake pretending the freezing hand didn't send chills up my spine. I couldn't have been entirely sure that was from his temperature though.

"I'll bring the board," Nicholas said. I didn't say anything; instead, I nodded and walked away from his table to the trash can. I could barely contain my excitement. Nicholas didn't walk me to class. I waited eagerly for him to come into the room. He eventually came, apparently in no rush.

Mr. Payne started the minute Nicholas sat down. There were no critical things that happened for the rest of the day. Savannah caught up to me and asked me all about lunch and why I was sitting with the Butlers and King's. I should've known she'd tell the whole school about our little-waged battle the next day, but I wasn't thinking; I wouldn't have considered it a big deal, it's only chess.

...

I could barely sleep that night, the excitement was too much to bear. I had watched a million chess videos I rented to prepare myself for the coming day. When Matt asked why we were watching chess, I told him of the following challenge. He approved wholeheartedly and even gave me a few pointers.

That morning drug on slowly and Kevin's flirtations didn't help my impatience. When lunch period came the news was buzzing; apparently, this was going to be a show. I d guess it was only popular because prominent people we're playing.

"I had no idea there would be a crowd," Nicholas said looking around.

"Scared?" I teased.

"Ha in your dreams Ver!" That was the first time he'd called me that- I liked it a lot. I had to give myself a pep talk to concentrate while he set up the board. 'Don't look into his eyes and don't even speak so he'd keep his creamy voice to himself.' People's chatters distracted me for a moment, but I refocused. 'you're going to crush him, you're going to win,' I continued my pep talk until it was time to play.

"I'm betting on Vera," Victoria said. Nicholas looked un-phased.

The game began- and ended fast. I had quite a few tricks up my sleeve; the game only lasted about 35 minutes.

"Queen to h4," I said in the last stroke of battle. "Checkmate," I looked up at him as my queen took her position. He looked like he might go into shock. He put his hand to his face with his index figure covering his perfect lips.

"You win," he said raising his eyebrows.

I started clapping "Nicholas King ladies and gentleman." The whole ensemble began clapping. You could hear voices in the background, I could pick out Oscar's, "Did you see that" "Is that move legal," "Write that down," "We need her on our team." I chuckled at the chit-chat.

Aiden grabbed me and gave me a huge hug, "I knew someone, someday would beat the snot out of him. Way to go Vera!"

"Aiden… I … Can't… breathe…" Nicholas flinched and glanced at him with a death glare.

"Oh jeez, I'm so sorry!" He let go of me immediately.

I smiled and laughed after I caught my breath he had knocked out. "Aiden you're like a freaking bear," I shoved him with all my might but didn't budge him at all; Olivia thought that was particularly funny. It was interesting to me how Aiden was just as cold as Nicholas.

I glanced at Nicholas- he was staring at me. "So," he began, looking as attractive as ever, "What do you want?" he pulled his hands to his chest resting his elbows on the arms of his chair and interlaced his fingers while leaning back.

I paused a moment, "I'll let you know when I've decided," then I took a bite out of my apple; I winked at him and walked to the garbage can. I took a look over my shoulder to see Nicholas's jaw to the side, pressing his lips together nodding. His eyes were scrunched a little as he stared me down. I also didn't break my gaze until I was out of the cafeteria.

I wanted him to dote on me and to wonder what it was I was going to make him do.

In Philosophy a boy named Theodor approached my table, his voice was breathy, and he exhaled a lot with a slight shake. He was very nervous, I felt awful for him; he was a member of the chess club.

"Ummm he-hey Vera," he stammered and cleared his throat. "I watched the game in the cafeteria, and umm, I think you're really good at chess; do- do you want to join the chess club?" At this moment Nicholas came in, he saw my predicament and smiled that Perfect smile I loved, he started walking slower to buy his time.

"You know Theodor, I'm a little busy right now with all my extra-curricular activities, but a little birdie told me that Nicholas King was hoping you guys would break his door down to ask him to join your chess club." I saw from the corner of my eye Nicholas retreating to the hallway. "And I have to give you a little tip, Nicholas likes to play hard to get. So don't take no for an answer."

"Oh, really? Well, I might have to hunt him down then. Thanks," Theodor said looking around for Nicholas.

By some 'miracle', Nicholas came in exactly when Mr. Payne did.

I was proud of myself for my victory and latest joke; the confidence was coming off my face. I slowly turned my head to Nicholas to gloat my prank.

He looked at me completely serious.

I whispered, "Oh are you a bad loser, Nick?"

He just shook his head.

I chuckled breaths "Or is it my volunteering you to the chess club?"

He looked at me straight this time with raised eyebrows.

"Oh, I see, ha Victoria is going to love this." I was beaming, I put my hand on his arm and pulled a fake face of sincerity. "Oh Nicholas, how can I ever make it up to you?!"

He couldn't help but crack a grin and breathed a laugh, then after a long pause, he looked at me with a look that was truly sincere. He stared at me with piercing eyes that smoldered, his lips opened slightly like he wanted to say something- or do something. Then he breathed out a sigh, never breaking our eye lock.

'Wow,' I thought to myself, 'I wonder what his indisputable favor would have been.'

Mr. Payne paused his lecture which caught my attention, it turned out he was just shuffling through some papers. I looked back at Nicholas, but he wasn't looking at me anymore his eyes were off in the distance, his hands lightly shaking. I thought about Peter and how similar they were.

When I got home, I realized I had forgotten to ask Matt if I could go to San Francisco with Victoria on Saturday. The exhilaration of the chess game had me too hyped up to remember. I decided I'd ask him during dinner.

I had dinner almost ready when Matt got home, we had chicken fajita filling wrapped in lettuce. Matt was excited to eat when I called him in until he saw the romaine lettuce wraps on the table. He let out a sigh of disappointment and patted his stomach like he was saying goodbye to his beer and bacon belly.

"I'm going to order pizza tonight," he said as he sat down to eat.

"That's just fine Matt," I said laughing.

He was on his thirds when I asked him if I could go this weekend to San Francisco with Victoria.

"Oh, yeah sure," He paused to take another bite, "Victoria Butler, right?" He asked with his mouth full.

"The one and only."

"I like her, she's a nice gal." He took another bite, "This is great stuff Vera, you should make it more often."

"Haha, you've got it, Matt." Matt always somehow beat me eating, even though he ate at least three times more than I did. I ran upstairs to give Victoria a call after putting my plate away.

"Hey, Victoria it's Vera."

"Vera, how are you! You know- you are my favorite person right now."

"Oh yeah, why is that?"

"Theodor came by today to ask Nicholas if he wanted to join the chess club." Victoria was laughing so hard she could barely speak " Ni-Nicholas turned him down, but Theodor said 'I will not take no for an answer.' Ha-ha-ha- Nicholas was shocked, and that must've startled Theodor because he retreated a little and said, "Vera told me you like to play hard to get." Ha-ha-ha, "Is that the case here?""

I could hear laughter in the background like I was on speaker phone. I threw myself on the bed laughing so hard my stomach hurt. "What I wouldn't have paid to see that!"

"You're in luck," I could hear her catching her breath, "Emma, my Mom, filmed it!"

"No, sir! When can I watch it?"

I heard a male voice speaking loudly so I could hear, "Never, thank you very much." I heard his voice was closer now as though he took the phone, "Oh and Vera, sweetheart, let's get one thing straight-- I am hard to get."

"Ohhhhhh okay, tough guy." I started laughing again, "Oh man, I got you good. Put Victoria back on I need to talk to her."

A female voice sounded again, "So are we set for this weekend?"

"We are I just asked Matt." I could tell I was still on speaker phone, "Maybe I should get Theodor some I'm sorry flowers. Poor kid didn't stand a chance."

Nicholas yelled again, "And it's all your fault."

"Oh yeah, maybe I should make my indisputable favor you joining the chess club. Just to make it up to Theo."

Laughter split my ear on the phone; there was clearly a crowd of people. I tried counting how many people lived there, 8 total?

"Don't I beg of you Vera, spare me, please?"

"I'll consider it." I hung up the phone to leave him sitting right where I wanted him-- thinking about me.

It was sunny outside, and I had a hankering to ride my motorcycle. I called Owen feeling on top of the world. I asked him if he wanted to go riding with me. I had to sneak out since I didn't have my driver's license yet.

Owen picked me up at my house. I figured the rumble from his bike would dissipate the sound of mine starting, which worked like a charm. I was dressed in black leather.

He took me to a secluded spot on a trail in the mountains. While my bike was a road bike, the path was luckily smooth enough to get up. The sight was to die for; Humboldt California had gorgeous cliff ranges full of trees and clear water.

"Owen, it's beautiful up here," I said as I pulled my helmet off.

Owen took his helmet off and smiled, "This is the spot I go when I want to be alone-though I'm usually on foot."

We sat on the ground dangling our feet off a drop-off.

I was getting bored of the silence, so I started some small talk, "How's school going?"

"It's great, I love going to college. The people there are more to themselves and care about making good lives for themselves. Plus I like not having school all day!" He threw a couple rocks off the ledge. "You know, you're tan enough to pass as a Native, I could smuggle you into my old school with the rest of my friends if you want?" He was almost hopeful sounding.

"Nah, I've already settled in my school. So I'm cool then eh?"

He smiled, "Yeah, yeah. Don't let it get to your head though." He looked at me sideways and flirtatiously.

"Too late," I smirked.

"I'd love it if you got to know my friends, and you'd be closer to my house."

"I want to meet your friends for sure. But I don't think I want to change schools now. Thank you though!"

The sun was going down, and I was getting cold. The ride took a long time, so we didn't have much time to talk. The quality time was spent riding together.

I snuck my bike next to the garage and covered it, and my helmet with a tarp. I waved and smiled at Owen while he watched me get inside my house.

I was thinking about Nicholas while I got ready for bed. I couldn't help but jump in my bed like a giddy little girl.

Chapter Four: My Biggest Mistake Yet

The next morning I secretly drove to the school and danced ballet in addition to running on a treadmill they had there. I was a good ballet dancer, my lines were always straight, and toes pointed. My long legs accentuated my movements, and my toned body emphasized the beauty of my dances.

Mid-dance I paused with the same eerie feeling that someone was watching me. I saw a shadow pass through the hall and it startled me.

I froze momentarily calming my terrified heart. Before I finished calming down, I chased after the figure. My heart was thudding as I rounded corners and slowly crept through the half-lit halls. I saw a door closing quietly that went to an unknown room. I wasn't sure where I was, or what I was doing. I should've turned around; this I knew but ignored it.

I took a breath and walked in. I saw a lot of tables with white curtains surrounding them, I turned on the light to see they were displays for the robotics competition. Suddenly Oscar popped his head around one of the curtains. I breathed light again.

"Oh Oscar, it's just you."

"Yeah, we all have to come here early to set up," he said checking me out. "Nice outfit!"

I was wearing a sports bra and leggings with ballet socks that went just above my knees. I ignored his complement after looking down at what I was wearing. "How long have you been here? I felt like someone was watching me."

"Maybe like 1 minute," he said with total honesty.

"Oh. Well, good luck with your competition." I waved and pasted on a smile walking away.

In the next classroom, Nicholas hid himself as he was slowly but surely falling in love with a certain ballerina.

I resumed my workout to completion knowing my paranoia was going to get the best of me. Nicholas wasn't at school today- I didn't understand why I was as disappointed as I was.

After Matt picked me up I immediately started on a feast; Lasagna, salad, breadsticks, mashed potatoes, gravy, buttered vegetables, and brownies. I wanted the Reed's to eat exceptionally well.

Matt was elated and kept coming into the kitchen to see when it would be ready. "You can invite everyone over, every day, for the rest of eternity if we're going to eat like this!"

I laughed, "Well I hope you know we're sending all the leftovers home with them."

He looked at me like I had killed his puppy, "This is cruel. You wouldn't...."

"They're starving kids Matt, they need it far more than we do."

"Oh, that's the mission huh? Well, I can't say I disagree with you. But I'm still going to pout."

I laughed as he left the kitchen. A half an hour later there was a knock on the door, it was our designated guests. Matt let them in and led them to the kitchen/dining room.

"Hello, all!" I said as they filed in. Stephanie fist bumped me, and I gave her a hug in response. Jason walked straight to the table following his nose. Their parents were also not very sociable, they tried, but it wasn't part of who they were. Mr. Reed looked precisely like a drunk would- liver spots, yellowed skin, big belly, and a bad smell.

Mrs. Reed was as skinny as Stephanie, with blonde hair done up in a bun, and a sad looking demur like her son. It wasn't hard to guess to whom the burden of Mr. Reed's actions fell onto. It pissed me off royally, but I sucked it up to make an enjoyable evening. And I sucked it up because everyone jumped at his every request, typical of an abusive home. So if I wanted to gain trust, was going to have to make myself as pleasant as possible.

The evening went off without a hitch. For once I was thankful for Matt's appetite, the more he helped himself, the more comfortable our guests felt to take multiple helpings. I insisted they take the food with them, and they made no real argument either. I was glad to be of some small help.

My plan worked, and Mr. Reed liked me a lot. I was welcome anytime to his house, and his family was welcome anytime to mine.

After the goodbyes, Matt looked down at the floor and said. "I wonder if there's anything else we can do for them."

"Well, I'm trying to figure out how to give the kids free lunches at school without it being conspicuous."

Matt thought for a minute and said, "The city has a few programs for low-income families like them. I think I'll make a special recommendation. I really like that Jason kid, maybe I'll take him fishing with me sometime."

I practically yelled my response, "Yes, you should! You should see him at school, Matt. He's so sad and burdened. Promise me you'll take him fishing with you?!"

Matt knew what I was talking about, Jason already had depression wrinkles, and he was only a teenager. "I promise. Oh by the way you got a letter from the DMV, I think it's your driver's license."

I flew to the miniature table next to Matt's favorite chair. After I sifted through a bunch of papers stacked unorderly, I saw my letter. Sure enough, I was free to drive legally.

…

Friday was a beautiful sunny day, and Nicholas met me at a new spot he declared to be our meeting place. It was under a large maple tree in the front of the school, it was plain but made beautiful by his presence.

 He was so handsome with the sun rays shining through the tree leaves and into his hair that lightened his light brown hair even more. The sun bounced off the grass and illuminated his big green eyes. He was leaning against the tree looking up at the leaves.

"Nick, beautiful day is it not?" I said walking up to him happily.

"Sure is, how did your little dinner party work out last night?" His eyes twinkled as though he already knew it was great. He looked like something heaven had sent my way.

"It was simply perfect, I sent enough food with them to feed an army for a week! And Matt figured out how to feed them free lunches." I smiled as we walked together to our first class.

"Of course it went well, I have a feeling you have the gift of poking your nose where it doesn't belong." He teased with eyes that smoldered.

"Hah espionage- I've never heard the one before. No, I'm afraid I'm the worst liar on planet earth. I couldn't even convince you my simple dinner party was harmless." I flirted.

He chuckled, "That is, perhaps, the truest thing I've heard all week." He smiled with all his might as if it was something he was worried about.

'Why would me being a spy, or something, worry him?' I wondered, 'Oh my gosh, first it's someone watching you, now it's thinking people are worried you're a spy. I'm losing my mind,' I thought to myself.

It was hard to focus all day, not only was it was Friday, but I had a shopping trip planned for tomorrow. Annnnnd, I was incredibly attracted to the man who I spent my days with.

Nicholas sensed my especially good mood, "Are you excited for tomorrow?" He asked already knowing he was right.

"Nicholas, I suspect I am going to have the best time of my life shopping with Victoria. On top of that, Matt's having another game night party on Sunday with some good friends of ours, the Multnomah's. And that's always a blast. So yes, I'm having a wonderful day thinking about it."

"You're friends with the Multnomah's?" He asked this confused and almost annoyed.

"Yes, do you know them?" I asked this with a hint of disbelief in my tone.

"How do you know them?" He pressed.

"Kit has been Matt's friend since the caveman days. They were actually the first people I met coming here besides Matt. They're really nice people."

"Yeah, nice." Nicholas squinted his eyes in frustration which was something I was befuddled about, but I didn't want his sour grapes to ruin my day.

After school I saw Savanna fiddling with some English homework, she looked stressed about it.

"Hey Savy, can I lend you a hand?"

"Oh, no you don't have to- I just hate English," She said shyly.

"Nonsense, the sun is still out, and I love Jane Austin, I'd be killing two birds with one stone!" I set my backpack down and started talking her through the questions.

I waved to Nicholas after I sat down with Savanna.

I hadn't realized how long it took us to finish the homework; it was 5:30 when I got to my car. On my way home I wondered what there was to do on a Friday night in Arcata, California.

There were Matt's car and a silver car parked outside the house. I didn't recognize the vehicle. After I got into the house, I dropped my backpack and yelled, "Sorry I'm late Matt, I was helping Savanna with her homework."

No one answered. I walked into the living room where I saw Stefan and Matt sitting, the feeling was tense for some reason. I ran to Stefan and threw my arms around him, kissing him on either cheek.

"Stefan, what a great surprise it's so nice to see you!"

He smiled and twirled me around in our hug. "Ver, I've come to take you home."

My face dropped, "What?"

"Oh it's just for the weekend, your Papa is throwing a giant party, and he wants you to be there." He was still smiling.

"Stefan I have school on Monday," I grappled at any excuse I could find. The thought of going back to another party had my stomach in knots. "And a shopping trip tomorrow." I finished.

"I'm sorry, but you have to come."

"Why, Papa holds parties all the time." I had walked my way to the couch to sit down. Matt took in my countenance which looked worried. Matt stiffened even more than he already was.

"Some guests have requested your presence." He said this with a tone of urgent force, as though I needed to drop it and go pack.

I was turned away from Stefan, I gulped, and I could feel my breathing getting heavier. I tried to think clearly- 'requested my specific presence, what could that mean? Has this ever happened before?'

My face was pale white, and my eyes were wide after I considered what it could ultimately mean. Matt stood up and moved between Stefan and me.

"I don't think she should go, this is way too short notice."

Stefan moved around Matt who he towered over. He grabbed my hand and pulled me up with a little more force than was necessary. "Vera, go pack- this is not up for debate."

Matt got upset by the sudden physical turn our conversation had. He looked livid.

I piped up immediately; there was no need for a fight to break out on my behalf- I was probably overreacting anyway. 'Okay, give me a minute," I changed my facial expression to look confident and determined for Matt's sake. I would have gone for happy, but there was no way I could pull it off.

Halfway up the staircase, Stefan yelled, "Oh and Vera make sure you're dressed in a dress, there's a welcome party for you when we step off the plane."

I rolled my eyes because I knew what that meant, 'wear something skimpy for you admirers.' It took me less than 20 minutes to load up my overnight bag. I didn't pack much because I was going for Saturday and Sunday ONLY. I'd made sure I'd have to be back by Sunday night. It took another 20 to redo my curls and put on more makeup, I wasn't too concerned with perfection because we'd get to Paris in about 14 hours. I'd have plenty of time to do more dolling later.

When I walked downstairs, Matt gawked and was unhappy with what wearing my 'dress' entailed. His face turned 5 shades of red, I wasn't sure he was breathing.

"Let's go," I said to Stefan. "Matt, I'll see you Sunday night, will you call Victoria and cancel my plans please," I asked keeping my determined face.

We had a red-eye flight for the Eureka to Paris route. By the time we landed, I was thoroughly exhausted. The 9-hour difference made it 5:30pm Paris time. We were greeted by my Papa, Baye, Petrov, and some friends of mine that I didn't actually consider 'real'. They only spent time with me for the reputation of being my besties- they didn't actually care about me.

"Baye!" I yelled and ran to her.

"Vera, oh it is so good to see you!" We embraced and kissed each other's cheeks.

I then went to my Papa and then my friends next, I wasn't going to acknowledge Petrov, but Papa made sure that greeting took place.

The sun was so nice, and I found myself missing Paris and Baye, I also missed Stefan a great deal-- he was the highlight of the trip by far.

The moment I got home I showered and packed a few more suitcases full of my autumn and winter clothes. I was fully prepared to leave the moment the party was over. I had one of our manservants take the suitcases to my Porsche.

I went outside for an hour to bask in the sun. Stefan was by my side, as usual, his presence was calming.

"Stefan, I've missed you like crazy," I said with my eyes still closed. Being all by myself these days was odd, I always had someone accompanying me growing up.

"Ha, so you haven't forgotten all about me eh?"

"Of course not!" I looked at him- his tone almost sounded serious, "That would be impossible."

 "Good, because I will never stop loving you." He stooped down and brushed my cheek with the back of his hand. It felt so good.

All I could do was smile and say, "Wanna join me cown here?"

"You know I wish I could," he said, finally light toned and happy.

My dress was already lying on my bed when I got inside. It was red and backless, the sleeves went down to my wrists, but it cut across my chest, there was no fabric on my shoulders. The dress was tight, and it came down mid-thigh. It was so unique; I hadn't seen a dress like this before.

My hair was curled and voluptuous, I had a smoky eye and well-contoured makeup style with long eyelashes. I even shocked myself when I took a final look in the mirror- I was beautiful. While I was happy and I felt gorgeous and confident, something was off, my heart warned me something terrible was coming. I didn't want to believe it-- I turned my intuition off as best as I could. I didn't want to think my Papa, the man who should love me the most would compromise me in any way.

I stepped out of my room and looked at Stefan. His eyes were bulging out of their sockets. He grabbed my shoulders and kissed me as though he could resist the temptation any longer than he already had that day. We kissed until we heard an 'eh-hem' behind us. I turned around to see Baye and her bodyguard; we were ready to go down together for the party.

We were announced as we descended the staircase, this was unusual, but of course, this was probably the biggest party we had ever thrown. My eyes spotted Peter first who naturally stood out from the crowd. He waited at the bottom of the stairs, as soon as we reached the base he asked me to dance. I was more than happy to- I now had some questions for the Canali mystery.

"Vera you look outstanding this evening," he said smiling.

"Thank you, Peter, you don't look so bad yourself," I teased.

"If you had told me you were looking for another home I'd have gladly taken you to mine in Italy." He looked at me over-confidently, "It's been boring without you here."

Strange, he said that quite seriously. "What, the girls are too easy for you here is that what it is? You need someone to kick you in the pants and tell you no every once and a while?"

He laughed heartily, "You know me so well, it's almost painful."

I laughed heartily too.

Peter continued, "Of course, when someone tells you no all the time when they finally say yes- it's the best thing imaginable." He said looking straight into my eyes piercingly.

I stared straight back into his, we had paused dancing lost in silence. "Your naked body should only belong to those who fall in love your naked soul," was all I could say. "And last I checked you're incapable of love." I joked trying to shake the heaviness of our conversation.

He pulled me close and said, "Well, I'll just have to try harder then," he moved my hair from my face. His eyes flickered to my lips, and it made his mouth part. He breathed in sharply and pushed me back slightly to start dancing with me again.

"To love me, or to lay with me?"

He chuckled, "To prove you wrong."

I looked into his eyes to try to gain the truth of his words. I couldn't tell, so all I said was, "I guess we'll have to see."

The dance ended and he bowed, I curtseyed. "How old are you Peter?"

"I'm 20," he said pleased I didn't want our conversation to end.

"For as long as I can remember, you have looked the same. Why is that?"

"I have good genetics."

"Why are you so cold all the time?"

He smiled and asked, "Why? Does it bother you? I can warm us both up to red hot, it can be fast, or we could take our time."

I ignored his innuendo. "No, I am just curious about you. There's something different that I can't quite put my finger on."

He cleared his throat and glanced to my side. I turned to see another suiter asking me to dance. This went on and on until Papa came up to me hours into the party.

"Vera, my beautiful daughter, it has been so nice to have you back."

"Oh Papa, it has been nice, it's so good to see everyone."

He whispered, "Your lipstick has smudged a bit on your cheek, why don't you go see to that in your bathroom?"

I was embarrassed, "Oh," I touched my cheek, "Thanks."

I started upstairs, and Stefan followed, something was wrong. Papa had never done this before, every cell in my body was growing cold-numb, the ones still alive were screaming at me to turn and run. I started thinking about it.... Should I run? My instincts told me, yes, but my heart told me no, I wanted Papa to be virtuous, ethical, and honorable. I stopped on the staircase and looked over to him, he was laughing with some of the guests. No, he is good. I overrode my intuition out of love and blind loyalty to the person I should be able to give it to.

I walked into my room, my brain was already beginning to turn off- it was weird- unnatural. After I finished fixing my lipstick, I heard my door shut, Petrov.

"What are you doing in here?! Get out!" I screamed.

"Be a good little girl and listen to your Papa," he said as he walked closer to me. I froze.

"You're not my Papa!" I said scrunching my face meanly.

"No, but who do you think sent me here? Shhhh....Quiet now, there's a party going on."

I finally unfroze but it was too late, he was only a few steps from me. *RUN* I heard myself say in my mind. I turned and ran toward my bathroom, it was in vain, I was in heels, and he was much faster than I was.

He grabbed my waist and turned me around. *FIGHT* I threw a punch in his direction and made contact, but it was in vain, I was no fighter. He struck me hard enough for me to almost black out, my eye started throbbing instantly.

He grabbed me from the floor. *SCREAM* I cried and yelled at the top of my lungs "Stefan, help!" But it was in vain, why wasn't he coming?! "STEF-" Petrov grabbed me by the throat and slammed me against the wall with the door right next to me, I kicked and punched the wall trying to alert Stefan. I heard light sobs on the other side and realized it was Stefan. I. Was. All. Alone. Petrov was still holding me up by my throat, I began getting dizzy, and I could taste blood. I was seeing black, I could feel my body going limp then hitting something hard. I had hit the floor and without even thinking I started gasping for air.

CRAWL I tried to crawl though I couldn't see yet. He k cked my side, and I could hear a crunch, this knocked my limited oxygen out of my lungs. I could feel my body being lifted from the floor. No matter how my body felt, my adrenaline refused to let me give up. I fought back in his arms as he walkec me to the bed, throwing me on it. My vision was starting to restore, and I saw handcuffs in his hands, 'if I can just prevent him from cuffing me he'll never get to me.'

DON'T GIVE UP I put my hands in fists, I had no idea how to fight. He must've known this by the way my fist was formed because he laughed. "Stefan!" I tried to yell, but my voice was completely hoarse.

"Go ahead, scream, no one can hear you," he gloated.

He lunged forward, and I decked him in the face; unfortunately, I couldn't hit very hard. I'd never hit anyone before, and the feeling was weird like my subconscious refused to hit a person with all my might. It still hurt him though because he lost his temper. He lunged forward again only this time with full force, his body crushed me as he put the cuff on one wrist. I pulled as hard as I could, and he was getting frustrated. He turned my body around, so my face was smothered in the bed, he twisted my arm around w th my body until it was backward, and I heard another crunch. I screamed out in pain- though no sound really came out. I didn't care how much it hurt I still didn't let him attach it to the bedpost. He punched my now injured shoulder a few times- my mind was stunned from the pain long enough for him to connect the cuffs to the bedpost.

My body was giving up on me, I hadn't slept well for over a day, and it must've been around midnight Paris time. I wasn't going to go down until every ounce of energy was spent in my defense. I struggled the same on the other side; his solution was to punch my bad ribs several times until he could easily attach the cuffs to the other bedpost.

I kicked him still, as hard as I could- and my legs were powerful. Their blunt force left him winded a few times before he was able to restrain my ankles on the footboard. The metal dug into my skin, it didn't help that it was too tight around my wrists and ankles, but I never stopped giving up.

A few hours later, and some punches and scratches later, he was finally finished. To make his signature on yet another victim (I suspected), he lit a cigarette and smoked it halfway, then put it out on my bicep like he was branding me.

I couldn't move, my mind and body wouldn't let me. He had been gone for over a half an hour when I could finally inch my body off the bed. I put on new clothes that covered me from neck to foot, though I couldn't hide the black eye starting to form.

I didn't want to leave in a way that I'd have to see anyone. I could hear the party still going on though it was around 3:30am. I was surprised my mind worked at all when I thought about the servants' exit. I had never been in there before; however, I did know that it lead to a separate entrance and exit. I could barely walk, but I made it down the stairs. It was narrow and moist, ill-lit, and it had nothing for me to lean my body weight on.

It was like a maze as well, I was lost until I heard Anna's voice in one of the hallways. She was talking to someone about hors-d'oeuvres. I limped to her voice, she took one look at me and dropped her serving platter. She ran to me picking me up from my bad side, I groaned hoarsely in pain.

"What happened to you?!"

"Anna, where's the exit?" I asked, but she couldn't hear or understand me.

I felt a cold hand on the small of my back, and ther Peter came around. He assessed my body and face with a look of horror.

"Who did this to you?! Peter asked angrily.

Anna said, "Sir you're not supposed to be back here." Then she looked down realizing the magnitude of what had just happened to me.

He ignored her and took me under my good arm, he started walking me to the exit. I leaned in and whispered in his ear, "Tell Anna goodbye please."

"Anna," he said looking at her, "She's telling you goodbye."

Anna ran in front of me crying, "Never come back." She was holding back sobs "I love you like my daughter, and I'll miss you with all my heart. Please, I'm begging you…. Don't come back."

I would've cried if I could've, but I was too wiped out to even walk. I passed out onto Peter's shoulder and collapsed. Peter pulled me into his arms and carried me like I was a baby. I fought the fatigue enough to stay awake, he walked me to the exit.

Once we were outside, he asked once again with more anger and force, "Who did this to you?!"

"Petrov."

"I'll deal with him later, you have my word that he'll never do this to anyone else again!"

"Take me to my car."

"Where are you going?"

"Home." I was surprised he could hear me, let alone understand what I was saying.

"Let me take you, please."

I would've customarily said no way because I wanted my new location to remain unknown to everyone, but I had no choice. I merely nodded to his request.

"Airport."

He was to my car faster than I thought possible- or maybe I was entirely out of it. We made it to the airport in record time, I slept the way there. Still fatigued I felt him gently shake me, I woke up feeling slightly better than before. He grabbed my luggage, and we went to the terminal to wait for my flight. He had bought himself a ticket on the way.

"United States, Eureka, California huh?"

"Ya." I leaned onto his shoulder, he opened his chest to me, and I snuggled into it as he put his arm around me. It took no time at all to fall back asleep. It felt like I was asleep for 5 minutes when he was waking me again. We walked onto the plane, and though I usually can't sleep at all on flights, I was out again for the entire ride to Eureka.

We landed in Eureka at 5:00 am Eureka time. I was feeling much better, I bought some food walking to the exit where a taxi car was waiting.

"This will be a long car ride if you want to go home now I completely understand."

"A drive? Ha, you made it so the KGB couldn't find you if they wanted to."

I laughed hoarsely.

"You're feeling better, that makes me happy." He said in his Italian accent.

"Yeah," my face dropped.

He watched me carefully and grabbed my hand, the cold felt so good I put his hand on my eye like a makeshift ice pack.

He laughed and said, "Well I'm glad to see every part of me be useful to you." He was incredibly handsome. "Vera- what happened to you?"

I shook my head like I refused to ever go there with anyone. He grabbed my hand with his free hand and started speaking when I shifted his Icey hand from my hand to my wrist. He looked dubiously then his eyes widened, and he asked: "Why is your wrist so hot?" Then took his hand off from my face and used it to pull my sleeve up to see black and purple bruises lining my wrist.

His face twisted, and then he composed himself. "How did he hurt you like this?"

I knew the man deserved to die, he was above the law. If I let him get away, he would just do it to another girl sometime, somewhere. "He beat and raped me."

If I thought Peter was pale before, I was mistaken. He was in shock.

 "Peter?"

"You won't have to worry about him anymore," he said again.

"Thank you," I knew I practically hired an assassin, but I didn't care.

We got into the taxi, and he sat next to me holding my wrist the whole time.

"Peter, how did you find me?"

"I don't want to say. You wouldn't believe me anyway."

"Try me," I insisted.

"I… Get nauseous if I smell blood, I had a feeling to follow the scent, and it lead to you."

"I was bleeding?"

"Yes," he lifted my pant leg, and sure enough I had scratched my shin on the narrow staircase. I could also feel the blood drying from Petrov's scratches.

"Oh, yeah I guess so. Well, either way, I'm thankful. Thank you, Peter, for everything."

"Call me if you need anything- I mean it."

"Okay," I said as I started putting my pant leg down he caught a glimpse of my ankle and pulled the sock down before I finished with my pants.

He just breathed in slowly and pursed his lips while adjusting his shoulders as if to try to shake it off physically.

We sat in silence until I laughed randomly at some guy who was worse off than I was- he was drunk and dressed quite well. But he was so hammered that he rummaged through the trash on the side of the road and found a half-eaten sandwich.

Peter looked at me like he never wanted to be apart from my laugh again even though it was hoarse. When we pulled into Matt's driveway it was 2:00pm, I had called Matt at the airport to let him know when I'd be home. When we pulled up I saw the Multnomah's car, I laughed beneath my breath wondering if Matt had called them for back up just in case Stefan was coming too.

"Well Peter, this is where I say goodbye. Thanks again for your help."

"I'll bring your luggage up." It wasn't up for commentary; he jumped out and grabbed my suitcases.

I paid the cab driver for my drive and for Peter's on the way back. I walked my way to the door, but I was so slow that

Peter beat me there. I was hunched over in pain from my ribs, as I reached for the handle I breathed in heavily a couple of times, straightened myself, and put on my mask of determination again- no pain traceable anywhere.

Chapter Five: Fighting For The Life I Want

I walked inside the house and Matt came running, "Vera," He smiled then looked at me more carefully. "What the hell happened to you?"

Apparently, my black eye had developed, "I got in a fight," I half-lied. "You should see the other guy," I winked.

I walked upstairs saying hi to the Multnomah's on the way up. Peter followed behind me with my bags, he dropped my stuff with a face of excitement- I couldn't figure why.

"You should introduce me to your friends." He was more elate than usual.

"Okay," I looked at him tentatively.

We walked downstairs and into the living room, "Owen, Kit, Matt, this is my friend Peter."

Once both Kit and Owen took a look at him from the T.V. screen, they nearly jumped out of their seats. Peter flashed a brilliantly white smile.

"Very nice to meet you all." He was cocky and stared down Kit, threateningly.

I sensed the odd drama that unfolded. "Well, I think you should be off Peter. Thanks again for your help."

Peter looked at me and bowed his head. I walked him to the door and closed it behind him.

I was already ready for bed, I headed upstairs to shower and unpack the winter clothes I had grabbed from my room in France. When I finished I brought my homework downstairs to do it with some company, I somehow felt alone.

I wore the only workout outfit I had that covered me from neck to foot.

"Oh good, so you do own some real clothes," Matt teased.

I was walking gingerly and slowly "Yep," I said as I sat down slowly.

"You okay, Vera," Owen asked.

"Oh yeah, I'm a little sore from all the traveling."

I was finished with my homework quickly because it was easy for me. We heard a knock on the door, I was alarmed and afraid it was Big Al-- or worse-- Stefan.

"Matt. Are you expecting anyone," I tried to sound calm, but I didn't do a good job.

"Yeah it should be the pizza guy," Matt said as he got up from his favorite chair.

I stared at the door with a face of concern; it felt like it took Matt hours to get to the door. When he opened it, I saw a pimple faced boy holding a few pizzas. I breathed deeply not realizing I had been holding my breath.

Owen looked at me like I was weird. I just turned and watched the screen emptily.

Matt came in with the pizzas, and I scarfed a few pieces down. This time Matt looked at me like I was a weirdo.

I went to bed early- around 7. Owen looked disappointed I opted to lie in my bed instead of his shoulder.

I fell asleep as soon as I hit my pillow because going up the stairs was a major chore, and it made me tired.

The next morning I ignored my alarm for my workout and slept in till 6:30. I showered and readied for the day wearing clothes that covered my whole body. Matt didn't notice, he wasn't keen on those kinds of details. I was able to hide my black eye well with my makeup; I figured people wouldn't be able to see it at all. I decided I'd wear the same makeup look as Saturday to help cover the heavy makeup on my eye.

It was an icy day today. It felt like my insides- cold and dead. I felt nothing, no happiness, sadness, nothing but physical pain. I was getting worried about my shoulder, I noticed I couldn't move it around like I should be able to, and it hurt a lot constantly.

I drove to school without even thinking, I walked to history automatically, tagging Nicholas along with me. At least I could walk straight with proper posture though it did hurt. I didn't want any unnecessary attention.

During lunch everyone talked excitedly about something I had no idea about, I wasn't listening. I was lucky that my makeup job worked; no one noticed my black eye. From the corner of my eye I saw Nicholas stare at me in frustration- or maybe it was studious or concern? I looked away immediately and got up early from my table to go to Philosophy.

"You're very quiet today," I heard a velvety voice say after class was over. "What's troubling you?"

I was shocked he noticed, I figured if anyone would have it would've been Kevin. I tried to deflect his question, "Monday blues I suppose."

"You don't fool me, Vera, please- why are you so sad today?"

'Ugh- great,' I thought of another deflection, "Only those who truly care about you can hear you when you're quiet." I said looking at my book.

He sat there in deep thought, apparently what I said worked. He wasn't saying anything else, he was lost in his thoughts, so I took my window of opportunity to leave.

Kevin walked up to me in class and offered to take my books, "No, thanks I'm not feeling well today, I think I'll skip math."

He looked more worried than he should have- of course.

"I hope you feel better. Let me know if you need anything," Kevin offered.

I fell behind the crowd of people leaving the classroom. Unfortunately, Nicholas had recovered himself and caught up to me. He pulled lightly on my bad arm. I grimaced in the sheer pain, but I faced away so he wouldn't see. My heart raced, and I started getting a cold sweat, Nicholas let go of my arm as though I'd smacked his hand away. He looked sincere and studied my face for a brief moment- I flushed worried he saw my black eye. I turned quickly and walked faster than average, somehow he was able to keep up with ease.

"I'm not going to my last class either, would you like to join me for the next hour?"

"You heard that?" another deflection.

"Please," he was not deterred.

"Okay, I guess so- what do you want to do?"

"Talk," he said lightly, but I knew this was headed for a heavy conversation.

I just walked beside him trying not to think about it. When we got outside the literature department, I looked over at the main building's entrance where I should be for my math class. I saw a colossal figure dressed in a black suit- Stefan. I gasped and thought for a minute- I took a sharp turn toward the parking lot.

"Ver-" Nicholas looked towards where I gasped and saw Stefan. His face looked knowing all of a sudden. He ran up to me.

"Sorry Nick, another time." Walking as fast as I had strained me a great deal, my recovering voice broke, and I was hoarse again. "Please just leave me alone."

He looked confused and asked, "Where are you going?"

"I don't know- away for a while I think." I had just reached my car when Nicholas pulled on my good arm.

Between my already pained body and the force of his pull, I yelped as quietly as I could from pain.

"Vera, did he do something to you?"

"No- well-" I stammered, and eventually gave up. I got into my car and revved the engine.

I backed out and left as fast as possible. I called Matt and let him know Stefan was in town and that I was going away until he was gone. After getting home, I threw together a suitcase.

I ran outside without paying any attention, there was a large man coming up the driveway. I gasped hard and nearly fainted, I quickly saw that it was just Owen. I put my hand on my chest and breathed a few times.

"Haha, sorry to startle you. Where you going," Owen asked.

"I need to stay somewhere else for a night or so."

"Come stay with us. We'd love to have your company," he smiled.

"Okay," I said in a rush, really I was just worried Stefan would show up any second.

"Sweet, let me grab Dad's jacket he left here last night."

"Hurry," I said as I turned and opened my car door. I scanned my surroundings to make sure Stefan wouldn't be around to follow us.

I hadn't realized Owen was still standing there staring at me with worry. I didn't acknowledge him and jumped in my car. He ran into the house gaining the gist of my actions. We took off faster than the speed of light, my heart didn't stop racing until I knew we weren't being followed.

When we got to the Multnomah's house Kit was helped inside by Owen. We had leftovers for dinner, and the boys watched more sports on T.V. I wondered if all Americans did this.

 Their house was the size of Matt's, quaint, but adequate for their needs. They only had one chair and a loveseat that was usually occupied by Owen. It was clean and decorated with Native American décor. I was bored of watching baseball, so I got up to admire the beautiful beadwork and other handmade woodwork.

I was careful not to expose any skin that might cause questions to be asked.

"Vera," Kit called out.

"Hmm," I said looking at him from the art I was just admiring.

"How well do you know Peter?"

"Not well, in fact, I was surprised he offered to travel back with me to the U.S."

"I know why," Owen retorted so quietly I could barely hear him.

"Well good," Kit said looking visibly relieved.

"Why do you ask," a fair question I thought.

"I have feelings about people, they're usually right, and I don't like him."

"Well, he's a nice guy I guess." I shrugged my shoulders; our conversation brought me back to the living room. "But I don't think much of him because he's quite full of himself in a bad way. Who knows though, that might be a premature judgement. Like I said, I don't know him that well. It was very kind of him to bring me home."

Both Owen and Kit liked my general opinion of him. "Well don't be too diplomatic, he looks like he's killed people before." Kit said confidently.

I was shocked he knew such a thing; I only knew that because he was a Canali. I grew curious, "And what was your opinion of me when you first saw me?" I asked this while moving Owen's feet up and plopping them on my lap as I sat back down on the couch; he had sprawled out while I was away. Owen liked that I was so comfortable with him. "And please, I prefer a hard truth than a soft lie," I finished. I was worried he would know the truth about me; I was bad and dirty. If people got to know the real me, no one would want to be around me, and I wouldn't blame them.

Kit was amused I trusted his 'instinct' so much, "Well I've liked you from the start, but there's something about you that's hard to read. I think you have quite a past." He looked at me with animated eyes.

I laughed, "That's as vague as a fortune cookie." I teased, though I only teased him because he was right on the money and I didn't want to give that away. I changed the subject immediately, "I hope you don't mind, Kit, if I ever see Peter again, I'm going to form my own opinion of him. To take your judgment at face value would be a little irrational of me. Please don't misunderstand, I'll keep your good opinion in mind."

"Of course," he said gloomily, "Just promise me you'll be careful. Deal?"

"Sure thing, Kit," I smiled at him with full force. "Well Owen, I do not understand this sport at all, perhaps you can enlighten me?"

He was more than happy to explain the rules to me.

...

That night was the first night in a while I got to bed at my usual time, but I was utterly exhausted. I slept in Owen's room. And Owen slept on the couch, with paper thin walls, I could hear him every time he tossed and turned.

I hadn't known this about myself, but apparently, I talked in my sleep when I had nightmares. I was having a night terror about 'that night.'

"Vera, Vera wake up!" Owen said shaking me awake.

I screamed and grabbed Owens' wrists I was gasping for air as though Petrov had just finished strangling me. I looked around confused "Where am I," I whispered.

"Vera you're safe, relax," he grabbed my rapidly turning face. "Vera, you're safe, it's Owen."

I relaxed and started gaining control of my breathing. I was petrified. I had never been so afraid in my life.

"Vera you're shaking," Owen said matter of factly. I removed my hold on his wrists.

"It was just a bad dream," he said ignorantly.

"Okay, okay," I whispered. I heard Kit's snoring, and I was thankful I hadn't woken up the whole household.

"Are you okay?" He asked kindly. I couldn't speak yet, and I think Owen took that as a yes because he turned to leave.

 "Wait, Owen, please, I'm really scared; can you sleep with me tonight?"

"Sure, Vera," he walked to the bed and pulled the covers back. I moved over, but there wasn't much space due to it being a twin mattress.

As soon as he was in bed I grabbed him, I was so afraid. He was on his back, and I snuggled into his chest. "You're still shaking," he said with sympathy. He started playing with my hair, which soothed me more than anything, his warm body calmed me, and I fell asleep pretty quickly.

The 5:00 am alarm came at a good time, I got up and went to the bathroom to change into the only workout outfit I could. I stepped outside- it was still dark luckily, I didn't want any chance of Owen seeing the bruises I sported. Most had come to full fruition and were totally black and purple.

I went to the school to dance, it was the best thing I had to self-express, and I needed to get some emotion out. I started the music and could barely move. I was frustrated, "Ugh! WORK YOU STUPID BODY!" I said out loud. I overexerted myself a moment later and halted abruptly at the jabbing pains at on my side and shoulder, I collapsed on the floor immediately groaning in pain holding my ribs. I could've sworn I heard someone there who had rushed to me then stopped him or herself and retreated.

'This school must be haunted,' I decided.

I went outside to go for a walk instead of running, I went into the forest-- everything was just waking up--the sun and animals. I stopped to observe some squirrels playing on the ground. I saw everything, but I wasn't present in my mind.

I left early from my usual exercise routine because I was in some severe pain and I could barely finish getting to my car. I put my hands and forehead on the steering wheel and groaned.

When I got back, Owen and Kit were still asleep. I hopped in the shower and hurried my routine. I put the same workout outfit back on, it was hard putting on my zip up jacket I used for a shirt because my shoulder still couldn't rotate around. I felt silly wearing elegant makeup and a sports outfit. When I stepped out Owen had just woken up. He was happy to see me.

"Do you always wake up this early?" He asked surprised.

"Yes I do, I have to get my workouts in you know?" I said smiling.

I decided I'd go to the school early to check if Stefan was there. I headed out after breakfast with a promise to Kit I'd come by anytime I wanted. The parking lot was clear- so I headed home for an hour to kill time.

Matt was happy to see me and asked where I decided to stay. He had assumed I just didn't want to go to another party and that that was why I was avoiding Stefan. When I told him I was at the Multnomah's house, he bit his lip trying to hide how joyful that made him.

I ran my clothes through a quick wash and dry cycle while I was home and spritzed on a little more perfume than I had at the Multnomah's. I was still able to leave for school a little early so I could scout out the parking lot again.

I didn't see Stefan, so I pulled into the parking lot confidently. I saw Nicholas heading my direction as soon as I parked. I lingered in my car pretending to busy myself with something so that I wouldn't have to see him just yet.

I was startled when I heard my passenger door opened- I was always on edge these days.

"Vera, how are you doing today?" Nicholas asked this not precisely as a question, but rather an opening to the start of a substantial conversation.

I sensed this right away, and I sighed looking down. "Is there something you wanted Nick?"

"Yes, in fact, there is. Thanks for asking- you see I want you to go to the hospital."

"THE HOSPITAL!? Are you out of your mind?" I asked angrily and incredulously.

"Nope, and I'm warning you that you will get there whether you want to or not. If you don't go easily right now, then I'll find some way to get you there, and it may not be graceful." He pulled his lips into his mouth to keep himself from laughing. It was more of a gloat, he wasn't going to budge on the topic.

"What brought all this on?" I asked loudly.

"Steven saw you this morning collapse on the ground in the gym, and he was worried enough to tell me about it." He said this confidently, but I could've sworn Steven started his shift at 7:30 am, not 5:00 am. Maybe he had to go in early today?

"I don't believe you, I'm getting out of the car because I'm calling your bluff."

"Have it your way," Nicholas said as he leaned the seat back and put his feet up on the dash.

Now I really was looking around like a crazed lunatic. Before I got to History, the nurse came up to me in almost a trance-like state and insisted I go to the nurse's office for a routine checkup.

"Who authorized this? Did Matt- my guardian sign off on it?" I pretended I was sure about what I was saying, as though it would inevitably work.

"Don't bother fighting it Vera, if you don't go easily right now, then I'll find some way to get you there, and it may not be graceful."

This is precisely what Nicholas said. I was startled and afraid, "No. I'm Sorry, but I'm not going." I ran into class and Nicholas was sitting there looking at me like I was his prey, and that he was going to get me one way or another.

'How did he get here before me, I didn't see him sneak past me.' I shot a look back like he'd better watch himself because I wasn't going to have it.

He snickered showing all his perfect teeth. He was clearly enjoying the challenge.

The nurse met me before every class of the day trying to get me to come into her office. And finally, Nicholas said, "I will get you to the hospital. I figured annoying you to death wasn't going to work." He was smug like his prediction couldn't have been righter. This made him look dauntless- it annoyed the crap out of me.

I bragged, "I have a strong resolve, Nick- you aren't getting me there even if I'm laying out on a stretcher."

He laughed sinisterly, "Well I guess we'll have to see about that."

I didn't budge. During lunch, I sat at Savanna's table as usual and prepared myself for whatever was coming my way.

"Vera! Hey you." Kevin said waving with his food tray in his other hand

I half smiled and waved.

"You have to see this."

'Oh, he'd better not try to get me into the nurse's station too,' I thought to myself. I stood up and walked over to him hesitantly looking over at Nicholas on the way.

Kevin held out a worm and laughed.

"You're joking, right? How old are you, Kevin?!" I said indignantly. I felt bad immediately because it was rude.

Kevin laughed like the dork he is, and then he changed suddenly-- he was still himself but trance-like, like the nurse. He instantaneously 'tripped' on nothing taking me down with him.

Kevin took the brunt of it because I somehow landed on him. I smacked my head on his face giving him a pulsating bloody nose. Some blood got on me, and it looked like I had just finished slaughtering a pig.

High school students, being high school students overdramatized the situation. People came running yelling for the nurse. I got up faster than I should have and I was really dizzy, I walked around quickly barely catching myself on Nicholas. He happened to be in the perfect place at the perfect time.

I looked at him like he was the guilty party- because he was somehow. He looked back at me with full force and seriousness and said, "I have so much more prepared. Just give in and go to the hospital."

I was really dazed; I grabbed my head and stood up straight, letting Nicholas go. Everything was blurry, I briefly passed out, and Nicholas grabbed me again, holding me up. He was more than happy to oblige himself to take me wherever I needed to go- especially the hospital.

I wouldn't relent. I told him to take me to philosophy. He grew annoyed, as did I, I had a splitting headache.

During Philosophy I had to get up to walk around or else I was going to fall asleep. I held my own till the end of the day, and I shot Nicholas a look of triumph, he just stood at the front of my car looking at me guiltily. Then held out his hand to stop me, I waited for a second. He let himself into my passenger side.

I started to rub my victory in. I pulled my car out of the parking lot and onto the main road when all of a sudden, WHAM! From behind me, Olivia had hit my car so hard I hit the car in front of me ejecting my airbags and scaring the living daylights out of me.

Paramedics were there sooner than they should've been like they were called in advance. Olivia, Nick, the student in front of us, and I all had to go to the hospital- on stretchers. Nicholas rolled on his side once we were in the paramedics' van and he smiled sinisterly at the situation.

"What were you saying about stretchers?" He smugly asked from his stretcher.

 I folded my arms and sighed, "You are so dead Nick!"

Nicholas laughed sing-songy and said, "I can live with myself if you never forgive me for this."

- I didn't want to see a doctor, he might notice things that shouldn't be there. We arrived at the E.R. quickly, a doctor was ready to see us all when we came in. I grew terrified; I looked at the Doctor, then at the exit sign. Nicholas caught on to my sudden change in emotions and followed my look from the Doctor to the exit sign, he looked confused and worried.

We were all taken to our own rooms; the Doctor saw Nick first but eventually made his way to me.

"Are you Vera Bianchi?" The Doctor asked.

"Yes."

"How are you feeling?" He was very kind and apparently a friend of Nicholas's family.

"I'm fine," I said.

He walked to me and lightly pulled my head back shooting a bright light into my eye. "This will be a little bright, I apologize." He flicked the light to and from my pupils. After he listened to my heart and a few other routine checkup items, he asked: "Does anything hurt?"

I lied, "No, really I'm fine."

He caught my attempted deception quickly. "Well, I believe you have a concussion. Your head doesn't hurt at all?"

He was so kind and caring, but I couldn't bring myself to say anything. He began feeling around my head when he saw my well-covered black eye.

"Did this come from the car accident?" He asked.

I wasn't expecting that question at all; I was stunned with a wide-eyed look he caught onto.

"Vera," he started looking at me sincerely, "Honesty is the only way freedom can be achieved, secrecy is the keystone to the evils that happen in the world today."

Whoa. I had never heard a truth so plainly stated. "No, it happened Saturday night." My eyes narrowed choking back tears.

"Did Matt hit you?" He was objective in his questioning but extremely kind.

"No, he has no idea. I've been covering it up, and I spent the night at a friend's house."

"Is anything else hurting you?"

I closed my eyes debating if I should divulge. My shoulder was aching I knew something was wrong with it. "Yes, my shoulder hurts really badly."

He walked behind me and examined my shoulder. "Oh," his tone surprised "it's dislocated."

I flinched when he touched my shoulder though his hand was barely feeling it.

"I think it's a little bruised," I said without giving anything away.

"I'm going to have to take a closer look," He said putting his clipboard down. "Can you remove your jacket please?"

"I'd rather not if it's all the same," I said looking down grabbing the edge of my sleeves to wrap my hands in them.

He grew suspicious, I hadn't realized that by pulling my sleeves down it had pulled my collar down with it.

He lightly gasped, "Vera, your neck…."

I flustered and looked down realizing my mistake. Crap.

"Are those strangulation bruises?"

"Yes, they are," I spoke matter of factly, trying to keep my poise.

He paused for a moment then in a trance-like way said, "You'll want someone to hold onto when I relocate your shoulder, it'll hurt a great deal, and I could also use another pair of hands. Should I go get Matt?"

"No!" I said too quickly "Matt doesn't know, I want it to stay that way if it all possible?"

"I'm not sure I can promise that. I know Nicholas very well, he was in the car you crashed in, so I can only assume you're friends at the very least. I can bring him in if you prefer?"

I sighed, "Is he good at keeping secrets?"

Dr. Yost was solemn and non-trance like, "Yes, he is."

I looked at Dr. Yost with my eyebrows furrowed, "Okay, but maybe you should ask him first if he's okay with it. And maybe you should apprise him of the… Situation. He shouldn't do anything he doesn't want to do."

Dr. Yost nodded and stepped out of the room for a brief moment and came back inside with Nicholas. Nicholas's face was completely calm.

Dr. Yost stepped outside again to order X-Rays. I took a deep breath and exhaled quietly. Nicholas looked at me.

"Don't worry Vera, you're in good hands. I promise you're safe." His eyes were so intent they could've spread his message themselves.

"Thanks, Nick," I said comforted.

Dr. Yost came back in and said kindly, "I need to take a look at the damage, so I don't injure you more." He was so genuine I felt as comfortable as I could have.

"Okay, just- don't freak out," I stammered. I removed my jacket- grimacing in pain and looking at them tentatively. With only my bra and pants on, they could see everything. They were both shocked, and couldn't move. Their eyes were wide and their postures stiff, Dr. Yost was the first to break the silence.

He first cleared his throat, "Vera, who did this to you?"

I sighed, "You wouldn't know him. He's from Russia; he was at my Papa's party last Saturday."

Dr. Yost shook his head incredulously, "Why don't you start from the beginning?"

I took a deep breath and looked at Nicholas who was still frozen stiff. "My Papa has established himself in a culture that isn't good so to speak. My sister and I are sometimes offered as cherries on the top of his business deals. I left and came here for refuge. Friday night Stefan, my bodyguard, came to Arcata and insisted I go to the party on Saturday in France. During the party my Papa sent me up to my room, Stefan was outside my door, he heard everything and did nothing. The man came into my room after I did."

Both men standing in front of me looked almost green. I pressed on slowly. "He beat me, and strangled me, and raped me…. For hours."

It was completely quiet. They were both looking down at the floor eyes still wide.

"I'm very sorry this happened to you, Vera. Let's take a look at your shoulder," Dr. Yost finally said.

Dr. Yost walked over to me solemnly. "I think you may also have something going on with your ribs as well. We might need another X-ray." Dr. Yost said looking at my blackened ribs. "How did this happen specifically?"

"Um, he kicked and punched this spot several times. I heard cracking," I said bravely.

"I see bruised welts, all over, what are those?"

"They're actually scratch marks," I said nodding. "I'm not sure why they look like that." Nicholas's face looked like he was ready to kill Petrov with his bare hands and anyone who stood in his way.

Dr. Yost began looking at and feeling around my neck, "Did you have any breathing problems or voice changes after the strangulation?"

"I breathed…Clearly, but I lost my voice."

"Do you know about how long he strangled you for?"

"No, but I also lost my vision."

Dr. Yost smacked his lips, "That's not good." Nicholas looked at me angrily, I wasn't sure if it was me he was mad at or not. Perhaps he was mad I made him come and listen to this awful story. I looked embarrassed and scared, I saw Dr. Yost shoot a quick glance at Nicholas. Nicholas shook off his posture and face and went back to looking down.

"What's this circular mark here on your arm?"

I exhaled this answer, "cigarette burn." Nicholas was in pain, and he walked over to me, looking like he wanted to grab me to comfort me. But he restrained and settled for just standing next to me.

"Vera, I have to tell Matt. He has to sign off on all this before I can legally do anything since he's here. I also need to get your shoulder and ribs X-rayed."

"I'm not being there for that. Can you tell him yourself?" I asked defeated.

"Yes I can, Nicholas is going to stay here with you, and I'll alert him when the X-ray machine is ready for you."

I nodded and looked down.

"Is there anything else that needs to be addressed, Vera?"

"No, I don't think so."

Dr. Yost took his leave.

"Who did this to you?" Nicholas asked.

"I don't think that matters. He'll be dead soon if he isn't already."

Nicholas didn't care if the man might've been dead already, "What do you mean?"

"My friend, Peter Canali found me and helped me escape through the servants' exit."

This piqued his interest like it was the most interesting thing I'd said. "Canali, you said?"

"Yeah…. I was bleeding and….He said he…Smelled my blood… That's weird come to think of it.…"

Nicholas clarified, "So you were bleeding and alone with Peter, and he took you home?"

"Yes," I said still thinking with a studious look. "Peter was livid of course, and said that he'd take care of him."

"Well its good you got home safely, I'm glad to have you back. Do you know Peter very well?"

"Kind of, he and his family usually went to Papa's parties. He always asked me to dance, and he dated my sister for a bit, but that's it really."

"Why did he bring you home then?"

"I don't know. I think he just wants to get in my pants."

Nicholas snickered, "Why don't you like him?"

"He's an elitist pig; he takes pleasure from playing people like their one big game. I'm not fully convinced he isn't a sociopath or something."

He thoroughly laughed at that comment, "Are you afraid of him?"

"Pttttt no, why should I be? I'm not afraid of anyone but Petrov." I realized what I said and felt broken again.

I curled up trying to self-soothe. I couldn't believe I spilled my guts again in front of Nicholas, what was my problem?! Nicholas couldn't stand it any longer and put his hand on my back, I rushed into his arms without thinking. I hugged him hard and close, he returned the full force back like this is what he really wanted to do. He intertwined his fingers in my hair on the back of my head and held me close with the other hand, I couldn't wrap my bad arm around him so that hand stayed on his chest grabbing his shirt while the other was wrapped around his body.

"It's okay, you're here now. And more people love you than you know, you're not alone," he whispered.

It was exactly what I needed to hear, and the floodgates flew open. I hadn't cried in so long, the sweet tears of hell emptied from the pit of my misery. If tears were dyed the color of the depth of your despair or the height of your joy; my cheeks would be stained black.

Something about Nicholas was perfect for me, I could be exactly myself, and I never felt more comfortable than I did with him. He took away my pain and filled the chasm of my wretchedness betrayal left me.

After a few minutes I dried my eyes but stayed right where I was, it was home to me for some reason. I could've sworn I felt his cold lips press against my head, but it was a swift movement.

"When you're ready, the X-ray machine is available," Nicholas said after a long time.

I somehow missed how Dr. Yost had alerted him. But I nodded anyway and let go of him first, he held on much longer, it looked like it was physically painful for him to let me go.

I squared my shoulders and took a breath as though my dignity was still intact. We were back to my E.R. room soon, and I was thankful Matt wasn't waiting for me there.

Dr. Yost was back soon after. "Well, it looks like your shoulder is displaced as I said and you have a few cracked ribs." He looked at Nicholas and back at me, "I can give you some shots to numb your shoulder if you want?"

I hate shots, "No, I'd rather just get it done and over with," I inhaled.

Nicholas came to my side and grabbed my hand, Dr. Yost stood behind and to the side of me. I let go of Nicholas's hand and grabbed the back of his shirt and dug my face into his torso. He hugged me back for support.

Dr. Yost grabbed my arm and adjusted it, "And one....Two....Three" craaaaaack. I let out a relatively quiet painful grunt into Nicholas's body. After the relocation, I heard someone in the hallway say some profanity.

Dr. Yost looked down and said, "That's Matt."

"He's in the hallway?" I asked angrily after gaining composure.

"Yes, I told him the full story, and we've worked it out so that you're free to leave when we're done here."

"Oh," I sounded as guilty as I looked, "I'm sorry, I just.... This is already going to kill him, and I didn't think he should hear it. But, thank you so much for... Everything."

Dr. Yost smiled, "Of course. Take a few minutes to readjust, Nicholas knows the symptoms of shock, he'll let me know if anything happens."

Dr. Yost left, and I sat on the table for a few minutes just looking down. I grabbed my jacket and started putting it on with more ease than before, but I was still sore. Nicholas took it and put the rest on for me.

"Thanks, Nick.... I don't know what I would've done without you."

He smiled and looked down, he clenched his jaw and smoldered looking up at me again. "Do you promise me to call me or come to find me if you need anything?"

I considered what he said, "To be honest I'm very prideful, and I probably won't." I tried to play it off as a serious joke, but it didn't fly.

"Then I'll be checking in on you day and night miss Bianchi," he said with his velvety voice.

I smiled to myself at that thought, "This may sound dumb to you but, thank you for caring."

He just smiled and looked at me happily. I got off the table, and he grabbed me just before I got to the door to give me one more hug, I was incredibly grateful.

I looked up at him and smiled then turned to open the door. Matt was standing in the hallway as he stepped forward immediately to half hug me.

Matt looked at Nicholas, "Thank you." Nicholas nodded as Matt took me to the side exit keeping one arm around me. "I have a prescription to pick up the whole pharmacy before we go home."

I laughed and said, "What about my car?"

"I can get Owen to help me get it later, they were coming over for the game. But I can cancel it if you want?"

"No, its okay I'll probably just sleep anyway." I was fatigued emotionally, physically, and in every other way possible.

I paid for the medication on the road going to the pharmacy so that Matt could simply run in and get them. I took a look at all the medicine and asked about most of them, my meds consisted of sleeping pills, painkillers, a cream for the burn, and cream for my bruises.

"I'm just going to go upstairs and nap a bit Matt, you don't have to stick around here if you don't want to," I said on the way upstairs.

"Are you sure kiddo? I feel bad that I can't help."

"Don't worry about it, Matt." I closed the door behind me for privacy, I knew I was ready to cry a lot more. Nicholas had helped to release my pent-up emotions, and there was no stopping them now.

I heard the T.V. turn on downstairs, and I let myself go. I slide down on the floor next to my bed grabbing myself to hold onto something, and for something to hold me.

I felt so empty-- like everyone I cared about suddenly didn't love me anymore. I felt as though they all only cared to use and abuse me. I cried hard and rolled onto my floor. Crying so hard, and so quietly hurt my ribs but I didn't care, the pain almost felt good, at least I was feeling something.

I cried about the physical pain he put me through. I cried harder until I couldn't help but let some noise out.

I cried about being violated, and I suddenly felt exposed; I got off the floor quickly and ripped off my quilt. I sat on my bed and covered every part of my skin that felt breeze like there was a poison in the air that was going to kill me if any part of me but my face was unprotected.

I sobbed thinking about the little sobs on the outside of my door from the man I loved. I couldn't believe he of all people hurt me like that. I dug my face into my pillow to smother my loud sobs.

I sobbed because of my Papa, the man entrusted by God to love and protect me, his DAUGHTER. How dare he invade ME like that, he had no right! I became angry-- more than angry-- hateful. I hated him for this atrocity! It was asinine!

I slowly lifted my head from my pillow: my face was stiff and vengeful. My eyes looked like I could kill him by looking at him. …How….Dare…He…. I was going to do something about this. I got off my bed and started pacing. What to do, what to do? He was going to suffer for this, he was going to pay. I still felt incredibly sad, but I was angrier.

I was never one to lie down and take it; I was a fighter, a warrior. I was going to have to do something about this.

Fight… Of course… I needed to learn how to fight! Who could teach me?! Just then I heard the Multnomah's walk in. "Owen," I said out loud, "I wonder if he knows how to fight?" This idea stemmed from him mentioning he was at drill once.

I sat on my bed with a horrible migraine. It was only around 3:00, no doubt the Multnomah's came here early to keep Matt company. I drifted off to sleep sitting there, too exhausted to dream. I woke up around 7 with a pounding headache and swollen eyes from crying. I got up and looked out my window to see my car in the driveway.

I decided to take a shower and wash my face, then try to go back to sleep.

I finished around 7:30 and laid in my bed for what felt like hours, I gave up and looked at the clock, it was apparently only 8:30. I got up sorely and ditched my robe, it wouldn't be able to cover my bruises. I wrapped myself in my blanket and waddled downstairs.

"Vera! How are you feeling?" Owen said excitedly, he obviously only new about the car crash.

It was hard to be sad around Owen, he exhumed happiness. "Fine," I lied smiling, it was apparently enough of a white lie for anyone to tell I was fibbing.

I went around the couch and sat next to Owen. It was football again, I understood the general rules, so it wasn't utterly boring.

We all sat there silently for a while, Matt kept looking over at me attentively. I was getting annoyed because I didn't want to be babied, I already felt like a victim. Matt looked over at me with every movement I made. Eventually, fatigue crept back, and I was tired again. Sitting next to Owen was too nice to leave, so I stayed. I lingered too long, and before I knew it, I was laying back on the couch fast asleep, but not deep enough to be dreamless this time.

"….No…. Please…. Stop…." I began talking in my sleep.

"She's having the same nightmare she did last night," Owen said confused.

Matt began choking up, "We should wake her up."

"What are you not telling us, Matt," Owen asked calmly but sternly. Matt's tone announced to the world something was wrong.

Matt looked down and let a sniffle out. "It's not mine to share." He said with his voice cracking.

I started breathing heavier and cried, "…. STOP…."

Matt couldn't take it he stood up and shook me violently, "Vera wake up!"

My dreams translated it to Petrov, I broke through my blankets and silently cried still asleep.

"What the hell," Owen said grabbing my arm with the welts, bruises and burn. They could see my neck, wrists, ankles, and part of the bruise on my shoulder.

Matt was stunned, it was the first time he saw it in person. He staggered back to his seat while Owen examined me.

Kit spoke softly, "Matt, whatever this is, you can't be the only one to hold onto it. For your sake, share your burden."

Matt told them the whole story as far as he knew it- and he knew all of it. Owen pulled my pajama shirt up to see my ribs, and it made Matt dry heave.

"I'll take her upstairs," Owen said sadly.

"Wait" Matt stood up and went to the kitchen, "Give her this if you can, it's her sleeping pill. Maybe she won't have to dream about it."

Owen put the pill in his pocket and carried me upstairs. He set me on the bed and wiped my tears and played with my hair like the night before. It woke me up because he was too warm and kind to be Petrov.

"Owen?" I asked before I was fully awake because I knew who it was that felt this way.

"Yeah, it's me," He said somberly.

"Was I talking again?"

"Ya, Vera why didn't you tell me?" He asked this kindly and gently.

"Ugh." I avoided his question, "Owen do you know how to fight?"

"Well yeah, but why?"

"I want to learn how to fight. Will you teach me what you know?"

He chuckled, "Maybe after you're healed up Chika."

"There's no time to lose, Stefan can show up any minute. And I seriously don't stand a chance unless I at least know how to throw a punch."

He stiffened, "You'll stay at my house when he comes around again."

I sighed knowing he wouldn't back down. "Oh, I almost forgot, here's a sleeping pill Matt told me to give you."

"Thanks, I guess. Will you grab me that pillow on the floor, I need something to snuggle tonight." I dry swallowed the pill.

"It won't be as good as me," He said with a cocky smile.

"It's true, but at least it won't take all my blankets," I teased back. "Good night Owen."

"Good night," he left slowly not wanting to go.

I didn't dream at all, the pill did its job. I got up at 5:00 and went on a jog I enjoyed running because it gave me time to think. I thought about Nichols and his strange ability to make people do what he wanted them to do, how fast he made it to class, and how cold and graceful he was. I thought about Peter and how he said he could smell my blood. It was all confusing, and I knew there was something supernatural about them.

When I got to school the parking lot was full, and everyone ran up to me to ask if I was okay. It was hard not to get perturbed after a while. People swarmed Nicholas too, especially girls.

At lunch, Savanna talked my ear off about who said what and when during the crash and afterward. I looked over at Nicholas who was staring at me. I smiled and rolled my eyes jokingly shaking my head as though I wasn't going to get a word in edgewise.

Nicholas seemed to know exactly what I was portraying and laughed to himself. Victoria caught me after lunch and rescheduled our shopping trip for this weekend.

Between periods Nicholas put his arm around me placing his cold hand on my sore shoulder, it felt so good. I hoped he wasn't just doing it for first aid.

Time seemed to sprint, and I was excited for the terrible week to end, at least I had a shopping trip to look forward to.

...

San Francisco was fun and much needed, Victoria was a true friend, and I drew a lot of comfort from her. It seemed like we were destined to be friends. I didn't care what she was or what any of them were, they were good people. Peter, on the other hand, I was cautious about and hoped to figure out what he was so I could avoid him.

Every day was a struggle; I had to fight for my sanity. My workouts grew more intense, and I listened to SVRCINA 'Meet Me On The Battlefield' on a regular basis to keep the fight in me. I wanted to give up, to give into disassociation, I wanted to feel nothing- but I knew that it was not the life I wanted.

I quoted Ralph Marston to myself day after day in the mirror; "Happiness is a choice, not a result. Nothing will make you happy until you choose to be happy. No person will make you happy until you decide to be happy. Your happiness will not come to you. It can only come from you".

I read about Elizabeth Smart and her infamous decision not to let her abuser steal one more day away from her. She was going to choose to move on. I went to counseling regularly to help me cope. I was going to fight for the life I always wanted for myself, and I was going to settle for nothing less.

Chapter Six: Kidnapped

My wounds were mostly healed, and I insisted Owen, and I start my training. He taught me the basics of fighting like how to tuck your thumb into your hand when throwing a punch. I was surprised there were so many things to remember when sparring.

Owen didn't take it easy on me; if I wasn't performing, he'd yell at me like a coach.

"Come on Vera, you can hit harder than that!"

One time he even right hooked me with his padded hand to catch my attention. I wasn't expecting it, and he knocked me on my rear end.

I laughed a little shocked, "I think I picked the perfect teacher."

He lightened up and offered his ungloved hand to help me up. "Sorry. You need to always be on your guard Vera." Right after he picked me off the floor, he tackled me gently back down and rolled, so I was on the bottom. "See what I mean," he laughed triumphantly.

"That wasn't a fair move Owen." I jabbed him in the gut and rolled him on the bottom. "You wanna play dirty? I'm game!" I got up--almost.

Owen pulled me down and by sheer strength rolled me back and pinned my arms to the ground. He laughed again, but I wasn't amused.

"Oh come on, you have to give me a chance!" I blew a piece of hair from my face.

"Who says I have to?" He leaned dangerously close to my face when he said this. He moved my hands together and held them down with one hand. With the other started stroking my face and lips.

I struggled out of his grasp quickly and jabbed his stomach again. I got up and laughed so hard I was bent over. "You shouldn't let yourself get so distracted."

He rolled onto his back with his hands in the air, "I surrender, I surrender."

We always sparred on Thursday's in his backyard early in the morning as part of my workout. We walked inside for breakfast, and I left for my house to get ready.

Seeing Nicholas was the highlight of my day. It was mid-October now, the season change made the tree we met under also change into this bright red color. It was the most beautiful thing to see him and the tree together.

He smiled as always, "Hey Ver."

"Hi Nick," I smiled back.

"What are you doing tomorrow tonight?" He asked mischievously

"Nothing, I think, why?" Playfully suspicious.

"Would you like to go to dinner with me?" He looked and me with piercing eyes dancing with excitement.

"Like a date?" I asked happily.

"Yeah, a dinner date. I believe you said dinner's 'allowed for conversation'?"

"I'd love to!" I said elated

"Great, I'll pick you up at 4." He seemed to be concealing more excitement than I was- and I was ready to run around the schoolyard with the happiness inside me.

The day drug on for what seemed like forever, I couldn't wait for tomorrow to come!

That night Matt hosted another game night party. I prepped dinner and dessert as quickly as possible; the Multnomah's always came soon after Matt got home.

Sure enough, Matt walked in with the Multnomah's. "Smells great kiddo!" Matt said kicking his shoes off.

"Thanks," I said as I ran upstairs to grab my phone from my jacket pocket. I was hoping Nicholas had texted me more details about our date night. Since he hadn't I took the initiative 'so where are you taking me tomorrow?'

"Whom, may I ask are you texting with such a big smile on your face?" Matt asked suspiciously

"Nicholas King. We're going out for dinner tomorrow." I said looking up from my phone to Matt.

No one was happy to hear that. Kit said, "I've never liked those Kings and Butlers." Matt grumbled about it too.

I was a little pissed off and told them all to mind their own bee's wax if they were going to be a buzz kill.

Owen looked the most upset at the news, but I didn't care because it wasn't like he had ever tried to ask me out. We finished dinner and watched the game- which was something I was really starting to enjoy. I was more competitive than all the boys put together, so I was also the most vocal.

"Oh come on, my Nana could've thrown better than that."

The game night went late as always, and I headed upstairs to get ready for bed. I had just finished from the bathroom and put my Pj's and perfume on when I heard a knock on my door. I walked up and opened it; I was shocked it was Owen.

"Hey, buddy. What can I do ya for?" I joked leaning against the door jam.

He walked past me into my room and sat on the bed. I closed the door looking at him worried.

"Are you okay Owen?" I walked up to my bed and put my hand on the footboard.

"Listen, you can't go out with King. I'm serious."

I threw my head back in frustration "That's what this is about?! And here I was so concerned; it looked like you were doing a death march to my bed."

He stood up and walked over to me touching my now folded arms. "Vera, he's bad news. You really don't know him-- but I do. And he's someone you don't want to get mixed up with."

I looked as worried as I did before, "Why, what's he done?"

"He's a-," he let out a sigh, "I can't tell you, but please. He is more than you think he is- and it's not good."

I wasn't buying it I started breaking free of his grip rolling my eyes smiling. He strengthened his hold and leveled his face to mine- "I'm serious. I care about you a great deal Vera, and I'm not going to let you get hurt."

Looking at his olive toned, smooth skin in the moonlight coming from the window was distracting. But I held my ground and said, "I haven't seen anything but good come from him. And until you either give me a good enough reason not to go on the date, or I see something about him I don't like, I'm going to date him if I want."

"Ugh, you're too stubborn for your own good Ver."

I stayed quiet.

He pulled me into his chest, he was bigger than I had realized. He reminded me of the Stefan I loved. Owen smelled good-- not in the same way Nick did, but a mixture of musky and clean like the trees.

He hugged me for a long time and said: "Well, I think I'm just going to have to take you out every other weekend to keep you busy." He laughed to himself at this thought. I was busy at that moment trying to keep myself from mauling him.

He continued, "Next Saturday is Halloween, I'll show you how us Americans celebrate. My buddy is having a costume party, come dressed as Little Red Riding Hood."

I nodded, he pulled me back and kissed my forehead. "It's a date then" he whispered and left my room. I walked to my bed and thoughtlessly pulled my covers back, laying down I tried to process my new emotions of passion I felt toward Owen.

…

Friday was also long; Nicholas and I could barely contain our smiles. We kept nudging each other too, I was frustrated he didn't touch me more as Owen did.

I raced home and put on more date-worthy makeup and clothes, I sprayed my perfume just in time to hear the doorbell ring. I ran downstairs, and I opened it excited. "Hey Nick, I'm ready when you are!"

He smiled, "You are so… Captivating."

I blushed a little, "You clean up good yourself." We walked out for me to see his Lamborghini, I was shocked. "I didn't know you owned a sports car!"

He laughed, "My school car is not my recreational car." He opened my door and grabbed my hand on my way into his car. He looked at me as he always did-- mischievously. Sensually mischievous. Titillating my emotions which wanted him already.

It killed me every time, his added measure of gentlemanly acts was also a huge turn on. Why did he have to be so hot all the time?!

He took me to a little local restaurant called 'Big Wheelers'. It was quaint looking building with old wagon wheels used as their main center of decor. When we walked in a waiter yelled from the back, "Sit anywhere you want."

I laughed at the casualness of the place. "So many options, how can we ever pick?"

Nicholas grinned, "My favorite spot is the far corner by the big windows. You'll see why."

I was surprised to hear he was a regular here. I followed him to the table where he held my chair out and pushed me in. I looked out to see a patio area full of flowery shrubs and colorful leaves. My breath was taken by its beauty.

"Wow, it's gorgeous here."

He smiled, "I'm glad you like it."

A young male waiter walked into the dining area with menu's and waters. "Hello, Nicholas!" The young man said.

"Hello, Parker! Have you had the pleasure of being introduced to Vera Bianchi?" Gesturing to me.

"I do not believe I have. Very nice to meet you miss Bianchi."

I nodded, "Good to meet you, Parker."

"What can I get started for you today?"

We both ordered our food, and the waiter left.

"How are you doing Vera, I mean really doing."

"I'm doing fine; honestly I'm happy."

He grinned, "I sometimes think about that day in the hospital, I have to wonder why you thought it was going to be so bad if someone knew your secret." He looked at me curiously.

I sipped my water, "Have you ever had a secret you felt if someone knew, it would ruin their sleep as it does yours? Scare them with imagery that randomly creeps into their thoughts?"

He looked down at his hands then back at me. "Yes, I have."

I squinted my eyes, "Then you can understand why I felt like my secret shouldn't be allowed to ripple effect on those I care about."

He sighed like he knew exactly what I was saying. "I can."

"But you know what I've learned?" I leaned forward to emphasize what I was saying and whispered: "It's all a lie we tell ourselves-- a smokescreen if you will. The kinds of bonds you want to form with people are hinged on the basis of reality. The good, the bad, the ugly. But I feel the deepest of your passions and hurts should only be shared with those who you want to form the deepest of love and respect. Traumatic experiences connect people in inseparable ways."

Nicholas leaned back and stared at his glass of water. "How do you know when the time is right?" He looked up at me suddenly and with desperation.

"When you share pieces of yourself like that the timing is never right. I should think it would be a hard thing to plan." I smiled as I said this. "Nick, what's on your mind?"

He looked at me like a deer in headlights. Just then our waiter came over with our food, we tried to act casual and thank him when he finished topping off our glasses.

I saw Nicholas tuck his lightly shaking hands underneath the table. "Vera, you are my undoing. You somehow say the right things, no one can possibly know me better than you do." He wasn't making eye contact with me. "I'm wondering if you're some kind of witch or something."

I laughed, "Well if I'm a witch I want to know the spell to clean my house!" I made my face serious and inhaled, "Listen, Nick. You have cared for the part of my soul that I shared with you so… Gently. I can't tell you how thankful I am for you." I blinked tears away, "I want you to know you can tell me anything, and I will do my best to return your favor and be your confidant. But you don't have to tell me either."

He looked at me startled, "You… Don't care that I have a secret that you don't know?"

"Nick- I'm not going to pry; this is your life to make your own choices. Just keep in mind that you can choose your decisions, but you can't choose your consequences." I eyed him carefully, keeping eye contact with his beautiful green eyes.

Nicholas looked like he was going to pass out he was breathing so hard. "Please, excuse me." He got up from the table faster than I could say anything, he walked to the men's room. While inside he paced and ran his hand through his hair. "How does she do this?" He plopped his hands on the rim of the porcelain vanity. "I love her, stupid word porn." He

145

exhaled, turned on the faucet and splashed his face with lukewarm water.

I waited patiently taking bites of my Greek salad. I hoped I hadn't crossed any lines I shouldn't have. He walked out of the bathroom looking like he ran a marathon.

"I'm sorry," I started, "I sometimes talk too much."

He laughed under his breath, "No, what you said was perfect, don't you worry about it."

I changed the subject to something lighter, "You should eat before your food gets too cold."

He smiled without the smile reaching his eyes, "It's great either way, rigatoni is just one of those dishes."

"Lucky; salad is something that gets super soggy."

He was different; he couldn't quite shake off whatever it was he was feeling for the rest of dinner. He took me to his car after dinner and took me home early. Walking me to the door, he said, "Vera, you blow my mind, and I really like that about you. Hah never a dull moment." He grabbed my face and stroked his thumb against my cheek, exhaled and said: "Have a good night."

I smiled and grabbed his hand, "Good night." I dropped his hand and let myself in.

I put my head against the door as soon as I closed it, I so wanted him to kiss me.

Matt was waiting inside watching some sport, as usual, I walked in and sat on the couch crossing my legs. I was surprised dinner took 2 hours, it felt like a half that. I excused myself and went upstairs to do some homework, think about Nicholas, and get ready for bed.

I wasn't sure he knew that he meant as much to me as it seemed I did to him- or so I guessed.

The weekend passed with little more excitement than just Owen texting me making sure I was still alive. I wasn't amused by his joke that I wasn't entirely sure was a joke.

Saturday I decided to spend with Savanna, Kevin, and Oscar. They were a lively bunch who were the epitome of teenagers. We watched movies, bowled, played night games- the works.

Sunday was always my rest day.

Monday Morning's workout was something I looked forward to, I couldn't get Nick off my mind, and the only time I could physically release my stress and curiosity was during my workouts. Since this was the first day, I'd see Nick since the date I wanted to look extra special.

When I was ready for school, I walked out to my car hurriedly to get to school faster, and because I was freezing- it was the first snowfall of the year. I pulled into the school parking lot and looked for Nicholas, I hadn't realized I was earlier than I usually was in my excitement. I stepped out of my car to see a man a few yards away from me, I was excited and walked faster to see Nick. Only when I was right up to him did I realize this man was far larger than Nick was.

…Stefan…?

I paused in my tracks, and I bolted back to my car. He sprinted after me. I slipped on the snow just before I reached my car, I opened my car door, and half jumped into my car when I felt a jolt around my stomach. Stefan had caught up to me and grabbed me mid-jump, he pushed me against the SUV I was parked next to.

I was terrified; I was shaking, "Stefan, please let me go."

"I can't do that." He said with desperation in his voice. "I have to make this right; I have to remind you that you love me."

"That isn't going to happen, Stefan." I tried to look bold. People started looking at us weird as they walked by. "I'll scream if you don't let me go."

Just then I felt a sharp jab in my leg-- my vision was getting blurry, and I realized he put something in my system that was going to make me fall asleep.

"You have to love me Ver…" He said determinedly.

I was going downhill, all I could think to say was another Shakespeare quote. "The saddest thing about betrayal is that it never comes from your enemies." The last thing I saw was how my words had affected him.

He carried me to his waiting car and gently placed me in his back seat. As Stefan drove out of the parking lot, the King's and Butlers pulled in.

******

******

Nicholas waited for me by the tree until class started, something didn't feel right to him. He went to the principal's office and asked that Savanna Smith be pulled out of American History as a matter of urgency.

Nicholas met Savanna outside her classroom. "Have you heard from Vera?"

Savanna looked confused, "Not since Saturday night. But we were planning on seeing each other today, why?"

"Oh she's probably just sick or something," Nicholas told her, but he wasn't going to stop trying to figure out where I was. He ran to the parking lot and realized my car was there, his stomach dropped, he couldn't believe he didn't think of this before.

From the parking lot, he said, "Olivia, Aiden, Victoria, come to the parking lot now." Before he could turn around, they were by his side.

"What's wrong," Victoria asked.

"Vera is missing, and I suspect Stefan's back in town." He was livid and shaky.

Everyone looked worried and rushed to their car. Nick pulled out fast and followed my dying scent. He was going faster than any normal human could safely go on slick roads.

"What if we don't make it in time?" Victoria asked unwillingly, "We're headed to Eureka, it'll be much harder to find her there."

"We have to find her car before we hit traffic; I hate it when we're tracking people in vehicles," Aiden added.

"We'll find her, her scent is getting stronger and stronger. I suspect we can intercept him at the airport." Olivia said matter of factly.

Nicholas was silent and focused, they drove for 10 minutes before they reached a blue car still en route to Eureka.

"It's Vera!" Victoria shouted.

Olivia furrowed her eyebrows and waited for a moment before asking, "What is that familiar scent I smell in the car with them?"

"I only smell two people," Aiden said. Olivia had the ability to smell the best, she was no tracker, but she wasn't too far off.

"It's a scent coming off of Stefan. Something's wrong." Olivia looked at Nicholas "Turn around. I think something's wrong."

The blue car randomly pulled off the interstate headed towards a dingy, sketchy looking Motel.

"I'm not turning around!" Nicholas shouted.

Victoria grew as concerned as Olivia, "Who else do you smell, Olivia?"

"I might be wrong, but I think it's a Canali, it isn't potent, so I suspect Stefan was around one or all of them before he left for Arcata."

"This could be a trap Nicholas," Aiden said sternly, "I do not advise we move forward."

"I don't care if this is a trap. Vera is not going back to France." Nicholas was firm.

"You're usually the one who's clear and intelligible. Are you sure she's worth it?" Aiden asked ignorantly.

Nicholas didn't respond-- which answered his question.

Aiden continued, "Alright if we're moving forward the least you can do Nicholas is stay in the car where you're more likely to be safe."

The tension in the car was so thick you could cut it with a knife.

Nicholas breathed in and out loudly and grunted: "I-I don't know if I can do that."

Victoria placed her hand on Nicholas's shoulder, "She'll be fine, we can do this."

"Let's just wait till we get there and assess the situation then I'll make my decision."

They kept their distance from Stefan's car so they wouldn't alert him to something coming his way. It had been 10 minutes after Stefan pulled into the motel that the King's and Butlers decided to pull into the parking lot. 10 minutes that felt like hours to all of them.

"Olivia, what's the situation?" Nicholas asked this in a way that sounded like a co-op mission; as though a vital battle was about to be waged.

Olivia sighed, "Nicholas- Stefan's connected to the Canali's this will end badly. Whether it's today or another day, we're opening something that is much bigger than a rescue mission. Are you sure this is what you want?

"Yes. I don't care. She will still have her choice when this is through. Though I cannot tell you how much I wish I could make Vera come with me." Nicholas sighed, "I love her, and I need her back."

The car was deadly silent with a new feeling in place of fear and concern, it was now happiness and calmness.

Olivia smiled, "It's been century's Nicholas-- I can't believe it finally happened."

"We need to stay focused," Nicholas commanded. "We need to keep Stefan alive or else the Bianchi's will come swarming Arcata. We also need to keep our scents off of Stefan as much as possible."

"We can tie him up, so our scents are forced to leave him by the time he gets back to France," Aiden suggested.

"Do the Canali's have a tracker?" Nicholas inquired.

"Not as far as our intel is aware." Piped Victoria.

"How many, Olivia?"

"Just Vera and Stefan."

"I'll stay in the car, try not to touch Stefan or tie him up. I'm going to sit in the back seat with Vera, Aiden take the wheel when you've extracted her."

Aiden, Olivia, and Vitoria all nodded and climbed out of the car at light speed. They tracked Vera's scent to room 104.

They paused for a fraction of a second nodding once again to one another to signify readiness. Aiden kicked the door off its hinges. By a stroke of fortune, Stefan was in the bathroom. At that same light speed Aiden crushed the doorknob to the bathroom preventing Stefan a quick escape, Victoria grabbed the unconscious Vera from off the bed, and they all left into the blizzardy exterior.

The 'operation' took less than a minute.

Victoria had jumped into the back with Nicholas since she had Vera; Nicholas grabbed Vera from Victoria quicker than she could hand her over. He wasn't expecting Vera to be unconscious, which worked in his favor.

Stefan was stunned; by the time he kicked the door down, they were long gone with Aiden speeding off quickly. Stefan ran outside and examined the strangely perfect footprints in the newly laid snow. Usually, it was more shuffled, but he could clearly count three people; two of which being most likely female. He ran back inside to see the cuffs that held one of Vera's wrists to the bed was snapped in two with specific indents that looked like the size of fingers. Same could be said of the doorknob. What a mystery.

…

On the short half hour drive, Nicholas stroked Vera's hair and face, and he sometimes pulled her close as he did in the hospital. Every time he hugged her he closed his eyes tightly shut and sighed, enclosing her face into his neck.

Nicholas's party discussed the best move at this point without Nicholas being present in the conversation. They decided the best place to take her would be their house.

The plan was that Victoria would gather my luggage and tell Matt I was staying with her in a hotel until Stefan left town. She was to have brevity to prevent unneeded details from being disclosed.

Pulling into their property was something of a maze of shrubbery, multiple pathways, and dense vegetation preventing any visibility past the paved and unpaved trails. This was for defense purposes. Aiden parked in front of the giant mansion to drop us off and then parked it in the garage which was to the back of the house.

The Butler's Mom: Emma and the King's Mom: Katerina met the kids in the living room surprised to see a beautiful young human in Nicholas's arms. The parents were less aware of Vera and the progressing situation between Nicholas and Vera.

After a brief explanation of Stefan and the danger he posed, along with the Canali scent and a tip of the iceberg explanation of the risk Vera was in; they all sat down and waited for the Father's to get home.

The Butler Father: Benjamin was an apothecary, he and the King Father: William were pulling into the garage as the kids spoke to the Mothers.

Once Benjamin saw my condition he ran up to evaluate. After a moment Benjamin said, "Her pulse is steady, her pupils are responding normally, and her heart rate is regular. I suspect she was injected with some kind of liquid form of a sleeping agent. I can smell some dried blood on her right leg, I suspect that's where she was poked. I think we should get an I.V. started to help her system drain the drug from her system.

"I agree," Nicholas said. "Perhaps we should check on previous injuries to make a complete decision."

Benjamin looked perplexed until Nicholas took off my winter coat and lifted my shirt to expose my previously cracked ribs. "Ah," Benjamin said, "It would seem these ribs have not been given the proper time to heal. How long ago did these injuries take place?"

"A few months ago," Nicholas answered solemnly.

Benjamin laughed, "She isn't too far off the normal path, but I'm guessing she's too active for her own good."

Victoria jumped in, "Not only does she workout, but she spars with a werewolf every Thursday morning. We've all been on spy on Vera mode since Nicholas first set eyes on her."

Nicholas laughed and rubbed his face in embarrassment. "Yes, she's a little overactive."

"Wait a minute," William put his hand up as he said, "Is this the same girl who beat you in chess and stuck that poor boy on you to get you to join the chess club?"

Aiden laughed, "Yeah she is, she kicks his butt in more than one way. For instance, Nicholas's compulsion doesn't work on her."

"What?!" Katerina asked incredulously. "How?!"

"I'm not sure, this has never happened before," Nicholas admitted.

"How do you know she isn't involved with the Canali's?!" Katerina was eyeing Vera like she was the spawn of Satan.

Before Nicholas could defend me, Emma said, "I couldn't agree more. I think she might be a danger to us all."

Benjamin spoke louder than all the voices starting to debate the question at hand. "Why don't I ask her?" Benjamin had the ability to get people to tell the truth, no matter how strong their loyalties.

Everyone looked at each other silently, "Okay," "Yeah," eventually came from the crowd.

Nicholas pulled Vera closer without realizing he was. "As long as there are no adverse effects your power would have with the sleeping pill, then sure." Nicholas cautioned.

Benjamin spoke in a deeper voice than his already deep voice, "Vera, what is your last name?"

She groggily answered "…Bianchi."

Everyone looked around at each other in amusement.

"Vera, are you connected to the Canali Family?"

"…What do you mean?"

"Are you a spy for the Canali's?"

"…No."

"Why did you come to Arcata?"

"…I'm running away," her breathing quickened, "I'm not safe here, I have to leave, Anna said so herself."

"Who is Anna?"

"…My maidservant, though she is more like my Mother."

"How well do you know Marcus Canali?"

"…I don't, I've only talked to him a few times."

Nicholas mouthed Peter.

"How well do you know Peter Canali?"

"…I know him better than any of the others, he asks me to dance at every party we're together. He took me to Arcata. He told me he loves me."

Everyone gasped in horror.

"Do you love him back?"

"…Hell no. I'll never love that… Pig."

Victoria laughed out loud, and Benjamin flashed a scowl.

"Why not, Vera?"

"…He likes to play games with people. Something about him makes me cringe with worry, he's killed people before. But I'm glad he killed Petrov."

"How is your Father connected to the Canali family?"

"…I don't know much about Papa's business, just that it's illegal and dangerous. I think Papa does business with Marcus."

"Why did you choose Arcata, California to move to?"

"… I wanted to be in the United States, the land of the free. And I wanted to live in a small town because I supposed I might find the answer to the question of life. Arcata somehow spoke to me, I considered other places, but I wanted Arcata."

"What is the question of life?"

"…How to find true happiness."

Nicholas smiled at my quest. Benjamin noted Nicholas's affection toward me.

"Vera, do you love Nicholas?"

Everyone seemed to hold their breaths.

"…No."

"Do you love anyone romantically?"

"…I used to love Stefan, and I'm afraid I still might. Nick is a growing love, I haven't known him long. And yet, I find myself drawn more to him than anyone else I've ever known. And Owen is a growing love, though his love is different than Nick's. I thought Owen would be more like a brother, but he doesn't treat me like a sister."

"How so?"

"...Nick's is a deeper love, with little passion. Owen's love is superficial with more passion. Both can develop what the other lacks, but Nick's love has happened in the correct order. I can be assured when I give myself to him, that he has fallen in love with my naked soul. I wait to see how everything unfolds." Nicholas smiled at this.

"Who is Owen?"

...Silence...

Benjamin stated, "My influence has worn off. We'll have to wait if we need to know more information. I think the rest will do her good, I'm not sure how long she'll be out, but she should really try to focus on healing her old injuries."

Nicholas said in amusement, "It's Owen Multnomah."

Everyone sighed like, 'oh, of course, she would be that mixed up with a Multnomah.' However, everyone seemed to be at ease with the verdict, Victoria put a movie on for Nicholas, they all did their own thing but lingered in the living room with the mysterious girl who seemed to hold their attention. And they stayed to watch the miracle of Nicholas loving the mysterious woman.

Vera slept all that day and all that night, Nicholas stayed with her barely taking his eyes off her. He never put her down and held her firmly.

Everyone felt a shift in the wind; both marvelous and terrible things were now coming.

Vera started stirring in the morning; Nicholas ran her upstairs to his bed and sat at his desk.

****

****

I opened my eyes, and my head pounded. I grabbed my head and looked around; I saw my luggage on the big chest at the end of the bed. Then my eyes focused on a figure of a man, I gasped and threw myself off the bed too quickly. I passed out for a brief moment; before I hit the floor Nicholas was cradling my body again.

"Nick?" I asked dazedly.

"Yes, it's me." He walked me back to his bed and set me down.

"But- Stefan.."

"I know, I saw him take you and followed his car to an old motel. When he left the room, Aiden and I went in and grabbed you."

I sighed and threw myself at him. "Thank you."

He welcomed my affection and kissed my forehead. "Anytime, anyplace." He meant that more than I was aware. Everyone downstairs was overhearing our conversation and understood precisely what he meant.

"Can I borrow your shower?" I asked drowsily.

"Of course, take your time." He grabbed my bag of toiletries and set them on the bathroom counter. "Victoria explained everything to Matt, you're supposedly staying in a hotel with her until Stefan leaves, but you're actually going to stay here."

I nodded and thanked him. Nicholas left closing the door behind him. I cried quietly from fear and sat on the floor putting my head in my hands. Little did I know this was something everyone could hear. I started the shower water and brushed my teeth wiping tears away all the while. After I was ready, I sat on Nick's bed and tried to process everything.

I eventually went downstairs and became startled at the 8 pairs of eyes staring at me on the way down. I stopped in my tracks and furrowed my brow, looking for Nick. Nicholas stood up and smiled holding out his hand.

"Oh Vera, I'm sorry I forgot to tell you about every member of my big conjoined family." I took his hand and held onto his arm, almost for support. I was very tired, hungry, and thirsty.

Nicholas said, "These are my parents, William and Katerina."

"Oh, it is so good to meet you at last," Katerina said ecstatically.

"Good to meet you," I smiled and dipped my head.

"And these are the Butler's, Benjamin and Emma," Nicholas said gesturing to the little woman and large black man.

"I think you'd better feed your girl Nicholas, she's been out for about 24 hours. No doubt she's weak and thirsty," Benjamin said. He and Emma were both smiling pleasantly at me.

I was confused by the way he spoke-- it was so different from anything I was used to.

"Of course," Nicholas said in a way that sounded like th s was something he should've thought of.

He led the way to the kitchen which was coincidently stocked with all my favorite foods. Nicholas made himself and me a salad. Nicholas didn't seem to be hungry, but he ate with me anyway. I'd guess it was so that I didn't feel bad for eating alone.

I sat at their bar drinking a full glass of water while he made the food.

"What day is it?" I asked.

"It's Tuesday morning, 9:00."

"Why was I asleep so long?"

"Stefan drugged you. Benjamin is pretty sure it was just a sleeping agent, nothing serious." He tried to say coolly.

"This is your house?" I was still confused.

Nicholas smiled as he chopped a tomato, "Yes it is, I'm sorry I haven't explained everything very well, have I?"

I smiled, "It's okay."

I looked outside to the winter wonderland, "Oh my gosh that's a lot of snow." I must've looked like a little child with my excitement. "Is that why you're all home, snow day?"

Nicholas laughed, he wasn't used to having to account for his attendance at school, "It is actually a snow day, but I think we all would want to stay to keep you company even if it wasn't."

I frowned, "Oh don't let me be of any trouble to you."

Nicholas smiled again, "Vera, I said 'we would all want' that means it's no trouble to any of us.

I didn't say anything at first, "Do I still have my coat?"

"Yes, it's hanging in the coat closet." He pointed to it with his knife, but the distance from the kitchen to the closet was too far for me to grasp which door it was.

Nicholas finished making our food and sat on one of the stools at the bar, he patted the seat next to him for me to come to sit by him. I walked over to grab my empty glass and filled it with more water, then sat next to him.

"Hmm, excellent salad Nick, wherever did you learn to cook like this?!" I quipped.

"Well, it's all in the raising of the garden- which I obviously do. Then it's in the hand motion to chop the lettuce just right." He tried to pull this off with a severe tone, but he couldn't help but have under laced sarcasm.

I laughed, "What's the funniest thing you've seen or heard this week?"

He paused and thought for a moment, "Aiden tried on Victoria's shoes to piss her off."

"You're joking right?"

"Yeah, I am. I only wish that happened."

"Well, I heard Matt singing in the shower Sunday night."

Nicholas chuckled, "No, now you must be joking."

"I'm not, it sounded like something was dying. But I think his encore was better."

I heard a laugh from behind me, Victoria had walked up to the bar. "I still have the video of Theodor if you want to see it?"

"Yes, please!" I yelled.

Nicholas looked blank. "Oh come on Nick, be a good sport!" I said enthusiastically.

"All right," He grumbled. We finished our meal and Nicholas put our dishes in the sink.

We all walked into the living room and took a seat while Victoria set it up. It was great watching it, it completely took my mind off of Stefan.

The day passed quickly, part of the reason it did was that I fell asleep mid-day on Nicholas's shoulder.

Stefan stayed in town till Friday morning. When I didn't show to the sparring match on Thursday, Owen called Matt who explained everything. Owen grew weary of the fact I was with Victoria in a hotel room all week.

I grew rather fond of Nicholas's family; we spent all day together-- all of us. I wasn't sure why the Father's didn't go to work to pass the time, or why no one did anything but stay together.

After the news spread the coast was clear I went upstairs to pack my belongings, Nicholas followed to help.

It was funny he 'came to help me pack' because the first thing he did when he got in his room was lay on his bed.

While crossing his legs, he looked off into the distance. I wasn't sure what he was doing, but he breathed in deeply a few times. His hands shook lightly, so he tucked them under his head.

"Thanks for letting me come, and thank you for letting me steal your bed," I said as I thoughtlessly refolded my clothes to fit in my suitcase.

Nicholas laughed, "You're welcome to it anytime."

"Where did you sleep anyway?"

"Oh here and there." He smiled in a way I wasn't familiar with.

"What?" I asked.

Nicholas walked over to me from his bed where he was laying. His face looked cautious yet determined. "Vera," he tucked my hair behind my ear, "Come back soon."

I smiled, "If I can find your house."

Nicholas laughed for a second then turned the full fury of his Green eyes on me. He took a step closer putting his hand on my cheek and brushing my lips with his thumb. He slowly pulled me into his icy grip and exhaled like he did at school. His breath was phenomenal, I found myself entangled in him in every thought. His hands never stopped shaking as he placed them under my chin and tilted it up to kiss me softly. My stomach churned in emotion, and I kissed him back in like manner.

I grabbed his hair on the back of his head and pulled myself even closer to him. He gasped at how it feels to be kissed- to

162

be loved- to be touched. He paused to make sure he could handle the feeling.

I asked, "What brought this on?"

He smiled, "From the day I met you, Vera, I have wanted you. In. Every. Way. And I tried to keep myself from jumping in too quick, but I've recently learned that holding back has been a detriment. I am so glad it has because now I can express myself more fully."

I smiled, "Well it's about time."

He laughed and put his forehead to mine, then sighed deeply letting me go.

"A little at a time," He told himself out loud.

"I couldn't agree more," I said zipping up my luggage. He grabbed it for me and took it to the car. After I said my goodbyes Nicholas and I drove to Matt's house, it was only 3:00, so Matt would be at work for 2 more hours.

"Would you like to come in?"

"I'd better not," he looked down and smiled to himself, "I don't think I can have any more self-restraint for the rest of the week."

I laughed and got out of the car grabbing my stuff. I waved to him at the front door then let myself in. I went upstairs to start unpacking when I realized I could still smell him on my clothes. I breathed each of them in on their way to their proper places.

When Matt came home, I treated him to some homemade lasagna and breadsticks. The timing on its preparation was luckily perfect.

"Vera! So good to see you." Matt said as he whiffed his hand from the lasagna pan to his nose.

"Good to be back, Matt." Though I felt like that was a lie somehow, perhaps I wanted to stay with Nick? No, I knew I wanted to stay with Nick, who was I trying to kid.

"You know you can get a restraining order on Stefan kiddo?"

"I doubt that would be any good if I'm being completely honest."

"I can see why you say that I just figured I'd let you know," Matt said scooping up heaps of lasagna on his plate.

"Thanks, Matt."

"Oh, the Multnomah's are coming here soon. It's another game night. Plus you missed your sparring match with Owen yesterday, so he's quite concerned."

"Oh great," I mumbled.

This amused Matt, for once he looked up from his plate to me. We heard a vehicle rumbling into the driveway, it was obviously the Multnomah's because their truck had a specific sound.

It was hard leaving my Nicholas box to enter the level-headed box where I was keeping my options open.

Matt got to the door before they knocked. "Hey, Y'all," Matt said happily.

"Is Vera home yet," I heard Owen ask concerned.

"Yep, she's in the kitchen."

I pretended I didn't hear and started the sink water to rinse my dish before putting it in the dishwasher. I was startled when Owen goosed me from behind.

"Owen," I smacked his giant peck.

Owen grabbed me and twirled me around laughing. "It's so good to see you, I was worried about you."

I sarcastically whispered, "Because I was with a Butler all week?" I was annoyed he held such an incorrect opinion of my good friends who had not only saved my life but were the kindest people in the world.

"That and Stefan. How did you find out he was in town? Matt had to watch closely to see he was sometimes outside his house and running around town in a sneaky and seemingly organized way. I mean, what happened?"

I shuddered at the thought, "It's a long story," I tried to blow it off.

"And I want to hear all the details."

I sighed and looked away setting my jaw to the side. Matt and Kit walked through the kitchen door into the awkward silence.

"Oh." Kit said, "Did we walk in on something- do you want us to leave?" He was half turned back already.

"Not at all," Owen said without looking away from me. "Vera was just about to share what happened when Stefan was in town."

"This is something I want to hear," Matt said.

I sighed, "Why does it matter? I'm here now. It's not a big deal."

No one spoke, and no one moved. Owen crossed his massive arms and leaned back on the counter to make himself comfortable while he waited for me to speak.

Matt started, "You're right, it's not a big deal. So why don't you tell us?"

"Because you'll make a big deal about it," I answered trying to put some kind of blame on their behavior, but really it was just that I didn't want them to worry about me so much. Why did I have to be such trouble?

Once again everyone just waited for me to speak. "Alright, but you all have to promise me not to freak out, okay?!" I made a face which said this was a point I wasn't going to budge on.

They all hummed a, "Yeah, course, sure."

"He found me in the school parking lot all by myself. I tried to run, but the snow made me slip. He caught up to me and drugged me- I was out before we reached his car. The King's and Butlers saw him pull out and followed him to a ran down motel. They waited for him to leave, then Aiden and Nicholas carried me out."

Owen was furious, "How do you know he didn't do anything to you?"

"Well, I still had my clothes on."

Owen continued in his frustration, "Oh that's reassuring! What does he want? Is there another party or something?"

"He said something about making me remember I still loved him or something. I don't know it's all a little fuzzy." I only wish it was a little fuzzier.

All three of them were livid. "I knew this would happen," I yelled, "I am never telling you anything else ever again." The guilt was eating at me, and part of my guilt came from pinning it on them.

Matt was also obviously mad, "Well it's a bigger deal than you made it seem Vera. I was not expecting anything like that!"

I sighed and lifted my body from the edge of the counter where it was resting. And walked into the living room, Owen wasn't far behind me and grabbed me before I reached the couch.

"Vera, please don't be upset- your anger is being misdirected."

"I know you're right. I'm sorry." Freak, how did he know?!

He pulled me into one of his warm bear hugs which were more comforting than I remembered. It was too natural to be physically close to Owen. Maybe it's because his stature reminded me of someone who I had a long history with. I was going to have to watch myself around him if I was going to try not to be singled off with one man.

I released our hug that was starting to get dangerously long. He smiled at me, grabbed my shoulder, and pulled me down on the couch right next to him where he proceeded to keep his arm around me. I changed my mind about why it was so easy to be physical with him; it was because he barely checked himself. He was communicating clearly that he wanted me to be his only.

Since the whole week was spent resting I found it easy to stay awake and go to bed at a proper time, which I was intending because falling asleep on Owen spelled exclusivity.

Chapter Seven: Who's Afraid Of The Big, Bad Wolf?

This morning I drove to Eureka early to try to find a good Little Red Riding Hood costume. Unfortunately, today was Halloween, and that was a popular costume. I went all over trying to find something. At 3:00 I was ready to give up when I saw one more Halloween store, crossing my fingers I walked in to see an overly helpful employee.

He was more than happy to show me his last Little Red Riding Hood costume. It had a black corset torso with red strings in a crisscross pattern, a White sleeveless sweetheart neckline, a short red body with white lace on the bottom and a mini white apron, and a long red cape with a hood.

I wondered if Halloween was created as an excuse for girls to dress like sluts or something. I groaned and bought it after trying it on- surprisingly it fit perfectly. The overly helpful worker said it was the last one because it was too tall for the rest of the girls who wanted it.

I got back home early enough to spend as much time as I wanted to doll myself up, so I did I. I decided on wearing my thigh high black boots with the costume. When I walked downstairs, Matt just gave me 'the look' but didn't say anything.

"Don't start on me Matt, it was the last one. I shouldn't have procrastinated." I said giving him the look right back.

"Who's saying anything?" He said as he sipped his soda from his chair and purposefully gave me 'the look' again.

Luckily it didn't take any time for Owen to come to the door. He practically jumped out of his own costume once he saw mine.

After we were out of earshot from Matt, Owen said, "Nice costume," in a tone that both approved and taunted.

"Ugh. It was the last one, I went to Eureka and shopped all day today trying to find something. Do you know how popular this costume is?"

He opened my door for me and after he got inside said, "Oh I'm not complaining," then flashed his pearly white smile. "I guess girls just like being wolf prey." He smirked to himself like this was an especially funny joke.

"Do you think that's so funny cause you're dressed as a wolf one night a year?" I gave him an unapproving look. "I'm not your prey, I'd kick your butt." I bluffed knowing it was entirely untrue.

Owen looked at me like 'you're joking' and said: "I'll let you think that."

We were a little late getting to the Halloween party, on the way I asked him what his friends were like. They were all apparently Natives that lived with him outside the Reservation in Grand Ronde, Oregon. Grand Ronde was about seven hours away from Arcata. The way it worked is there was a small band of Natives who lived in Arcata apart from the reservation in Oregon, but they were allowed the same privileges as though they were on a reservation.

He walked straight into his friend's house, it was decorated to the max with celebrations of the dead. I about died when I saw 11 guys and no girls. After brief introductions, a couple of guys moved from the couch, so Owen and I had a seat. Of course, most of them gave Owen the 'nice dude' look. Just then I saw a few girls emerge from the kitchen with Halloween themed appetizers. I relaxed quite a bit.

Monica laughed at Owen and gave him a fist bump, "Owe, I love your costume!" The whole room broke into laughter, and I was totally lost why it was so funny. I looked at Owen confused; he just put his arm around my neck and kissed my temple.

If Owen weren't going to tell me I was sure someone would. "What's so funny?"

Everyone fell silent with a few of them snickering, "She doesn't know?"

"Know what," I looked at the one who said that.

He looked at Owen, and his face dropped then looked down, "We're just messing with you-er- Vera. There's no joke." The suddenly shy boy explained poorly.

I was not convinced, but I also knew no one was going to tell me.

We started the night by playing minute to win it games Halloween style. Because I was extremely competitive I was a great asset to our team. Everyone loved my enthusiasm and the fact that I was entirely willing to chest bump when we won.

By the end of the night, I knew everyone by name. There were two guys that had the same build as Owen, they're names were Liam and Elijah, then there were about 6 with a smaller stature, but still quite muscular named Jack, Greyson, Dylan, Chris, Levi, and Adrian, then three who were once again still muscular, but the smallest of the group named Leo, Josh, and Mateo. The smallest also were the most rambunctious and immature, they made for more fun company because it was so easy to get under their skin.

The three girls there were Monica, Katie, and Laura, they were all down to earth good girls. They were the girlfriends of Levi, Chris, and Elijah. Us girls went to the kitchen to scrounge up some more food after some of the games. I swore teenage boys were half goat, they ate everything in sight.

"Do all these guys spend all their time together?" I asked.

The three girls all smiled at each other, "Pretty much," Katie laughed.

"In a weird way they're all like in sync or something," I continued.

They all laughed at the joke I wasn't intending on making, 'maybe they are all just really easy to please' I thought to myself. I finally said, "I feel like there's something you are all laughing about that's right under my nose. What's the big joke?"

After our conversation started everyone in the other room was quiet like they were listening in. But there was no way that could be possible since I was speaking quietly, and we were in a different place with Halloween music playing loudly.

The girls all shifted uneasily, "There really isn't a joke. You're overthinking it, Vera, really it's nothing to worry about," Laura said smiling. Of all the girls, Laura was the most maternal and kind.

"Maybe you're right," I said out loud though I was thinking, 'you are all lying to me, and I'm going to figure out what it is.' I was perturbed they must've thought me to be as dumb as they were treating me. Although it seemed uncondescending like they were more concerned about keeping a secret.

We brought out a ton of finger sandwiches which were eaten up faster than we could've made them if there were 10 of us.

I had to make up a game plan- who was their weakest link- who would tell me the secret they all loved but were too proud, or too scared to say? Josh. He was worse than a pregnant woman on steroids in the temper department, and he was incredibly immature. Game on Owen, there's something here. I know it, and you're sticking it in my face then calling me crazy. IT IS ON!

I picked on Josh the rest of the night. While everyone else thought it was all in fun and loved the spunk, I eyed Josh with the deepest of communication telling him I was onto him, and that I was going to win. He only grew more and more frustrated as the night progressed.

"Jeez Josh, calm down," Elijah said after Josh lost another game. With every victory, he grew more boisterous and with every defeat more flustered. I had him right where I wanted him, Josh was on the brink of mental breakdown. It was getting late, and he complained he was getting hungry again.

I had a speech prepared that would bait him to spill his guts, the trap was set, all I was waiting for was Owen to leave. I had an instinct for these things, for some reason I knew that if Owen were there, Josh wouldn't say a word.

The party was going to end with a scary movie, we all moved to the living room again. I had been fluid pushing Owen all night, and it finally paid off, as we all sat down Owen left to take a bathroom break before the movie started.

I opened my mouth to start my speech when instead Mateo teased Josh about his inability to grow facial hair or something. Josh was losing it, and it was physically visible, I thought there was something wrong with him like he was having a seizure. I got up and ran a couple feet toward him to help poor Josh, but Liam bolted off the floor and grabbed me tackling me down. Everyone stepped a few yards from Josh calmly like it was routine. Elijah commanded him to calm down. I couldn't believe what I was seeing- no one was helping him. I wrestled with Liam to make him let me go so I could help Josh.

Liam was way too strong for me, though he seemed to enjoy my attempt. He picked me off the floor and faced me toward Josh, but he still had his massive arms around me. Josh started calming down when Leo, the third of the smallest teased, "Don't even get us started on his inability to get a girlfriend." Elijah commanded Leo to be quiet.

Josh let it slip by him without an effect. Then Levi, who was a middle-type guy hit a little below the belt and said: "It's probably because his balls haven't dropped yet, or his wiener's too small."

Such childish chides.

Josh lost it and hunched backward then forwards in a snapping motion and growled a snarl. I was terrified! "Does he have a mental problem?" I asked Liam quietly.

Liam and everyone else in the room laughed hard, and Josh snapped the rest of the way. He broke out of his clothes and transformed into a wolf. Josh lunged at me from my last comment, and I screamed. Liam threw me behind him and held out his hands, he commanded Josh to control himself.

I ran for it. Liam caught my cape, but I slipped it off quickly by untying the bow around my neck. I ran to the bathroom where Owen was whistling and washing his hands. I slammed the door behind me and locked it. Owen, of course, heard everything but played along.

"We have to get out of here!" I yelled while throwing the large window open.

"Why?" Owen yelled back.

"You won't believe me-- just come on!" I was halfway out the window when he pulled me back in and pinned me against the wall.

"What, are you afraid of the big bad wolf?" Owen asked in a low, teasing, sensual tone.

"Owen," I started, "This is hardly an appropriate response.." Then the light bulb went on, and I figured out what he was saying. "You-?" My face must've looked like a million bucks, a mix between fear, figuring it out, and trying to think of what to do next.

"Does Matt know?" was all I could think of saying.

"Yes, he does. My Dad told him ages ago since they were best friends."

I was borderline pissed off or ready to cry. Owen laughed heartily and gave me a hug- like that would help. "Owen!" I hit his giant peck.

He laughed again and said, "You asked for it. I saw what you were up to the moment you singled Josh out. But your brilliant deduction encouraged a reward, plus I didn't think it would work."

I tried not to be amused, though I was. "Does anyone else know about this?"

"Everyone in our tribe does," I could tell he was picking his words carefully now "no 'civilians' know. So you have to swear to secrecy."

I still didn't know how I felt about all this. "I won't tell anyone." I finally managed. I wondered to myself who didn't count as a civilian.

"Good, now let's start that movie." He said while grabbing my hand.

I was stiff, I didn't want to see Josh for the rest of the night. Owen pulled me hard enough for me to know he wasn't going to take no for an answer. Before I left his presence, Owen had to be sure I was comfortable with my new knowledge.

I looked at Josh hesitantly he was in clothes too big for him now.

He laughed at me and said, "I'm so sorry Vera," completely sarcastic.

That pissed me right off, and here I was going to run to his aid. "Josh if you ever lunge at me again like that I'll rip your puny balls off with my bare hands."

Everyone ripped into laughter. Owen led the way to the couch and sat me down next to him.

Josh countered, "I'd let you try."

Now Owen was pissed and shot him a disapproving look that shut that fantasy down fast.

"Now I get the Little Red Riding Hood joke!" I said elatedly.

Everyone laughed again. "Yeah that was a funny pun Owen," Liam said approvingly.

Owen said, "Yeah, well that and Vera looks great as my prey." All the guys laughed at that, but the girls rolled their eyes.

"My, my grandma, what a big head you have," I said in all seriousness.

That comment was the highlight of my night. It stupefied Owen.

I was entirely wiped out- it was way past my usual bedtime, and I always felt tired after a jolt of fear. Not even the blood and gore of the movie kept my adrenaline up. Owen was warm, and comfortable as usual and falling asleep on him was getting too easy, luckily before I was entirely asleep on his shoulder my phone rang.

It was Matt, "Hey Matt," I answered standing up and picking my cape off the floor.

"Hey Vera, I just wanted to let you know that I'm going to bed." I loved Matt, most of the time he saved my bacon like a real Dad.

I smiled, "Okay we're just watching a movie, and I should be home after that."

"Who's saying anything? Good night."

"Night."

I walked back to the couch and leaned forward to keep myself from falling asleep again.

After I got home, I was barely able to walk myself up to my bed.

Sarah was in the kitchen polishing off a bowl of cereal. I hadn't seen her for a long time. I wondered why it was that she chose this life.

"Sarah, how are you?" I asked enthusiastically.

She looked tired, "I'm very good dear, how are you?"

"Tired, haha!"

"Yeah me too, I'm glad you're happy here, Vera."

"I couldn't have asked for a better place to live, to be honest."

"I'm sorry I'm not around very much." She looked down sadly, as though she was ashamed she couldn't spend more time with her 'daughter'.

"That's okay, Sarah. I just don't understand how you and Matt can do it."

"He sees me every day, we have lunch together."

I smiled almost relieved, for some reason I worried about them like a child might for the relationship with her parents. "I'm glad, I know it isn't really my place, but I've been concerned about that."

She looked proud, "Don't worry, dear. Matt and I are meant to be. Nothing about us is changing anytime soon."

I was happy and content with that. I said my goodnights and walked upstairs slowly. I pulled off my shoes before hitting the sack.

I spent most of Sunday sleeping. The Multnomah's came over for Sunday night game night as usual. I had so many questions, I was glad Owen was coming over.

Once they got inside, I asked for Owen's help in the kitchen, which I admit was a little conspicuous.

"So what exactly are you?" I asked once the T.V. was blaring.

"Well, we call ourselves wolfs because we're not like a werewolf who can only change at a full moon. We can change at will. But we can only change into a wolf, and not all of us can."

"What do you mean by us?" I asked as I slapped the top of the sandwich I was making together.

"Native Americans. We all have the bloodline, that's why it's common to see wolfs associated with Native Americans, though no one actually knows that besides us."

"Hmm." I stooped down to pull a salad from the fridge. "It looks like there's a pecking order, but I can't figure out who is chief-you, Liam, or Elijah."

"You are very smart, I'm the acting chief when my Dad isn't around, and Liam is my number two, Elijah my number three." He was leaning on the fridge with his arms crossed. There was a hint of shyness when he admitted to being the alpha like it was something he was proud of in a humble way and would never brag about it.

"Oh, I like pickles on mine," He interrupted.

"You can put them on yourself," I said.

"But I hate getting my fingers pickle juiced. Please do it." He whined.

"Oh bite me." I shot a wink at him, this was going to be the start of a lot of puns and jokes in the werewolf department.

Owen smiled a full smile and chuckled. "I've created a monster."

"No, I made myself. You just let her out, and you are doomed. I'll let you sink your teeth into that for a moment." I smiled and grabbed three plates of food and left the kitchen all smiles. Kit could hear everything; of course, he was also softly chuckling when I handed him his plate.

Owen came in with his sandwich and sat next to me. During the game, Owen complained about being tired over and over. I told him to suck it up most of the time, but the last time he complained I said, "Hey Owen, what do you call a sleeping werewolf? An unaware-wolf."

Owen thought it was funny but pretended he didn't and gently smacked my face with the decorative pillow he was leaning on. I chuckled and said, "Good luck sleeping now, I have your pillow."

To prove me wrong, he threw his feet on my lap and curled into a ball on the couch. "Maybe you're half cat," I whispered in his ear right before he was asleep.

"If you don't shut up I'm sleeping in your bed." He threatened. And just like that, he was out.

...

Monday morning came early. It was the first day I was able to work out for a week, plus my sleeping schedule was way out of whack. It felt like I hadn't seen Nicholas in ages.

I hustled to school to see Nicholas waiting under our tree. I ran up to him and gave him a huge hug, which wasn't our norm- so it took him off guard in a good way.

"How was your Halloween," He asked with an odd tone.

"It was weird. I went on a date with a guy and, we had fun, but it was not what I was expecting." I said as we walked to history. "How about yours?"

He was more interested in my Halloween, "Weird in a good way, or weird in a bad way?" He seemed to be fishing for an answer he really wanted to know.

"Good, I think. I guess time will tell."

He smiled at my answer apparently happy about it. "My Halloween was --fairly-- uneventful."

"What did you do?"

"Espionage."

"Oh come on, seriously." I set my books down on my desk.

He laughed a beautiful, smooth laugh, one that made me gush. It was hard not to dote on Nick. "There isn't much to do when you're too old to trick or treat. I found things to do here and there." He glanced at me with a playful look. Kind of like the one he gave me when he said that he slept here and there when I asked where he slept as I stole his bed.

"Oh, sad tsk-tsk next year I'll have to show you a real good time."

"And who might you dress up as? Dracula's bride?' He smirked.

"I can't decide that a year in advance." I countered unaware of what he was saying. I logged it into my Nicholas file because it was one of those things that had that particular feeling. 'Hmm, Dracula's bride? Why that?'

The class was called to attention, and I had a whole hour to decipher his coded message.

During class he kept sneaking peeks at me, and I returned them with my 'thinking face.' After History Nicholas asked what it was, I was thinking about.

"You. And what you said." I answered generally.

"What specifically?" He probed.

"There's something about you that I can't quite put my thumb on Nick. And whatever it is, I had decided to let it go. But after certain events this weekend, my curiosity has been piqued."

Now it was him who was thinking hard.

"What are you thinking about?" I asked.

"To be, or not to be; that is the question." He smiled looking down.

I understood all too well what it was he was saying, it was his big secret. "It's your choice whether or not to tell, but just know that I will be on the other end of the dark tunnel trying to figure you out."

"I'll let you know if I'll meet you half way." He smiled again.

It was so exhilarating trying to discover the unknown, to touch something unimaginable. I could feel it in my bosom that I was on the verge of a world I've never known. Little did I know I was already in the realm of the unknown- I was already seeing, touching, hearing, and breathing the unimaginable.

During lunch, Savanna was talking about Christmas and Thanksgiving. I was already in Christmas mode because I hadn't celebrated Thanksgiving before.

Savanna was appalled, "Vera what do you think Thanksgiving is?"

"The day Americans eats turkeys," I answered straight.

Everyone at my table chuckled, and Savanna continued, "No, no, no, it's so much more than that! It's a holiday to give thanks for everything you have by eating a lot of food."

I laughed, "American's would think of a holiday to eat as much food as humanly possible!"

Savannah rolled her eyes, "Just wait until you try pumpkin pie!"

In the parking lot Victoria ran up to Nicholas and me, she was winded, but somehow it didn't seem like she actually was. "Vera, I'm so glad I caught up to you. My family is staying in town for Thanksgiving this year, I was wondering if you, Sarah, and Matt wanted to join us?"

I smiled and said, "I'd love to; I'll make sure Matt doesn't have something planned already."

"Great, also you guys should come over for dinner this Friday," Victoria added.

"Are you up to something Victoria?" Nicholas chided.

"Who, me? Never." Victoria winked and giggled wa king off before I could answer.

I didn't care if she was or wasn't up to something, I just wanted to see Nicholas all the time.

Before I left Nicholas in the parking lot, I grabbed his arm during his usual split from me to his car, "Nick, I hope you meet me half way."

He looked at me almost pained and said: "Vera, I'm afraid to run you off."

"Can I take you home?" I offered.

"No, thanks." He hung his head and walked off.

I was confused, he knew my past. What in the world could run me off? I pulled into my house and put together some 'rabbit food' for dinner. I wasn't paying much attention to my surroundings. After I chopped the chicken I felt a chill run down my spine, there was a chill in my surroundings. I stopped what I was doing and looked around.

Something about the house was dark… And my body was filled with goosebumps. Someone was here…

There was some kind of shadow bolting around, it looked like the same looking shadow in the school while I was dancing. I walked slowly toward the living room cautiously.

I saw no one, it was too hushed… Too quiet. There was death in the air. I peeked into the coat closet and around the furniture in the living room. I felt a shadow stop behind me. I gasped and turned around to see a perfectly still Peter Canali.

"Ahh," I yelled putting my hand on my chest. "Peter you scared me!"

He smirked, "Yeah I know."

I was scared, he was acting weird. I stepped away from him, "What are you doing here?"

"I'm here to take you home Vera."

"Why you?"

His still face turned angry. "I don't understand, why not me? Am I not good enough for you?" He started to yell.

"What are you talking about? Why didn't Papa send Stefan or Big Al or something?"

His face lightened to amusement. "Ah, I see, you misunderstand. I'm here to take you to my home."

I looked disgusted, "No you're not. You don't even know me, I don't know you."

"And yet I find you are always on my mind. You owe me for bringing you to this pathetic place safely anyway."

I folded my arms, "I owe you nothing! Get out of my house!" I yelled pointing to the front door.

"You say that like you have the ability to enforce it." He laughed sinisterly. "You'll learn to love me, Vera, after all-- we'd have eternity."

"I don't know what you've disgustingly fantasized about us, but I'm warning you to leave and never come back."

He laughed again and took a step towards me, "Or what?"

"I'll kill you, or Matt will." I was firm but secretly afraid.

"That's what I like about you Vera, you can't be tamed. You're bold, and you speak your mind. Even when you know, I can run circles around you." He took another step towards me. "But, I like domiciling wild ones… It's somewhat of a hobby of mine." His head slightly tilted and returned upright, "I like breaking people."

I took a few steps back.

Peter continued, "My only regret was ever letting you go. Ha, twice!" He looked up and clenched his fist in disbelief.

 My breathing accelerated, I ran for the spot I knew Matt hid a handgun. He didn't move and let me get to where I was going. I held the gun with both hands and aimed it at him. "You have no right to assume authority over me. Get out, you're posing a threat to me, and I will kill you out of self-defense."

Peter looked at me incredulously pulling his eyebrows together. "I have every right to your insignificant life, I can do whatever I please to you or anyone else." He paused momentarily, "I can't figure out why I need you so badly. It's no matter now, I will have you all to myself from today on."

He lunged at me. I pulled the trigger and it went straight through him, in another moment the wound closed in his chest and he looked up at me. He was upset.

I stared at the freakish phenomenon I'd just witnessed. He ran at me at light speed and grabbed my gun yanking it out of my hands.

I was scared, "How did you do that?" I whispered with tears welling up.

He was still angry. "I can't believe you actually pulled the trigger!" He adjusted his head like he was cracking his neck, "I guess I have more breaking in to do than I thought." He crushed the gun to powder and grabbed me.

I stared at the powder that laid at my feet. I gulped then looked into his big green eyes, his cold hands as bone-chilling as Nicholas's. It all clicked into place.

"Wha-What are you?" I managed.

"I'm a vampire." He leered.

It made no sense at all. How was this real?! My mind was racing… 'Dracula's bride' I thought to myself. "Leave me alone Peter."

"I can't, that's the problem." He looked down at my whole body, "I wonder what is better, you, or your blood?" He pulled me into him and smelled my neck.

I tried some fighting moves Owen had taught me. But they had absolutely no effect.

"I hope you know that to me, that feels more like little tickles." He smiled and nibbled my earlobe.

I didn't know what to do. He picked me up and threw me over his shoulder like a ragdoll. I kicked and punched to no avail. When we reached outside, I heard a familiar noise, a growl of some sort. My hope was renewed. "HELP!" I yelled. Peter took off fast. Everything around me was moving more quickly than I could process it, it was a blur of green.

Something hit us hard, and I was knocked to the ground. I looked up coughing windily to see a pack of wolves. And Peter a couple of yards from me.

Peter's eyes grew wide, looking at the pack. They looked scarier than I had recalled in the partially dark room I was in when I first saw one. They were all black with pale white eyes and pointy ears. Their lips were pulled back exposing sharp jagged teeth.

Peter looked at me seeming to calculate if he could get away with me or not. I tried to get up to run to the wolves, but my leg hurt severely.

Another snarl rose from the most massive wolf, and Peter jumped straight up into the trees. "I'll be back Vera! There's no place you can run or hide! And to all you wolf boys; I'll be back with an army if you don't leave Vera to me. Consider whether one woman is worth all your brothers." He jumped from tree limb to tree limb until he was out of site.

I grabbed my leg and stood up with concerted effort. I sat on a rock and hid my face crying. The biggest dog whimpered and nudged me until I was crying on him with my arms wrapped around its horse-like neck. "I-I don't understand. Why me?! I barely even know him!"

I looked up again to assess our surroundings. "Where are we anyway?"

The big wolf just helped me to my feet, and I walked around until I could step comfortably on my leg. It was a good several miles from my house, walking in silence was nice, it gave me time to think.

The herd of wolfs by my side stopped at the edge of the forest. I looked back and sighed walking up to my house. Matt was home by that time, and I was relieved I wouldn't be alone- I didn't want to be alone.

Chapter Eight: Fund Raising

I walked inside in all my glory; cry faced and scraped up. Matt ran up and gave me a hug. I sobbed into his shoulder. He sat me down on the couch and asked what happened, pointing to the gun and bullet hole in his wall.

"Matt, what all do you know about the mythical world?" I asked seriously.

He was shocked "Umm I know that werewolves exist."

"Anything else," I asked.

"There's more?"

"Yeah, apparently there are also vampires. And bullets don't work on them." I said nodding to the bullet hole.

"Who is it?"

"Peter Canali, you know the guy that brought me home? I had no idea until today, I didn't even know about werewolves until Saturday night."

Matt looked like he'd seen a ghost. Who knows, maybe they're real too. I made every excuse to stay downstairs until the very last minute.

I eventually walked upstairs to get ready for bed, I went into my bedroom terrified of what I might see. Peter? Stefan? Nick? Owen? Nothing?

I opened my door carefully. After I looked around and didn't see anyone I closed the door, ran to my window to check the lock and close the blinds, then I bolted to my bed where I pulled the blankets over my head. If someone was going to get me, then I wasn't going to see them.

"Vera."

I jumped when I heard my name called. I yanked the covers from my head and looked around. I saw nothing. I was breathing heavily as I kept scanning my room, from the shadows I saw a man come forward.

"Who is it?" I asked with a slight tremble.

"It's Nick. I heard about what happened, and I'd like to talk you through it." He stepped closer to me.

"Are you a vampire?" I asked quickly.

"Yes, I am. But I mean you no harm." He said putting his hands in the air.

"Why didn't you tell me?" I had tears welling up in my eyes though I wasn't entirely sure why.

"I was worried you'd be afraid of me. Are you?"

"Am I what?"

"Afraid of me," he answered

"I'm not sure yet. I know that you differ from Peter, significantly." I answered honestly.

Nicholas moved closer to me then caught himself mid-stride, "Please don't fear me."

We sat in silence for a moment then I sighed and got out of bed, I walked up to Nicholas and folded my arms. "Maybe you should tell me your version."

Nicholas exhaled and said, "Vampires are vampires, like how a human is a human and a dog, a dog. But I have chosen a different lifestyle. I don't view people as my pawns in our eternal struggle for power. I have killed before, and I don't necessarily regret it either. But I haven't lived that way in decades."

"How old are you?" I asked.

"I was born in 1609."

I was dumbfounded. "Do you intend to go back to your old lifestyle?"

"Not if I can help it."

"What do you mean?"

He walked away pulling his hands through his hair and rubbed his face. "For you, Vera, I'm afraid I would do anything."

"Why, why me Nick?" I was ready to cry now.

"You… Intoxicate me, you… consume me. My emotions are true, but you should know it's a gift you have to draw those around you close to you. That's why everyone has a need to know you, romantically, friendly, as a parent, as a sibling, so on and so forth. Everyone, mortals and immortals alike all have specials gifts."

"How can you know you love the actual me?"

"Vera, that is a part of you, and I love more of you than just as a friend, or just physically."

I was ready to go back to bed. This was too much for me. I walked to my bed and climbed in.

Nicholas sighed in defeat. He walked dejectedly to leave out the window. He turned back to me after he reached the window. He walked up to me, sat on the edge of my bed and put his hand on my face.

"I wanted all this to be different, to come out different."

I huffed a laugh, "The timing is never perfect."

He looked down, "Have I lost you forever, Vera? If you so say, I will leave you be, and I won't push myself back into your life."

I waited a moment until he looked at me, "No, Nick you haven't lost me. I'm falling in love with you too, though I don't know if I 'love' you just yet. You are good, I know that, and you speak to me differently than all the rest. It's as though you speak to my soul."

Nick grabbed me and pulled me onto his lap in the same instant. He hugged me passionately and caressed my face looking into my eyes. "I love you, Vera. With all of me, and you can take all the time you need to figure out what you need, and what you want." He kissed me with the same passion as his hug.

"I don't mean to hurt you, Nick, I wouldn't want to. Why would you ever allow me the space to explore other men?"

"It's because I want what's best for you."

"What if you get hurt?"

"Ah… 'but he that dares not grasp the thorn should never crave the rose.' –Anne Bronte. You'd better get to bed, it's getting late.". I thought about what he had said, and it moved me deeply.

"Okay," I said as I got up from Nicholas's lap and walked to my desk chair where I had my pillow to snuggle with, I grabbed it and went into my bed. Nicholas tucked me in and laughed at my extra pillow.

"What's this for?"

"I'm afraid to be alone tonight," I admitted embarrassed.

Nick smiled bright and said, "Why didn't you say so?" He pulled the pillow from my arms and placed himself in its place.

"Will you be able to sleep with your pants on?" I asked this without insinuation.

"Vampires don't sleep."

"Really??"

"Shhh, go to sleep now," he played with my hair. Even though Nicholas was cold, he was comforting and soft. I buried myself in him and fell asleep quickly without a thought of the danger I was in.

…

Waking up to Nicholas was even better; he was indeed the most beautiful person I'd ever seen.

"Good morning," I smiled after turning off my morning alarm.

"Good morning, beautiful. I am truly amazed you're just as beautiful in the morning as you are in the daytime, and while you sleep."

I chuckled, "Thanks. You want to work out with me today? I can only assume you have eternal endurance?"

He smiled, "Well, not eternal, but pretty close to that, yes."

"Awesome I'm feeling some yoga today. I always stretch and run too." I sat up and stretched my arms when I said this.

"Yes, I shamefully admit that I-or one of my family members has been keeping our eyes on you day and night."

"I knew someone was watching me! I'd normally be creeped out, but since I'm so infatuated with you, I find that endearing." I got out of bed and stretched the rest of my body and yawned.

Nicholas huffed an approving laugh. "I'll go change into something that looks more like workout clothes. I'll be in your front yard before you are."

"You're on!" He was gone before I got to my dresser, I threw off my pajamas and dropped them in the hamper. Faster than ever I had a sports bra on and spandex. I tossed my hair into a ponytail, popped some gum in my mouth and hopped out my bedroom putting my shoes and socks on. I ran outside and there he was… Waiting for me. I couldn't believe it, I couldn't have been more than two minutes.

"You win," I said unhappily as I retied my laces. "That was incredible!"

He smoldered and said, "Maybe one day, you'll be just as fast as me."

I laughed feeling flattered someone as patient and kind as he would want me in such a way. It was crazy, the threat of immortality the day before this enticing invitation stirred entirely different emotions.

We were quiet as we worked out, but I couldn't concentrate on thinking. I was too aware of him and what he looked like, and it didn't help that he kept staring at me.

When we finished, I got ready for my day. When I was in the shower, all I could think was a quote I couldn't remember where I'd heard from which said: 'in life, there are three shapes you should avoid… Vicious circles, love triangles, and squared minds.' I was going to have to tell Owen I wasn't going to date him. There was no need to hurt anyone else, I knew I was most attracted to Nicholas, so Nicholas was who I was going to explore.

I called Owen on my way to school to tell him I wasn't going to date him anymore. He was convinced it was what Peter had said about amassing an army against the wolves and that I shouldn't give into my fears. I tried to tell him it was because I was going exclusively with Nick, but he wouldn't buy it. I was going to have to hard nose convince him.

Going to school with Nicholas was now different; it was more exciting and energetic. I could feel his constant presence, and I was glad he was there in my life. We held hands as we walked together and I sat at his table most days, about one day a week was spent at the Reed's table, and another at my old table.

As the weeks passed, I wouldn't even watch game nights with the guys so that I could separate myself from Owen, and more importantly so that Owen would have time to digest our new situation. After three weeks I joined them again for the football games, I was bored, it was Thanksgiving break, and I still wanted to be friends with Owen.

"Well look who's back from the dead," Matt said barely looking from the T.V. screen. Owen acted smooth, but I could tell he wanted to jump from his seat.

"And here to stay I think." I said as I eyed Owen who was sprawled out on the couch, "Can you make room for a zombie?"

He rolled his eyes at my supernatural joke. 'Back from the dead.' "What are the passwords?"

I thought for a brief second, "Try this one on for size: how do werewolves eat? They wolf it down."

Owen chuckled, "You're worse than Mateo. Nope, that's not right."

"Give me a hint?"

"Agree to come hang out with us tomorrow, as friends, of course. The guys have been asking about you since, well, you know."

I looked down involuntarily, "you got it." Owen sat up, and I sat down. "What are we going to do?"

"I don't know yet, but bring your coat and clothes for inside because we could do anything."

"How is everyone?"

"Same as always, but we have an addition to our crew; Scott."

"No way, that's awesome! How old is he?"

"14, so if you thought Josh was immature.." He made a wide-eyed face like it was the worst torture he's had to endure.

I laughed, "Oh boy, thanks for the heads up. What time?"

"I'll pick you up around 9:00."

Matt shushed us so he could watch in peace. It was a fun evening, and I made sure not to make any physical contact. I went to bed at a reasonable time so I wouldn't be tempted to sleep on Owen.

Wednesday morning I spent with Nicholas working out, though it was only a work out for me. Then a little after 9 Owen picked me up, he was a little more than excited. He opened my car door for me and hugged me before I jumped in. I loved the happiness exuding from him, as always, it made me very happy.

As we pulled into Liam's house, I recognized it as the place we were at on Halloween. It was probably their hang out spot because it was the biggest house of all of theirs.

Walking in I received a warm welcome from everyone, wolves have such happy characters. They sure know how to make you feel welcome.

"So Vera have you heard from the vamp in the woods yet?" Dylan asked, but everyone was wondering the same thing, they probably talked about it a lot.

"No, it's like I said in the woods, I don't know him very well. He lived in Italy with me, and I only saw him when my Papa would put on parties. Well, that and Peter brought me to Arcata once."

That made Owen tense up because he knew why I had to have help to come home.

"I hope he makes good on his threat!" Levi shouted excitedly with everyone in the company agreeing wholeheartedly.

"Are you guy's crazy?" I asked seriously. "You don't know who you're dealing with. He has connections from here to Tim-buck-two. I doubt he's ever been denied what he wants, he's going to be livid. Who knows what he's conjuring up."

"I say let them come. We'll put that entitled child in his place!" Elijah yelled, with concurring cheers following his.

"I'm not going to let you guys get hurt if it means saving one person. Be rational!" I argued.

"Vera, we know what we signed up for being on 'active duty' as we call it. We've all made oaths, and we've all been told the dangers. Vampires like Peter don't deserve to live." Liam said calmly but firm.

"Not for me you aren't, I refuse your help. I… care about all of you, and it isn't worth it to me." I retorted.

"Well, it's a good thing we don't take orders from you," Josh said snottily.

I stood up in frustration and went outside for a breather. Owen followed me out and wrapped his arm around me.

"Ver, look we care about you too. Do you really think this 'Peter' is going to stop at you? How many other people has he hurt, or will hurt if we don't stop him now? Think about it, it's bigger than you, and it's bigger than all of us. It's our privilege to fight for what's right."

"I can't help but feel responsible. I understand this is your choice, but if I hadn't moved here, you wouldn't be in the line of fire." I said looking out from the porch.

"Are you scared?" Owen asked kindly and reassured his arm around me.

"Yeah. I'm… Terrified actually." I looked down trying to keep my tears in their ducts. "Why can't he just come already, the wait is the hardest part."

Owen pulled me into his chest and kissed the top of my head. "Nothing is going to happen to you, or any of us. This nightmare will end, I promise."

I hugged him back and wished I hadn't ever known Peter; the jerk, what a douchebag!

After a minute we walked back inside and of course, who greeted me but Josh who said: "Oh are you done with your temper tantrum?" Everyone looked at him in contempt.

I rolled my eyes "Josh, I hope you know I do not feel one ounce of guilt letting your cohorts tease you about your puny balls."

Everyone snickered but Josh. But I didn't mind him being the butt of the joke after his stupid comment.

We started the day with a hike, of course, all the wolf boys showed off different tricks and talents, the girls just looked at each other like 'what are we going to do with them?' Owen never left my side even though he could've gone way faster, I wasn't slow, but he was a supernatural wolf.

We took a lunch break back at Josh's house where the boys ate the whole kitchen. All the youngest boys teased Scott to the brink of insanity, but every time he started shaking they'd tease him about how his Mom wasn't going to buy him another pair of shoes. I was interested in this, more concerned than anything.

After the games and movies, we played and watched all day Owen took me home. When we were out of earshot from the wolves, I decided I'd ask more about Scott.

"Owen, promise me you'll answer this question honestly okay?"

…."Okay?"

"What is the financial status of Scott's home?" I asked this looking forward out the windshield trying to be impersonal about my personal question.

"Not good. In fact, several of our families are struggling. We'd have more in our pack if the men could afford not to work."

"I'm going to help. I'm going to hold a 'save the wolf' fundraiser. No one will really know what kind of wolf they're saving." I smiled at my deviousness.

"That'll never work," Owen said matter-of-factly.

"Oh please. You do not give me enough credit, my friend."

Owen hated the last part of my sentence almost as much as the fact that I was spending the next day, Thanksgiving, with the King's and not with Matt and the Multnomah's. "Do what you want; I'm not opposed to help." He said quickly.

I smiled smugly, I knew I could make a substantial dent in their needs.

After I got home I ran upstairs and started putting together a guest list full of dignitaries and deep pockets, I knew plenty and I anticipated the King household did as well. The plan was the famous wine and dine them, if there was one thing I knew about rich people it's that they liked to spend money, especially on tax write-offs like charitable donations. Rich people wanted to network with other rich people- and to show off their financial capacity to them.

By the time I had finished putting together an outline of the party events and a rough draft of the guest list it was past 9:00. I got ready for bed excitedly, I couldn't wait for the fundraiser, and I couldn't wait to see Nicholas and his family.

I had to call Nicholas every time I was outside his long driveway to have him lead me through their maze. After I pulled up I didn't have to knock on the door, Katerina was already there and hugging me along with Emma. I forgot how beautiful they were.

I could smell good food cooking in the Kitchen, and I heard the Macy's Thanksgiving Day Parade playing on the T.V.

"Can I help with anything?" I asked.

"No, you can either play football with the family or watch the Macy's Thanksgiving Day Parade. I've got the cooking under control." Emma thoroughly enjoyed this American tradition and was particular about how things should look, be cooked, and taste.

I looked at Nicholas who threw his head in the direction of the Parade. I think he was trying to save me from a game I would be overly competitive about that I would suck at because I was playing with people way out of my league.

Everyone was seated in the living room though they weren't necessarily watching the parade.

"How long have you been in the U.S?" I wondered.

"Oh about a century or so," Nicholas answered.

"Have you always been with each other?" For some reason, my question was slightly amusing to William.

William answered, "It seems we have been together since the beginning of times." Williams threw a smile in Nicholas's direct with a certain amount of love I hadn't seen from him yet.

"Why do you all choose to live together?"

Benjamin got in on the conversation at this point, with his deep voice he answered, "A lot of Vampires choose to live together in covens. We can't procreate, so most of us gain the needed feeling of love from our covens."

"So this is a coven?"

"Our coven is actually quite larger than this, but we're taking a little break from the whole family," William answered smiling like what I was asking was, once again, pleasing him.

"How can you guys stand the sun, aren't you supposed to die from it?"

Nicholas laughed that smooth and creamy laugh that seemed to roll, "Oh Vera, you are so curious. The sun doesn't affect us, think about the logic behind it. We are the living dead, why would photons hurt us?"

"If I'm completely honest, I haven't tried to make sense of mythical rumors." I nudged Nicholas.

"But now that we are not mythical.." Nicholas started but didn't finish.

"Exactly, and it regards people whom I love." I finished for him.

Victoria looked up from her book to give me a look that told me she loved me too.

"Awe Vera's getting soft on us," Aiden said.

I ignored his 'joke' and moved on to other questions. "So if Vampires can't procreate, are you all actually related?"

"Yes and no. Victoria and Aiden are Emma's and my biological children, but the Kings are not related." Came a vague answer from Benjamin. It seemed like a touchy subject, so I let it slide.

"How can you eat real food if you survive off of human blood?"

"As long as we have enough blood in our system, our organs work normally," Olivia answered.

It was interesting for me to hear how they all talked the same, or very similar. It must be because they have been together for so long.

"So you have a heartbeat?"

Nicholas grabbed my hand and put it on his chest, "We sure do."

"Can you drink animal blood to keep yourselves alive?" I wondered.

Aiden laughed at this question, "Oh come on! No!"

Nicholas expounded for him, "Animal blood is different enough from ours that our humanoid heart can't process it. But since we are technically dead, antibodies aren't apart of us anymore, so we don't have to worry about the blood type we're putting in our bodies."

"Do you have to kill to eat?"

"No." Victoria stated, "We have lived a long time, and we have people we know who supply us with as much blood as we need. I think they're phlebotomists or something."

"Oh thank goodness! So here's another odd question, why do you smell and look so good?"

"That's part of the vampiric germ, we have adapted to look good to our prey, smell good, be faster, and stronger. We're immune to the bacteria, viruses, and germs that cause disease or decay. It's all in our evolution." Nicholas answered honestly.

"Oh, okay. Do you have fangs?"

"Yes, retractable," Nicholas said watching the parade.

I ran out of questions, and one of my favorite artists was performing so I decided to halt my chit-chat. It was around 2:00 when Emma came out of the kitchen announcing Thanksgiving dinner was ready.

Before my eyes laid the most beautiful display of dishes and a cornucopia, you could tell this was something she thoroughly enjoyed doing. She had decorated with Fall colors and Red berries around the plates. There was more food than I could recognize, all perfectly cooked and each dish looking like a piece of art themselves.

I felt like the turkey afterward-- stuffed; lethargic from eating too much and the tryptophan in the turkey. Nicholas and I went to the couch where we watched 'It's a wonderful life,' and I fell asleep on him.

After my mid-afternoon nap, we played games together, games more about intellect rather than physical abilities. I was still way out of my league playing with vampires that were 100's of years older than me, but it was still a great time, and I fell more in love with 'the family' than before.

…

I still felt like I was wobbling the next morning when I got up for my workout.

"It's officially Christmas time," I yelled to Nicholas on the front lawn where he always met me in the morning.

"That is truly something to celebrate. What did you usually do in France for Christmas?"

"We actually lived in Italy for our Christmases. We didn't have any specific traditions, but I'd like to start a few of my own this year." I said as I stretched.

Nicholas didn't need to stretch, so instead, he stared at me just to try to embarrass me. "What do you have in mind?"

"I want to secret Santa people, like the Reeds for instance. This year I want it to be all about service and giving." I stopped stretching and pushed him away to signal to him his game was working and to knock it off- I was thoroughly embarrassed.

Nicholas Chuckled and grabbed my arms, he pulled me into him mid push. "I like it, I'll bet you my parents know some people who have needs." He locked me into his grasp and started kissing my neck.

He was way too good at this. I hadn't told him I wasn't seeing anyone else because I still wanted us to take it slow, but if he were still watching me, he would be able to see that my affections toward Owen had changed. This made him bolder.

"You are making it really hard for me to concentrate, Sir Nick." I tried to keep my wits about me, but my neck is incredibly sensitive.

"I don't care, I want to spend our time 'working out' in a different way than your usual. They say a kiss burns 90 calories an hour you know?" Nicholas flirted.

"Not after Thanksgiving. I'm feeling like one of my workouts is exactly what my body needs." I gave our bodies separation and smiled at him.

"Alright, we'll do it your way today." He groaned but stole a kiss before letting me go.

I laughed and continued my Christmassy plans. Now I had two things on my planning plate; the fundraiser and service projects.

After our hard work I called Katerina to invite the Parents to the fundraiser and asked if they had any deep-pocketed friends who would be interested in coming, they did of course and told me to expect about 20-30 extra guests.

I couldn't believe the guest list looked so promising. I plopped myself on the couch and hand wrote invitations to the fundraiser making the official date two weeks from Saturday. I had a lot of work to do, but I figured if I kept it before the end of the year people would be more likely to donate due to the tax year ending soon.

Writing the invitations took a couple of hours. I texted Nicholas to ask if he knew of any suitable venues that could house so many people and could hold the level of class I was aiming to achieve. Luckily there was, there was an auditorium in Arcata that was beautiful and was usually empty because renting it out was expensive.

I called the owner of the beautiful building and reserved a time for me to go see it. He was available that day; he was obviously not busy enough.

On my way to the auditorium, I called Kit to make sure the date and the potential venue would work for him and the wolves.

"Oh, we're actually doing it?" Kit asked dubiously.

I scoffed, "I told Owen we would. Honestly, you two should know me better by now."

"Hah, I guess so. I think that time and place would be fine for us."

"Good. I want all the wolves there, it's a formal occasion, so Savanah's in Eureka has been very generous and will donate dresses, accessories, shoes, and tuxedoes to all the distinguished guests. The distinguished guests are all the Natives. Is that going to work?" That was a lie, really what happened is I set up a deal with the store owner to settle any accounts at the end of the day to anyone who charged to the 'save the wolf' account.

"Wow, that's amazing Vera! We might have to figure out a taxi situation for some of the families, but we'll figure it out for sure. Thank you so much!" Kit was elated and thankful.

"Perfect. I have a few trips to take to Eureka for the decorations if they all don't mind some additional time in Eureka?"

"I'm sure it would be fine."

"Great, I'll call you later; I'm at the auditorium now.'

I met the old real estate owner outside the beautiful building. It was white and mimicked the neo-classical Roman architecture. The pillars were majestic and ideal for what I was going for. The inside was just as eloquent. When you walked in you could walk up to a railing that overlooked the central space below. Descending the staircase, you walked into the main room that was circular and was lined with the same pillars on the exterior. The chandelier walking down was breathtaking; it was made only of faux crystals. There was a patio from the back of the building that you could open up from triple French doors. There was a water fountain and little tables and chairs on the patio.

"I'll take it." I said instantly, "Is it available December 8th?"

The owner was a little shocked, "Oh umm, I'll have to check the schedule." He opened up his phone and in an instant said: "Ah, yes I do have an opening the 8th."

"Can I block out the 7th and 8th for set up purposes?"

He was excited, "Well it just so happens it's going to be open both days!"

I paid the retainer and left the parking lot. I parked next to the postal service and finished the invitations to include the venue. I mailed all the letters on an overnight order.

I picked up my first car full of wolves and family later that day, so I could get started on the décor sooner than later. Taking the families to get their attire was the most fulfilling thing I had done since figuring out how to give the Reeds free lunches for the remaining school year.

The Families were all excited, the formal wear was probably the most beautiful thing they all now had in their closets.

It took no time to find an interior decorator who would understand my vision, she showed me a few mockups, and we had a theme set in stone before I left.

I took another trip the next day as well to Eureka. I decided to rent a van so I could take a lot of people with me. Between Owen and me everyone was covered for rides and everyone was suited up within a day before the party.

I skipped school Friday the 7th so I could navigate the decorations to make sure everything was perfect. I had an entourage of strong wolves helping me as well as Matt and Kit. I looked like a well-dressed frazzled mess because my designer was sick and couldn't set up the party.

With a clipboard in hand, I directed each piece of décor to its proper place.

"Liam, that goes to table 7. No, I said 7. Elijah, they go on top of each other like this." I instructed.

The wolf helpers had everything inside from the vans that held the decorations by 3 o'clock. Afterward, they all left except for Owen, Matt, and Kit.

"So Dad and I will come by to pick you and Matt up at 4 tomorrow," Owen said holding up a curtain while I t ed it in place.

"Wait, don't you have a date?!" I asked frustratedly.

"No, am I supposed to?" Owen asked calmly with a hint of annoyance.

"Didn't you read the invitation? This is a couple's party for all those 15 years old and older."

"Does it really matter?" He asked sarcastically.

"Yes, I don't want any odd people out! Most of the party is couple dancing."

He walked off upset like this was his last string. I walked up to Kit and Matt, "Can you think of anyone he can ask last minute?"

"No, to be honest, I don't even have a date." Kit said sheepishly.

"Do I have to fix everything?" I looked up at Matt, "I m going to have to ditch you the day before our Daddy-Daughter date Matt, I'm sorry." I said smiling. "You can take Kit on a 'friend' date instead."

Matt looked over at Kit, "Well?"

Kit's eyes sparkled, "Never, I'm way too good for him." He chuckled.

"Kit!" I yelled dragging his name out.

Kit looked at me, "Haha, for you, I suppose I can drop my standards for a night."

"Oh hardy har har, you think you're so funny." Matt rebutted.

I left the boys bickering to find Owen. In the background, I could hear "we're calling this a hangout." "I hope you don't expect a doorstep kiss," I kept walking until I couldn't hear them anymore. I wasn't sure where I was, but I saw Owen heading in this direction.

"Owen" I called out. "Owen?" No one answered. 'This place is bigger than it looks on the outside' I thought to myself as I kept walking the long hallway. I considered trying a few turns or doors but decided against it.

Everything was completely dark on this side of the auditorium. "Owen?" I yelled one more time before I decided I'd turn around.

Out of the blue big hands grabbed me and pulled me into one of the little rooms and pinned me against the wall. I went ape on my attacker, the big man was fighting my struggle- he was as big as Stefan. I started yelling, "Stefan?!"

"No, no." a voice called. "Relax Vera, it's just me, Owen."

I couldn't see him, so I reached for the light switch and turned it on. "Oh, Owen you can't scare me like that!" I smacked his chest.

"I'm sorry," He answered chuckling, "I can see you perfectly; I forgot you normal humans can't see in the dark."

I was finding my breath still. I scoffed, "I came to apologize, I was a little snippy back there."

"It's alright. Don't worry about it."

"I think I have your date problem solved."

"If you insist on me bringing my cousin I'm not going to your party."

"No, no." I started, "You could ask me… If you want, I mean."

He looked at me in shock. "But I thought you were going with-"

"Matt." I finished his sentence. "I figured the fewer the vampires, the better. Well..?"

He just looked at me. He grabbed and kissed me passionately, I wasn't expecting this at all. His warm hands caressing my face and back was more than I could handle. I hadn't allowed so much physical intimacy with Nicholas because I wanted it to be for the long haul. But that doesn't mean my body hasn't known these feelings previously- and I missed the excitement.

A mixture of nostalgia and a love renewed towards Owen came flooding back. I resisted the feeling and pulled away long enough to say, "Just as friends, a friend date."

Owen resumed kissing me without relent of any kind. Then breathlessly said, "You can call it whatever you want, I don't care anymore." He pushed me us both against the wall and kissed me again. I was putty in his warm hands.

I had never felt unrestrained lust acted upon by anyone. Owen was naturally passionate and carefree.

He pushed his body against mine until there was no space between us. Then he tickled my neck with his nose and warm breath. I couldn't believe how it felt and what it made me want to do. My mind suddenly hyper-spaced back into reality and I thought about Nicholas.

"Okay, okay," I said breathlessly.

He didn't understand my meaning; he thought I was giving into him like he wanted me to do. He moved forward now with more confidence. He wedged his hand between my shirt and lower back and gasped a breath from my warmth.

His hand was soft on my back, so much so that it gave me goosebumps throughout my whole body. I wanted him to keep going. My mind said no, but my body said yes. I didn't give into my bodily desires instead I pulled back and rested my forehead on his.

Owen kissed my lips one more time. "I've wanted to do that for months." He said closing his eyes and hugging me. "It was as great as I thought it'd be. I don't care what you call us; I'm always going to have feelings for you. And I'm always going to try to win you."

"Owen, I-"

"Shhh. As I said before, Dad and I will pick you and Matt up at 4." He bent down slightly and stole another kiss before putting me down and leaving.

I stayed there leaning against the wall, I had to process what just happened, and what I had felt. Was it love or lust, did it matter? 'I'm sure either can turn into either with time.' I thought to myself. Owen was so much of what I wanted, but maybe I wasn't being fair to Nicholas by denying any vital physicality. Oh, heart…. Oh, brain…. What do I do?

I peeled myself off the wall and sauntered to the main room. It was getting late, and I was ready for a hot shower and warm blankets. We all called it a night, and I knew I had quite a bit of work to do the next day.

I automatically washed my hands, then brushed my teeth and washed my face. I was only thinking about my dilemma. What do I do, what can anyone do when their heart has feelings for two people? I thoughtlessly hopped in the shower and continued my train of thought. They both know about one another, why couldn't one of them just bow out of the race and make it easy for me?

I pushed that thought out as soon as it entered. I was strained emotionally when I wobbled out of the shower. I walked to my bedroom with my towel wrapped around me as usual, and I put on my silk pajamas. After spritzing myself with my perfume I climbed into my bed wearily, I dreamed of Owen all night.

…

In the morning I walked out of my house ready to confront a saddened Nicholas. Instead, I found the opposite- he was ecstatic to see me.

"Hey there, beautiful," he said cheerily.

"Well hello back," I said confused. "What has you in such a great mood?"

"You."

"How so?" I asked as I stretched.

"Never mind it. Just know that I love you and I hope you have a good time tonight with Owen."

Now I was bewildered. "I can't understand your excitement."

He laughed but didn't say anything.

He obviously knew I was now going to go out with Owen, so he probably heard about the kiss.

"Do you still have people stalking me 24/7?" I said as I started Pilates.

"Yep, I sure do. You never know when Stefan or Peter might pop out of the blue and try to retake you."

"I don't like being watched you know?"

"I could imagine why, but it's imperative I keep you safe."

"What if I'm with the wolves though, wouldn't I be safe with them?"

"Not necessarily, and I'm not planning on taking any chances."

I scoffed in frustration. Nicholas wasn't exactly sympathetic either.

After we finished our run and 2nd stretch Nicholas gently wrapped his hands around me and whispered, "You are free to make your own choice, but keep in mind that if my competitor is going to pull out all the stops, then so will I. There will be nothing that he does that I will not match and supersede." He smiled, as his eyes smoldered. He let me go and ran off into the woods towards his house.

I was shocked, he completely had me, leaving at that moment was… Hot. 'Hmm' I thought to myself 'I don't mind that at all.' 'No, no Vera' came another voice 'don't mess around; these are feelings that are on the line here. Think about where that got you last time.' I shuddered at the thought of Stefan and Peter as I threw on some stretchy clothes I could finish decorating in.

It was 2:00 when I got home with everything in place, the catering would be there on time, and the central space looked stunning. I had plenty of time to get ready, but I hurried through so that I could make sure I spent adequate time on my hair and makeup.

I showered and did my hair in an eloquent up-do. It was curled and parted in the middle in the front letting my long bangs shape my face, the rest was voluptuously pulled backward and coiled into a low bun.

My makeup was a darker party look weighing on the side on navy blue to match my dress, my eyelashes were full and dark. I had my lips stained with a light apple pink color.

My dress was one I bought from France, it was Navy blue, form-fitting, with a slit up my leg. It had long sleeves and a plunging front and back lined with 6 layers of pearls connected to the dress. The first string of pearls ended in a loop at the small of my back, the subsequent layers following the leader, the last strand lined my dress ending in a deep V. In the front my dress though it had a plunging neckline had built in push-up and padding in the bust, so there was no need for a bra.

I took the full 2 hours to get ready finishing my look with my perfume. I heard a knock on the door and headed downstairs.

I was shocked to see how handsome Matt looked when he tidied up and wore a tux.

"No comment," was all he had to say about it.

I laughed when I opened the door, it seemed he was a little embarrassed to be the one who answered the door. Owen was standing there with a rose star struck.

"Is this for me?" I asked happily.

"Uh, yeah." He had just finished composing himself when he handed me the rose. I went to the kitchen to put it in water and Matt walked himself to the car. Owen opened my door for me, we were in the back seat together.

I had hired a party host, valets, and servers to distribute the appetizers before our dinner. One of the Valets helped us and parked our car. When we walked in, I took everyone's sight as Owen, and I descended the stairs.

Owen had his hand on the base of my back just above my first layer of pearls. I had a clutch purse that matched my dress in my right hand. Kit and Matt took longer to get there because of all the stairs.

We walked straight to our table which I had nameplated. There were quite a few faces I didn't recognize, I dropped my purse and led Owen and me to the King's and Butlers. I assumed the faces I didn't know were their guests. They were talking to friends of theirs when Owen and I approached, Katerina and Emma both broke the circle to let us join and kissed our cheeks to greet us.

After we mingled and networked with everyone, the host announced it was time to take our table for dinner. Everyone ate merrily, and it took about an hour for everyone to finish, we followed dinner with a dance. Owen was more than happy to pull me close to dance, the mini-orchestra played traditional classical songs. As we swayed back and forth, Katerina and the host cut in apologetically.

"I'm so sorry to disturb you two, but we have a friend here who dances ballroom professionally, and we thought it might be a fun program addition to have you two dance for everyone. Would you be willing to do that?" Katerina asked kindly.

"Oh, um, well I'm no professional, but- I guess so," I answered cautiously.

The host got on the little stage we had made just for him, and he spoke in the microphone, "Ladies and gentleman if I can have your attention, please. We have a couple here who have graciously allowed us to impose on them a dance for us to enjoy. Give them a little grace, this was unplanned, and they've never danced together before. If we can all make a circle on the dance floor, it would be much appreciated."

Some people came in from the patio while everyone else moved to the sides of the room. That is, everyone but myself and another young man, I was surprised to see he was so young. I would guess he was about 22-23, strangers would think us the same age. He was handsome and well-polished, he turned and nodded to me in a quick introduction.

"Thank you, everyone, Mr. Kent and Miss Bianchi ladies and gentleman." The host finished.

This 'Mr. Kent' went to the orchestra and asked them something no one could make out. It seemed they knew the song he was referring to. Mr. Kent walked over to me smiling holding his hand out. I grabbed it, and he pulled me in quickly, telling me this was going to be a fast-paced dance.

Everyone applauded.

The orchestra started, and so did we, he led so impeccably I knew exactly what to do and when to do it, only on occasion did he deviate and pull a surprise- I always seemed to take it in stride keeping my lines straight. He also offered little pauses so I could add my own creativity into the dance.

The music was old jazz and sexy. It started slow and sultry, he held me close, and we began some in-sync dance steps never breaking eye contact. The tempo of the music changed and he threw my hands in the air with it right on time. He slowly pulled his hands down my arms and followed the curvatures of my torso until he reached my waist. He spun me out where I inserted some hip action that mimicked the slithering of a snake.

He smiled and pulled me in close where we spun and twisted in perfect harmony, I wasn't quite sure what dance he was aiming for, it seemed to be a mix of sorts with no rules. He took me quickly and spun me so quick my legs took flight; I took the opportunity to spin midair and land perfectly in stride with him. For once I had surprised him as much as he was surprising me.

He turned me and got up into my backside, I leaned my head back on his shoulder, and he caressed my neck with his nose. People were applauding apparently loving the palpable chemistry between us. He placed his hand on my stomach, and we swayed our hips together. I could feel his thumb and pinky working in opposites in conjunction with his hand telling me where to move next. We stepped together with him behind me, then I rolled my neck into a body roll that placed us facing forward again. We danced a few more steps together before I broke off again on my own volition and walked a circle around him rounding my hips.

He loved it and grabbed me, our legs were intermingled, and we stepped together, then suddenly he pushed me spinning away and spinning back to land on his lap. I knew this meant the end of the dance and by happenstance, I threw my leg straight up in the air at the last note. Mr. Kent grabbed my leg and smiled at me. Yes- I'm sure I was as surprising to him as he was to me. It was as though we had practiced before. Even Mr. Kent and I were surprised. Everyone applauded and yelled, some saying encore, but I shot that down fast. I was sure we wouldn't get as lucky the second time.

He pulled me in for a curtsey and bow. After that, he pulled me close to his face and said: "I'm Alec, nice to meet you."

"I'm Vera, likewise. You're a very talented dancer." I said with my French accent.

"And you!" He smiled.

I smiled courteously and walked back to Owen. I couldn't tell if he was beaming or jealous, probably a little of both.

Owen held his arm out to recapture me. I could feel the stares of a million eyes including Alec's. The mood of the party cooled down again as we started another slow dance. In a typical situation, I would have gotten to know Alec, but I didn't want there to be any chance of a new lover in my pool of lovers.

"I didn't know you danced?" Owen said happily- like this was something he didn't mind in the least.

"I do, I do all kinds of dances too, not just ballroom," I answered him flattered.

"I like that," he said unashamedly. "What other hidden talents do you have?"

"My Mama was a stickler about all things etiquette and eloquent, so you can assume all the traditional talents have been incorporated in my tool bag of talents."

"That's awesome! I can't wait to get to know more about you. I thought you were more of the motorcycle, sparring, bad-A kind of girl. But you've really taken me by surprise!"

I laughed, "Those interests came later, and only because my best friend was a boy."

"Who was it?"

"Stefan, actually." Then it got awkward, he was confused but didn't touch the subject further.

"Would you like some punch," Owen offered after a minute of silence.

"I would!" We walked to the punch bowl where he dished me a cup. "Tell me about your Mom," I said after a sip.

"I don't remember her much, she and Matt's daughter were shopping with my sister and Dad when they got in a really bad car accident. Everyone died instantly but my Dad. And that's just because of the wolf genes he had. I was too little to remember her."

"I'm sorry."

"That's okay, I've always had other women who have stepped into the role of Mother for me."

"That's good. At least it wasn't just your Dad raising you." I said sympathetically.

"Yeah my Dad couldn't have done it without them; Liam's Mom, Linda, in particular, is who I would consider to be my surrogate Mom. What happened to your Mama?" He asked with the same sympathy as mine.

"It was a mysterious death. No one actually knows what happened, the story I was told is that Papa tried to wake her one morning and she was unresponsive."

"How weird. Have you been curious about that?"

"Oh, yes! But I doubt anyone would tell me a straight answer." I said rolling my eyes downward.

"Do you have another dance in you?" Owen asked upbeat and excited.

"I sure do."

The night grew late, and the auction went better than I expected. Of course, our gracious host threw in a date night with me as one of the items to bid on, to my embarrassment it went for a few thousand dollars. It was sold to Alec Kent.

Matt drove us home, and on the way to our house Owen grabbed my hand and held it the whole time. I laid my head on his shoulder which he immediately opened up his chest where I ultimately stayed. I was so tired I couldn't care less if it was a friend move or not.

Matt opened my door and put his arm around me, this saved me from a potentially awkward door scene with Owen. I took my shoes off the moment we got into the car, the cold pavement felt good on my sore feet.

When I got to my bedroom to put my shoes away, I saw Nicholas lying in my bed crossing his feet, and his hands were behind his head resting.

"Nick!" I whispered suddenly awake.

He looked at me and whistled a low tone, "Katerina told me about the night and how you looked- I had to see it for myself." He smiled sitting up and moving to the edge of my bed.

I smiled, "Hold on a sec. Can I get ready for bed real fast? It'll only take me a half an hour or so?"

He smoldered and zipped up to me, he ran his hand against the edges of my pearls on the back of my dress all the way to the last one. "I suppose so," he said reluctantly as he traced his fingertips along my collarbones. His cold hand made the light touches even more ticklish than the norm. You could tell it took considerable effort on his part to pull himself away from me. But he eventually did.

He looked at me top down then said, "I have to admit, I lied before, I saw you in your dress already. It took my breath away. And I watched you dance with Alec. Whooooo." He breathed out.

I chuckled, "You enjoyed it?"

"I loved it. You tempt me more than anyone else has. I can't even tell you."

"Haha well, maybe next time I can dance it with you?"

He stared at me intensely, "I would love that." He then peeled himself away further and said: "I'll be back in 30."

I smiled and nodded. He was out my window in a jiffy. I stripped my dress off and hung it up. I ran to the bathroom in my robe and did my routine quickly. I came back in plenty of time to put my pajamas and perfume on.

 I was pulling the covers down when I felt a gush of cold air behind me. I turned around smiling, and so was Nicholas. He grabbed me and jumped on my bed. I laughed quietly, we were in no danger of getting caught, Matt was in his room snoring.

"You are so handsome," I complimented looking into his beautiful green eyes.

He smiled and huffed in a way that was almost like, 'I'm good looking, look at yourself'. "Thank you." He tucked himself under me and smiled again mischievously. I leaned over and kissed him, then I snuggled myself into his chest for bed. I was so tired. "I love your human qualities, like your weakness in sleep. I love watching you sleep."

I was already mostly asleep and yawned a barely coherent, "Thanks."

Sometime in the night, Nicholas had grabbed me a heavy quilt, I must have been shivering being against his cold body. I couldn't believe he could stand being there the whole time without getting bored.

I woke up to his beautiful face at my 5am alarm. I was so tired my head hurt, "Let's skip our workout this morning, yes?" I said with a froggy voice.

He looked at me seriously, "My metabolism requires our daily workout to keep up this body. I don't think it would be fair to ourselves to give up now." Then smiled at his little joke.

I pushed him back down to the bed and curled myself into him.

He smiled bigger, "Well when you put it that way…."

I slept in until 8, which was something I rarely did. This time I woke up to Nicholas holding out a bowl oatmeal and a cup of milk to for me to grab.

"Oh my gosh, thank you!" I sat up while swinging my legs off the mattress and grabbed the dishes to set them on the little nightstand next to my bed. "I feel like a queen."

"As you should, you really are cut out for royalty." He winked, "And my last name is King." Nicholas looked at me playfully and leaned down placing his hands on the bed on either side of me. "So you should pick me."

"Oh because my last name would one day be king?" I said one eyebrow raised.

"Yes, and because I can do this.." He trailed off and kissed me a few times.

"Now I'm tempted!"

"So if I did this," he threw me back on the bed and jumped on me kissing me a few more times.

"Yeah, now I'm almost convinced!"

"Why didn't you tell me the way to your heart was through my sexy body?" He smiled and winked. "Well, you can't have all of it." He said playfully waiting for me to beg.

"Oh no," I said sarcastically, "I'm going to have to steal your virginity aren't I?" I grabbed his wrist forcefully.

He laughed his perfect velvety laugh. "Eat your oatmeal rookie."

I rolled on my side and grabbed my bowl, "This is good, what did you put in it?"

"Human blood."

I almost gagged, "What?"

"Yeah, I wanted to see if you'd be a good vampire fit." Then he looked sideways at me and cracked a grin.

"You- gah! Such a tease!" I smacked his arm softly.

After I ate, I held my finger up and left the room to get ready for the day. He was gone when I got back which made me very disappointed. Then Matt knocked on my door.

"Good morning sleepy head!" I said opening the door.

"Yeah, that was the longest and most fun party I've ever been to. Are we still going to the Multnomah's today?" He asked rubbing his eyes.

"Yeah, we're going over all the financials of the fundraiser."

Matt added, "And the game… Of course. Can we leave early, like in 30 minutes or so?"

"Sure!"

I closed the door again after he left. Nicholas was hiding in my closet and came out quickly. "We only have 30 minutes to make the most of this morning!"

I laughed, "I'm so glad you didn't leave!"

He played with my curled hair, and we both talked and kissed for the next half hour.

…

After Matt and I got to the Multnomah's we all sat in the living room, Matt brought a chair from the kitchen to sit on.

I started the meeting. "So after accounts payable, the total funds we received from the fundraiser are just over 5 million dollars."

Everyone jumped a little at what I had said, Kit answered with, "You're kidding me!"

I thought it was a little sad, in my world raising that amount is nothing. I was shocked by their happy reaction. "It's not that much guys," I said sincerely.

Everyone looked at me in disbelief almost doubting my sanity.

"That money is going to go faster than you think. Now what I recommend is we place the majority of it into cash-flowing investments. That way you can over time make the 5 million into a self-sustaining money source for the wolves that are on 'active duty.'"

Kit looked at me like I was speaking another language. He asked, "How do we know we won't lose it?"

I understood they would need some education about investments. Which were the safest but not so safe that the money sat and did nothing but depreciate.

"My Papa is a brilliant money man, I learned a lot from him. If I wanted to, I wouldn't have to work a day in my life- from my own accounts. That's because I came from a privileged home and I had excess money for days. Instead of buying up whole departments and islands, yachts, and private jets, I invested. Don't get me wrong, I also spent a lot too. But my point is; in a savings account which earns you 0.0001% interest rate annually you lose money. Inflation is around 4% in the U.S., not only are you losing money that way but you also lose on the money you could've been making."

Kit's light bulb turned on, as did Owen's, poor Matt was left in the dust.

"So let me get this straight, if we invest it, then we can make being an 'active wolf' a full-time job?" Owen asked.

"From the resources, you possess currently, no. But over time, yes." I was proud they were starting to understand. "I think we should consult a CPA who has a lot of experience with investing. And I'll recommend my personal financial advisor to you."

The room was silent as everyone thought about what to do. Kit was the one who broke the silence, "I think this is something we should pursue. I think we should exercise patience to grow this money so that we can have our wolves receive compensation for being on active duty."

After our meeting, Owen stared at me like I was an alien from another planet. "What?" I asked offended.

"Nothing, I just didn't realize how much I don't know about you. I like what I'm learning, but it makes me very curious…. Who are you, Vera? Where did you come from?" For all, he knew I was just a clunker driving, pleasant smelling, hot biker chick.

I looked down wishing this was a conversation he hadn't brought up. "I told you I had a bodyguard did I not?"

"That's true, but I never thought about why. Why do you need a bodyguard Vera?"

This was a fair line of questioning, and he deserved to know-especially where he had saved my life from a problem of my past. I looked up to realize he wasn't the only one talking to me anymore, Matt and Kit were also looking at me for my answer. I felt like I had to explain this a lot.

"You all deserve to know, especially you Matt. I was hoping not to bring my past here, but it seems it followed me. My Papa is not a straight arrow so to speak. He has mixed himself in the world of black market trading, I don't know much about that side of his business. He became more and more selfish as time moved on; this placed more pressure on my family. We all had bodyguards wherever we went. And there were bodyguards to spare who would be stationed all over our complex. It was getting to the point where the danger no longer posed from my enemies but from Papa himself. So I left. And that's the whole of it."

"Okay." Matt said after a minute of digestion, "I don't really care you know? I'm glad you came here."

My heartstrings had been pulled, Matt truly loved me as a parent- a Father. I kept the tears from falling, but I did look down at my hands and smiled. I got up from the couch to get away from the thick air and got a glass of water.

Life is great, life is beautiful, and even though some people make bad choices, the human race as a whole is excellent. I felt that light hit my soul and peace flooded into me, I had people who now loved me unselfishly. Was this the happiness I was seeking, pure love? I think so, there is something divine about it. It doesn't matter if your life is spent a 'mimicry of other people's passions' like Oscar Wilde so disgustingly noted. What matters is to be happy, and the correct kind of happy. The joy that mixes peace and happiness because you're making choices you know is right. You can get happiness from doing bad things that release endorphins, but it isn't free happiness, one day you'll pay the price.

I sat there for a minute relishing in my peace, and then I happily joined my family for a game on T.V.

Chapter Nine: What Death Feels Like

After Matt and I left the Multnomah's house, it was snowing. I was giddy about it because it was a thing of Christmas. Matt, Sarah and I had decorated for Christmas the first week of December. Our house was like a classically decorated gingerbread house. We were all ready for Christmas both of us with our gifts for each other under the tree.

We had planned with both the Multnomah's and the King-Butler clan several homes to secret Santa. I was especially excited for today because Sarah had it off.

All the girls- except for Olivia had spent a day shopping for decorations and gifts for the families while the boys of all the families cut down some trees in the forest for Christmas trees to give away. Olivia opted to stay with Aiden and help with the trees. She was more tom-boyish than I gave her credit for.

We all got together at the King's house to wrap and label the gifts. We watched 'How the Grinch Stole Christmas' while we wrapped.

"Matt," I said in a serious tone, "You are fired from wrapping," I said as I eyed his piece of....art.

Olivia rolled her eyes, "Why does it matter, it's just going to be ripped open?"

Victoria answered for me, "It's part of the decorations the whole season long!"

"Who cares," Olivia continued. Kit seemed to be on her side though he was still just trying to get used to being around vampires.

"I think someone's heart is two sizes too small," I said as I finished tying a bow on my beautiful present.

Aiden piped in, "I don't think she has a heart."

Everyone laughed at this, but Owen laughed the loudest.

Sarah loved the kinds of jokes where someone was the butt. "Y'all are just like my kids in school."

We all jumped into the rental van with the gifts and tree for one of the families. And we completed our crafty deed in time to do another one that night. Everyone- even Olivia- had a great time.

We did this every night for the next week and a half. It was only a week from Christmas, the ground was snow white and beautiful, plus Christmas break was starting. Nicholas and I made plans to go snowmobiling on Monday to celebrate the break.

Monday morning was just as beautiful as ever. I received a text from Owen telling me I had to meet him in a unique spot he had found the day before. I had time before my date with Nicholas. So I gowned up in my snow gear and headed out to see Owen.

I parked my car at the trailhead and hiked to the spot he mentioned.

He was in his wolf form, "Hey Owen!" I shouted. He had some kind of harness on him. Like something I could sit on for a ride.

"If you think I'm riding you, you are sadly mistaken!" I smiled as I walked closer to him. He just stood there like 'wanna bet.'

I crossed my arms, "I'm not joking! I left my phone at my house. Do I need it? I figured we wouldn't get reception out here." He just stood there.

"I don't have all day you know, I have a date. Will you please just change back and show me whatever it was you were excited about showing me?"

He started to transform, I turned around to give him privacy since wolfs obviously don't have clothes on.

He put his big arms around me after he transformed, I laughed, "I'm pretty sure you want a shirt don't you?"

I turned around, and to my horror, it wasn't Owen, didn't recognize this man. I tried to back away, but he already had me in his supernatural grip.

"Who are you," I yelled.

"I've come as a favor to Peter Canali." He said with a southern accent. He smirked when he saw the terror unfolding on my face as I processed his words. I then realized he wasn't black like the Multnomah tribe, the fur I saw on him was a light grey color.

I heard a branch snap, and I looked to see if it was Owen or a friendly vampire. It was a massive wolf clan; they all snarled and snapped at me. I knew I was in danger, and there was nothing I could do to stop it. These wolves were pudgy and fat.

I tried to fight this big werewolf who had me so tightly in his grasp I could feel his individual fingers through my coat. But to no useful employment, he was too strong. He gripped me tighter and said, "Listen, pretty girl, we have orders not to touch you, but we're rule breakers. And I do bite." I could hear the other wolfs smirking even in their wolf form.

I spit in his face, "I don't care who you are, or what kind of monster you claim to be, I'm not going to lie down and let you take me!"

He wiped it off angrily, and I saw the anger in his eyes, it was scary, but I had a poker face on, and I stared back unflinchingly.

He threw me on the ground towards his wolfs and transformed. Behind me two men also transitioned and grabbed me, I kicked and screamed, but it did nothing. They tied me to the harness, it was very uncomfortable. I heard them transition again, and we started running. It was clear these wolves weren't trained like the Multnomah tribe; they seemed to be disorderly and out of shape.

An hour into the run I couldn't feel my face. Two hours in and my hands were going numb from the tight binding. "How far are we going?" I asked the wolf I was riding. Of course, he couldn't answer, not that he would have anyway.

The running never stopped.

******

******

Nicholas was at my house to pick me up for our date; he rang the doorbell and waited patiently. After a few rings, he opened the door himself and walked in. It was quiet--too quiet.

"Vera?" He called out. When I didn't answer he super speed ran through the house. When he didn't see me he panicked and took his phone out.

"Matt, its Nicholas. Did Vera mention she was going anywhere this morning?"

"Yeah, Owen texted her to meet him somewhere for a bit before your date. Why?"

"She isn't back yet, I think something might be wrong. I'll call Owen though, thank you."

Nicholas called Owen, but he didn't answer, it went straight to voicemail. Miraculously because of all the service projects we did, Nicholas had Kit's number.

"Kit? It's Nicholas, Do you know where Owen is?"

"Yeah, he's right here on the couch next to me."

Nicholas sighed a breath of relief, "Is Vera still there?"

"Umm, Vera wasn't ever here." Kit looked at Owen concerned. Owen was already starting to sit up, he could hear everything Nicholas was saying.

The panic returned, "Matt said Owen texted her this morning to meet him somewhere early today."

Owen stood up and took the phone from Kit and put it on speaker phone. "Nick, I lost my phone yesterday."

Both fell silent for a moment, their faces looked terrified. "We need to find her," Nicholas said as he hung up. He ran outside and tried to sniff out my trail, but it was too faint. He called his family who were there in less than 30 seconds.

"Vera's missing, we need to find her."

Without a word, Olivia closed her eyes while everyone stared at her. She took a deep breath through her nose, "She went this way."

They all zoomed into the woods, they came across my car and let hope come back for a brief moment. Then when they saw my car was empty, they sighed in dismay.

The Multnomah wolves were already there scouting out the smell. Owen transformed standing behind a boulder. "It's another wolf pack. They're an enemy pack to us. I can smell Vera was here too with them."

Victoria growled, "Is this some wolf dispute?!"

Nicholas interrupted calmly, "Why would they have taken Vera though? No, I think the Canali's are the ones who have orchestrated this."

Everyone knew he was right. "Where does this wolf pack reside?" William asked.

"All over the bayous in Louisiana," Owen answered.

"That's over 2300 miles away!" Aiden shouted.

"What's the likelihood they might take her there?" Benjamin asked.

"Ultimately your guess is as good as mine. But if I were a betting man, I.. guess I'd say so." Owen said blackly.

"Well, what are we waiting for," Butted in Olivia impatiently.

"I think it would be best if you were to stay here." Owen said, "We'll have quite a few numbers because the Multnomah tribe is Chief over many tribes. As a warfaring tribe, we can call upon our brothers to help us with whatever we need."

"No way!" Nicholas said irritated.

"Think about it. We'll have an army of werewolves, and if you guys get bit once…. You'll be dead. I'm not interested in babysitting."

Benjamin- the voice of reason spoke to that. "I think he's right Nicholas. Getting killed by werewolves is way too easy for our kind and if you died, how would that help Vera?"

Owen smirked like 'I think she'd live.'

Nicholas's face looked wrenched. "I-I don't know if I can stay."

Liam came back with 100's of wolves all different shades. Owen turned to Nicholas, "I'm leaving now, she'll be in good hands."

Nicholas whimpered, "I can't lose her. I don't know if I can stay." Owen was already gone with his army of wolves. Nicholas ran his hands through his hair and whimpered some more staggering toward a tree which he punched to the ground in one swoop.

"We need to tell Matt and Sarah," Victoria said shyly. It seemed everyone empathized perfectly with Nicholas's emotions and walked away melancholic.

******

******

After the first day of riding, I was sure I was going to pass out, not only was my body numb from being in the same position, but it was cold and hard to sleep on this moving beast. We were lucky not to hit any storms, but we were moving so fast it felt like I had jumped out of an airplane without a parachute.

Another day passed of this misery; I couldn't believe they could run for two days straight at the pace they were going.

We seemed to arrive at our destination, and I looked around to see it was swampy. The water had iced over, and there was a solid concrete building on the outskirts of a piece of land. It looked like something from a horror movie. We slowed to a walk as we crossed the ice, not that we were being careful, it just seemed we had reached their base.

More wolves were standing around the compound as sentinels. When we got into the concrete building, it was smelly, dingy, and dark. There were no heaters, it was incredibly cold inside. I was stuck to the wolf I was on, the same two men transformed again.

When they pulled me up it ached, I barely grimaced in pain however because I didn't want to show any weakness. They could tell it hurt though, one of them seemed to like to inflict the pain, the other took sympathy and volunteered to untie my cords. I could barely stand, my legs were asleep and tingling. He was incredibly gentle and picked me up and carried me to one of the many small rooms. It looked like this was some kind of dungeon, there were chains on the walls, and there were a lot of doors- with no exterior windows.

He set me down and left locking the door behind him. I could hear someone- or something else in prison. It made screeching noises and laughs. It scared the heebie-jeebies out of me. My throat was dry, and my stomach growled, but I didn't complain.

I didn't move from one spot on the concrete floor, there wasn't a bed, so I had to make do on the ground. Every place around me was a bone-chilling temperature. Even through my layers of clothes, I was freezing cold, my body started convulsing in uncontrollable shivers.

I finally fell asleep to try to numb the pain, I'd rehearsed the same Shakespeare quote in my head to keep my sanity 'and sleep that sometimes shuts up sorrow's eye, steal me away a while from mine own company.'

I dreamt of the awful thing that must have been in the other cell, I was both glad I didn't see… *it*… And unhappy because it let my imagination run wild. I wanted to cry but I was too cold, and I doubted I had any water left in my body to cry out. I estimated it had been three days since I had drunk water.

I guessed that part of the 'breaking me in' that Peter talked about had to do with this shoddy treatment. I saw the prison door open, the light was blinding, and it gave me an instant headache. I couldn't move, I didn't know what they were doing. I then heard my door open- it was the kind wolf, he gave me a cup of water and eyed me apologetically then left.

I drank it down in a single gulp, it was painful not to receive more. I figured they were just giving me enough to keep me alive. I would return to the cup and tip in as far as I could and pat the bottom for imaginary drops that might flow into my mouth.

I eventually threw the cup across the floor. My body was utterly numb which I was thankful for, I would be grateful if I got out with all my toes and fingers. I was starting to wish for anything but this- even if it meant living with Peter for the rest of my life. Sweet sleep came to me again before I genuinely went insane.

******

******

Owen and his army had arrived at the bayou, my scent was strong, and they knew they were getting close. Adrenaline burst through their veins, and they felt the intensity of their mission had come to its peak. It was now time to find the girl wrongfully kidnapped by these mutts.

On the way, they had plenty of time to work out a plan and strategy. They took care of all the wolves on the 15-mile mark acting as sentinels, they moved quietly and quickly.

In an instant, they were spread into an arrowhead and went straight for the compound.

******

******

 I woke to hear snarls and growls, whimpers and silence. I was too numb to be afraid. 'Whatever comes, comes' I thought to myself.

The fighting went on for hours it seemed, but then again I had no light to reference time. The prison door flung open, and I vaguely heard my name. The light hitting my closed eyelids still burned them. I woke up to prison doors slamming open. Then mine flew open, and I could see a familiar face I couldn't quite place.

He picked me up and ran outside yelling, "I have her, I have her!"

"Well done Liam!" I heard coming from another familiar voice. "Vera, can you hear me, are you okay?"

I couldn't speak, and my eyes could barely focus. "She's slipping" I heard come from a voice I didn't recognize.

"You're right, Chief Apisi. Get me some water!" Owen shouted-- Owen, that's who this was. I felt the brim of a canister being pushed to my lips, my instincts took over, and I gulped the water too quickly. I started to choke.

"Thank goodness," Liam whispered.

I was awake and mostly alert. I grabbed the canister of water and gulped it all the way down. I took a few deep breaths and looked around to see many faces I both recognized and didn't, all shirtless with cut off sweat bottoms on.

I realized what was happening, I was being rescued. "Owen," I said as my confused search landed on his face. I threw my tired arms around him.

"It's okay; we're going to get you home." He said softly stroking my hair.

"It was Peter- he did this!" I sobbed. I was uncontrollably letting tears fall from my face and wet his bare chest.

"We thought so." He answered gravely.

I continued, "The Wolfman, he said he owed him a favor or something."

"Shhhh, it's okay now."

"You're so warm," I continued to sob, "It kind of hurts because I'm so cold." I started to laugh at my last words.

This helped to lighten the mood for everyone who, without realizing, was leaning slightly forward.

Elijah came forward with yet another harness. He nodded to Owen like it was time to go.

Owen sighed, "Vera it's time to go home. Do you know what this is?"

I looked like I was looking at something demonic. I nodded.

"Good, we have a long way to go, in order to beat some storms we need to leave as soon as possible."

I sighed. "Who else was in that dungeon with me?"

"I don't know," Owen answered confused and looked at Liam.

"Once I found you I just left," Liam reported.

I looked around and tried to stand up. It was painful, and I staggered until I fell over with Liam catching me. I grabbed my spinning head, "I want to free her." I said after a minute.

All the wolves who hadn't transformed yet walked with me back inside the dungeon.

"Hello?" I called out.

One of the doors were kicked and rumbled. I was afraid, what was it? I decided I was being stupid so I pressed forward leaning on Owen for support. I looked into the barred window on the door of the cell without seeing anyone, or anything.

Owen opened the door- nothing. There wasn't anyone or anything in the cell.

I looked up at Owen, "You saw that too right?"

He was scowling, "Yeah. Let's get out of here."

"Umm yeah," I said quickly. Something wasn't right, and my instincts were screaming at me to get out of there.

I turned around to give him privacy while he took off his pants to transform. He had put his harness on beforehand so I mounted him; he was quite larger than the other man- this made for a more comfortable ride because he was more of a horse size than a dog.

On the way out of the prison, there was a cloaked woman. She was tattooed on her face and hands from what we could tell she was tattooed everywhere, she had razor sharp teeth and pale eyes. She was holding some kind of beaded necklace. "Thank you," she said.

"You're welcome," I said boldly though I was so scared I could've pissed my pants. Something about her was sinister and uninviting.

She smiled balefully. "If you wish I will tell you a fortune for your kindness." Her s's drug out like a serpent would.

"Thank you, but I don't think we have time. The future will come when it comes." I smiled diplomatically.

She looked at me ominously and laughed. She bowed her head and left slowly.

Before she was wholly out of the way, Owen started a full sprint dodging her. I saw all the carnage that had taken place;

this looked like a real battlefield. I was sad to see so much death, though it made me feel a little better when it looked like the only deaths came from the Louisiana tribe.

Suddenly there was something loud that came from behind us, a ricocheting bang. I looked back to see an angry woman about 100 feet from us holding a shotgun. I highly doubted she would hit anyone. The shots continued from behind us. We were pretty lucky she only had a shotgun, it seemed like she was a good shot.

We were surrounded by the many wolves in our party.

Out of the blue one of the shots almost hit us; instead it cracked the ice underneath us. Owen pushed harder as did all the other wolves without hesitation. The cracking continued louder and louder until I could see the jags underneath us. Owen howled, and the wolves all spread out like a fan to distribute the weight.

By this time we were far from the woman, so I was surprised when the ice continued to crack. In another howl, Owen started walking slowly and carefully, along with everyone else. I could feel a shift beneath Owens' feet, in less than a second his back feet were in the water that was now exposed. It threw him backward bucking me off. In the same movement, Owen was putting weight on his front paws for balance.

I somehow slid beneath the sheet of ice into the sub-zero water. I hit the ice ceiling as soon as I fell in but Owen was standing on the ice sheet. Liam saw me slip in and barked something that instantly made Owen transform and punch the ice sheet open again. He reached for me and found me immediately; lucky for us Bayou's don't have much of a current.

After I was pulled out, I laid on the ice freezing cold. Owen transformed again and barked at me to move. I fought every instinct in my body to stay, I forced my body to move- to fight for my life. I mounted Owen, and we were off again, not only was I cold now, but I was wet, and the wind seemed to penetrate my coat with ease.

Once again I felt myself slipping, my body wanted to give up, but my mind was well trained to resist the urges of my body. I started seeing things that weren't there, like Baye, and Mama. I didn't complain thinking I was toughing it out.

20 or so minutes had passed, and I was full on fighting blackness that was entering my eyes. I started swaying on Owen and passed out on top of him. His broad back caught me between his shoulder blades. I couldn't feel the warmth of his skin anymore. I could hear the systemic patting of Owen's paws and the breath leaving and entering his body. The rhythmic sway of his run made it harder to fight the pressure on my brain to cave into my bodily desires.

I could faintly hear barks and growls; it seemed even to my dying mind, that there was a decision being made.

We quickly cut to the side almost knocking me off of Owen. We were heading in a different course while others continued the same.

I could barely hear now, it was all mumbles. I felt a great deal of peace, it was comfortable, euphoric. I couldn't see anything but darkness. I felt light and weightless; it was enticing to explore this feeling. Though I had no control of my faculties, I could still control my thoughts.

Nothing… There was nothing. No sadness, no pain, no joy, just being. I saw a little light, I knew what it meant; it meant I was going to die. Did I want to die? Was I ready to die? I somehow knew the choice was mine to make.

The light came closer and closer. No, I didn't want to die I realized. So I turned back and walked away though the darkness wasn't welcoming like the light was, I felt a sense of peace. I suspect I would have felt this with either choice—the light or the darkness.

I could hear again, we were indoors, and voices were trying to decide how to save my body.

"We need to warm her up!" I heard one voice say.

"Let's get her in a hot bath!" Cried another.

"No!" Shouted another, "I think that would put her body into shock!"

"We have to do something- she's dying," said another in desperation.

"Let's put her in a lukewarm tub!"

"Yes!" Everyone agreed.

I sensed my body being pulled in different directions like my clothes were coming off. I again sensed my body being lifted into some smaller chamber of sorts with the sound of running water. I was placed down. Then I heard nothing but periodic draining and rerunning of water.

It seemed I had been gone for days. I fluttered my eyes open to see a blur.

"She's awake!" I heard a male voice call out.

"Vera, can you hear me?"

I was staring forward to try to get my vision back. I could finally see a silver spicket staring back at me. Then I looked to my right which was little white tiles of a shower surround. I touched it, the contrast of smooth tile and rough grout was fascinating. Then I saw my hand which was still a ittle red from the minor hypothermia. I saw that my fingertips looked like prunes. I looked down at my body which was also splotchy red and white, I had my bra and underwear on. They were red, I liked this pair I had. When I looked to my left, I saw three pairs of eyes staring intently at me.

It took me a minute to figure out who I was looking at. It was something that dawned on me suddenly- Owen, Elijah, and Liam.

"You all look terrible," I half smiled.

They all relaxed their faces and chuckled. Liam said, "You should see yourself."

"I'm sure I'm a vision of beauty with these splotchy red spots all over my body." I pulled myself forward with some degree of effort. I smacked my dry lips, "I'm thirsty."

Everyone laughed, and Elijah joked, "You look like you need some food."

"What day is it?"

"Friday," Owen said sounding relieved.

"Well, then I haven't had food for four or five days," I said as I pulled myself up to standing. "Can I get a towel?"

Owen handed me a towel without saying a word. I wrapped it around myself and stepped out grabbing Owens outreached hand. I walked outside the bathroom to see a fairly nice hotel room; there was food ready for me on one of the beds.

I jumped on the bed and asked if it was anyone's- it was of course for me though. I grabbed the remote and turned on the T.V. while scarfing down my food. I wasn't listening to the T.V. at all, "So where are my clothes?"

"They're getting cleaned and dried," Owen said sitting next to me.

Elijah took the couch, and Liam took the other queen bed. I sensed this was going to be our sleeping arrangement. I realized it was late, and dark outside I looked at the clock for the first time that week with gratitude for the simple things in life. It was 9:00 PM, the dark circles under the boys' eyes told me this had been a long week for them too.

"You guys should get some sleep, you don't have to watch me anymore."

"We've been able to get some naps in between shifts," Liam said from the other bed. "But I'm sure we'll all sleep better now that you're awake."

I could hear snores coming from the couch. "Go to sleep. I'll take care of myself" I told Owen who was still worried about me.

I turned the T.V. off and called the front desk for a toothbrush and toothpaste. I went into the bathroom to check myself and brush my teeth. My face looked normal, which I was surprised about. I washed my face and brushed my teeth.

I decided to shower for real, so I could wash my hair and feel clean again. My underwear was still wet, so I hand washed those too.

I felt good again, though my fingers still felt strange and partially numb. I walked back out to hear three snoring men, my body was tired, and I had chugged probably about a gallon of water. I crawled into bed next to Owen who naturally rolled my direction and grabbed me pulling me close.

Owen was too warm for me to fall asleep so I opened one of the windows. The cold was nippy, so I only cracked it and climbed back into bed.

I awoke in the morning when I heard a knock on the door. Everyone was still asleep, so I put a robe on I had found the night before. It was the dry cleaner with my clean clothes. I was tired, but I got dressed anyway and went downstairs to eat the continental breakfast.

When I walked back to the room Owen, and the other two were all racing to put clothes on.

"Is something wrong?" I asked worriedly.

Owen sighed, "Vera! Where the heck have you been?!"

"I was hungry, and you all were so tired, so I left."

Owen grabbed me and kissed my lips, "Don't scare me like that again."

"I'm sorry, I didn't mean to scare you all." I hated having everyone watch me like a little child, but I knew why this was more than necessary. So I told my prideful self to be thankful.

I walked down with them so they could eat. They ate almost the whole breakfast offered by the hotel all by themselves.

We all left after their breakfast back into the cold which hurt my hands, ears, and nose more than usual. After we got into the forest, the boys transitioned, and I saw the rest of the Multnomah pack emerge from the trees.

I mounted Owen who spoke a lot with his tribe to get the gist of what happened over the day and night. We still had about a day and a half travel home. There weren't any further complications. The pack all dropped off once they reached home. Once Owen reached his house he slowed to a walk then stopped so I could get off. My butt was sore, but I was sure it wasn't as sore as Owen's whole body.

He transitioned once he got into his bedroom to put some clothes on. Kit looked at me like the boys had in the bathroom; I figured this was just the start of the long faces I'd see.

"I'm fine Kit, how are you?" I asked as best as I could with my frozen face.

He lifted his long face and smiled, "Oh, same old, same old. It's good to see you!"

"And you, Merry Christmas." I felt my body getting comfortable in the warm house with the plush couch.

"Merry Christmas to you too." Kit speaking to me made me jolt awake again.

Owen came out looking as tired as I did now fully dressed; we hadn't slept the rest of the way home. The drive to my house was comfortable too. But I made myself stay awake. "Owen?" I asked.

"Hmm?"

"Thank you," I said almost crying.

He looked over at me then pulled over and moved next to me, "Vera, you are worth all of this, plus more. I love you."

I started crying, "You've saved me from a horrible fate worse than death. I'm so thankful to you and your brothers."

"Don't cry, don't cry. We were happy to do it, to be honest, we were getting bored." He laughed as he moved his hand up and down my arm to warm me.

"I can't help myself, I'm trying to do what's right, but I'm falling in love with two freaking different people!" I yelled. 'I'm so sorry. I don't deserve you, and you deserve better."

Owen laughed, "Oh Ver… It's going to be alright. Don't you try to figure this all out right now, you're far too tired to make any sense."

"I love you too," I cried.

"I know you do, let's take you home, and we'll visit this after we've both slept. Yes?"

I nodded my head groggily. He slid over and took me home the rest of the way.

We staggered into Matt's house together. I'm not sure who was helping who get inside. There was a party of people waiting as I expected: Matt and my vampire family.

Matt was the first to grab me, he practically ran to the door once Owen opened it. He cried, "Oh… Thank goodness. oh Vera!"

I hugged Matt back as tight as I could. Benjamin helped Owen to the couch to lay him down.

Next was obviously Nicholas who hugged me tighter than Matt ever could. "Nick!"

He was shaking while he held me, "Are you hungry? Thirsty? Tired?"

"All of the above," I said realizing my meal count that week was dangerously low.

He didn't let me go, I'm not sure he could've.

Sarah and Victoria both 'ehh-hemmed' and snuck themselves in for a hug as well, Nicholas's hand was always on me. He helped me to Matt's favorite chair and brought out a plateful of food for me and one for Owen. We both ate like we hadn't eaten in weeks.

After chugging water, I declared I was going to take a shower and go to bed. Owen was already passed out on the couch, snoring loudly.

I showered quickly and dressed just as fast, with my bed calling out to me I audibly heard my name.

I turned around to see Nicholas. "Can I please stay with you tonight?"

"I would love it," I answered tiredly.

He was in bed before me and pulled the covers up. He even remembered to add the extra blanket. He held me close and tight like I was a memory he never wanted to give up, as though I could disappear and never be seen again.

"Vera, I can't live without you anymore. I physically can't. Please don't ever make me lonely for you again."

"It was Peter all along. I missed you so much too Nick!"

He started half crying while he smelled my hair.

The next morning was Christmas Eve, I couldn't believe it. I woke late, around noon or so. My body's clock was severely messed up, I knew this was going to be something that would be hard to change.

Nicholas was holding me as tightly as he was when I fell asleep, he smiled and kissed my face. I smiled back but it wasn't a genuine smile, it was a reaction to his. His face told me he sensed my sadness from the start and wanted to fix it— but what could he say?

Everyone bustled around me with happiness and joy, but I couldn't feel anything. All I could think of was how cold the concrete was, and how true hunger felt. My mind wandered to the scary lady in the dungeon.

"What are you thinking about?" Nicholas asked. Standing next to the couch where I was sitting.

I pressed my hot mug of cocoa up to my lips for a sip, "My hell week. In particular, however, a strange woman who was in the dungeon with me."

This caught everyone's attention who might have heard me, "What do you mean?" Nicholas asked.

"There was a woman who was also locked up; she seemed like some kind of witchy demon. She had a red cloak and a string of light blue beads." I said looking straight ahead.

The vampires all tensed up, and William asked: "Did she have tattoo's everywhere?"

"Yes."

"Pale eyes?"

"Yes."

"Sharp teeth?"

"Yes, what is she?"

Benjamin was anxious as he spoke, "Did you accept her gift?"

"No, I didn't."

They all sighed heavily in a bad way, "That is an Efreet, do not ever speak to one again. They mark people for death. If one was with you in the dungeon, it could only mean one of the wolves in that pack had mixed himself in some pretty bad stuff. The Muslims take them very seriously. Ignore it if it comes back, if you don't, and if you accept a gift, you're going to doom your soul." Benjamin said.

"Wow," was all I could muster. "Can they be killed?"

"Yes they can, but it's challenging to do."

Knowing there was an Efreet in the same dungeon as I seemed to make Nicholas very worried. "What all happened this past week Vera?"

I looked down automatically without wanting to, "I don't want to talk about it- it's Christmas Eve. We should all be having fun." I plastered on a smile that was unconvincing to everyone, but Victoria took the reins of the party in an effort to respect my wishes.

Owen seemed to be completely unaffected by the week, he had a gift to let things go and enjoy the present. I envied that quality of eternal optimism, I knew it was something I could develop too if I put effort into it. So I decided I would try. 'Happiness is a choice,' I thought to myself.

I grabbed Nicholas's hand to hoist myself off the couch, he smiled and put his arm around me in a blissful embrace. He made me feel whole again, something about Nicholas's presence made me feel like my troubles were nothing compared to the world of good I had in my life. Yes, I would be the one to choose to get off the couch, but Nicholas would be there every step of the way. He would never have made me get off the couch, that was a decision I had to make on my own, my own free will and agency. Perhaps that was a show of a beautiful love- to allow your lover to make their own choices, and if good, to patiently and lovingly stand by them. To never force progression or digression; yes indeed, I knew the love Nicholas had for me was real.

We played Christmas games, played outside, and baked cookies for our designated Santa. Usually, Matt and Sarah just spent Christmas with the Multnomah's, but this year we all decided to have Christmas all together.

The vampire family had spent the grueling week with Matt and Sarah as much as they could, their friendship was much more profound than before. They were together when they told him I was missing.

They were together when the gut-wrenching news came from Chief Apisi after he transformed and reported I had been found and rescued, but that I was in bad shape, moreover that I had fallen into ice water in their retreat. He said that I was dying when they split off so that I could get inside somewhere to warm up; he didn't guarantee I would come home alive.

They were together when I arrived home, still intact, and miraculously- still me.

I was happy by the time Eve came. We were all at the King mansion with our own rooms- though Nicholas and I decided to share a room.

After I was ready for the night Nicholas was waiting for me on the bed, he had a big smile on his face as he held out a little box for me.

"What's this?" I asked grabbing the box from his hand.

"It's just a little something that I wanted to give you in private, open it!" His eyes danced in excitement.

I opened it to see a beautiful necklace, it was a large circular emerald surrounded by diamonds on a gold chain. "It's beautiful!" I said stunned.

"It was my real Mother's. She received it from my Father to remind her of him forever." He said this in a happy but pained way. "I want you to have it, to remember me by forever, no matter what."

The gesture meant even more to me than the gift itself. "I won't take it off," I promised him.

He smiled elatedly and stood up from the bed to give me a hug and kiss. He took the box from me and turned me around to put the necklace around my neck. He swept my hair to the side and caressed my neck with his fingertips. "No matter what happens to me- or to you, and no matter what you choose, I will always love you."

I wanted to cry, but I choked my tears back, I turned around and kissed him with all my might. He was far too generous to me. "Thank you," I said though the words fell short.

He walked me back into the bed and calmly kissed me, he put some light classical music on with the remote on the nightstand. And we swayed back and forth enjoying the touch of our bodies and the energy between us.

Christmas morning was beautiful- he was beautiful. I forced myself to get up at 5am though I didn't work out. I just talked with Nicholas for hours until I decided to peel away to get myself ready for the day. He joined me in the bathroom after I was dressed, we talked and talked while I did my hair and makeup.

We walked downstairs around 8:30 and waited for Matt, Sarah, and Owen to wake up. We made breakfast hoping the bacon would permeate the air and wake them, but it didn't. I tended to be impatient on Christmas morning, and 9:30 was about all I could handle.

"I'm going to go jump on them." I finally said. I ran up the stairs quietly and found Matt snoring, I started running from the door and jumped on his bed yelling, "Matt, Sarah, wake up its Christmas morning!"

They jumped, and Matt groggily said, "What's wrong?"

"What's wrong is it is Christmas morning and freaking 9:30! It's time to open presents!" I said excitedly.

"Okay, I'll get up."

I left their room and hoped I hadn't woken Owen up so I could jump on him too. Owen was on the third floor, so I ran up that flight of stairs and did the same as I did to Matt. I started at the door and jumped on Owen, "Wake up its--- ahhh" *thud.

He was in defense mode and threw me off of him and the bed. "Oh jeez, I'm so sorry Vera." He got out of bed and turned me over, I had landed on the floor like I was trying to do a belly flop. I was laughing hysterically.

"Get up Owen, it's time to open presents," I said when I finally caught my breath.

"What are we, 5?" He asked sarcastically.

"I don't care what you call me- Christmas morning is nothing to mess around with." I turned toward the door and started walking out.

Owen grabbed me and playfully said, "I have a better idea, let's go back to bed together and sleep for a few more hours?"

"Owen Multnomah, if you are not downstairs in 15 minutes, I'm opening your presents for you!"

"Ugh. Fine," he said resignedly.

I left the room before he 'insisted' on an early Christmas gift in the form of a kiss, which I could tell was starting to churn in his brain.

We all opened gifts from our own family members, plus a special gift from Victoria, aka Santa Clause.

It was a perfect day filled with laughter, pranks, and love.

As I climbed into my own cold bed, all I wanted to do was be with Nicholas.

I whispered, "Nick are you here?" I so hoped he was around like he usually was.

After a whoosh of cool air, I saw the most handsome man stand before me. "I am, want some company?"

"Yeah," I smiled and opened my covers to him.

He happily obliged and climbed in grabbing me and pulling me close.

"Nick, have you ever loved anyone else before me?"

"I haven't."

"Why not? I'm sure there have been girls more beautiful and more talented than me who you've crossed paths with." I asked as I traced my fingers up and down the collar of his V neck sweater.

He sighed and kissed my forehead. "No, I haven't met anyone quite like you before. But it isn't because of any of those reasons. It's because my Father loved my Mother with every part of him, they were inseparable. It isn't common to have your biological family intact when you change into a vampire. The Butlers were our good friends at that time--they were the ones who changed us. Anyway, my Mother died about 10 years after our change. Her loss drove my Father mad in grief. I watched a grown man-- my Father-- cry every day. He loved her more than words could tell, and a huge part of him died along with her." Nicholas paused and hugged me tighter. "I didn't think love could be worth that. I swore myself not to love anyone unless platonically until I met you. Knowing and loving you would be worth any sorrow my heart will one day most likely pass through."

"Why me, I'm not that different from everyone else." I didn't ask this laced with insecurity, but rather with sheer curiosity.

"Oh you beautiful girl, you cannot know the good you put in people's lives. You have compassion yet you're also spunky with an insatiable zest for life. You make your own story no matter what's thrown your way. And you love to learn- I love that! You are perfect for me-- and... I love you!"

Nicholas made me feel so special, so good about myself. Why would I choose anyone else? There was a pit in my stomach, not bad in any way but good and desirable. I wanted him-- all of him, right here, right now. What was I waiting for? My head laid on his chest, I pulled my body up to meet his eyes. "Nick I'm not going to pretend to understand how deeply you feel," I laughed, "I'm not old enough or mature enough. But I know how I feel about you... And I love you too. I want you, Nick, I want your love, and I want you to be all mine."

Nicholas exhaled profoundly and kissed me with full love and compassion. He moved his hand along my silky clothes all the way down to my soft legs. He stroked my thigh up and down while I played with his hair. I whispered in his ear "I love you, Nick, I choose you." He gasped and looked at me with big eyes. He rolled himself on top of me.

"I won't let anything happen to you. You can never leave me again!" He whispered before kissing me again.

I tugged on his sweater to feel his smooth skin; his back was soft and cold and glistened like perfectly smooth skin in the moonlight.

The light caresses of my hand on his back tickled and aroused strong emotions in him. He pulled back until sitting up and breathed heavily with his eyes closed.

"I have to be careful. I want you too in more than one way. I need to be able to practice allowing myself the pleasure of you in one form, not sucking your blood." His hands were lightly shaking.

My shirt had come up a little, he reached down and felt the small section exposed. His breathing started getting heavier, and his hands began shaking more, he pounded them down next to my head on the pillow on either side of me.

His eyes changed-- the whites of his eyes were now exposed red blood vessels. From his mouth grew fangs and he hissed deep breaths trying to control himself.

He jumped off my bed and landed on the floor. I would be lying if I said I wasn't scared of him, I jumped from my bed and ran to my door.

He put himself between me and the door and managed a, "Wait, please."

I paused my retreat but only because I had no other choice, he wouldn't have let me leave if I tried, he had changed emotionally and physically. It was like a dormant wild animal was woken up inside of him.

His hands continued to shake, and he was half hunched down ready to attack. He stared me down like vultures on their helpless prey.

"Nick," I said with a shallow voice walking backward slowly.

He took a few deeper breaths and relaxed his posture, he pulled his head back and closed his eyes. Then it was like he snapped and he pushed me hard on the bed knocking the wind out of me.

He put his hand against my mouth tightly so I wouldn't scream. His eyes were still red, and his body felt rock hard. There wasn't one strand of muscle that wasn't flexed- he was now the predator.

I closed my eyes afraid of what he might do to me. I was shocked when he removed his hand quickly from my mouth and kissed me again with hard, passionate lips.

He moved me at light speed to sit on his lap and wrapped my long legs around him on the bed. He stood up and pushed me against the wall-- there wasn't so much as a light thud.

There was a different part of Nick, and this side of him was aggressive and passionate. I could see why he kept control most of the time.

With one step we were flying through the air, and we landed on my bed again. He ripped off the covers and threw them back onto us.

I wondered if he had any control at all. His shirt was off quickly, and I saw his perfectly sculpted body. It was hard not to touch him, but I needed to see if he could control himself.

I said, "Wait, wait." Putting my hands in the air between us.

He pushed his face into my pillow and screamed quietly enough not to wake Matt. He pounded his hand on the other side of me hitting my other pillow. Soon his breathing was under control, and he looked up at me apologetically. The redness was gone in his eyes, and his body was no longer tense.

"I'm- I'm so sorry," was all he could muster.

"It's okay-- I think," I said as I looked at him carefully.

"Don't… Please don't be scared. I didn't mean to lose myself." He uttered still looking apologetic.

"I am scared. You changed; I don't mean how you look I mean who you are."

"I know, I know. It's what happens when our hunting instinct overtakes us. I haven't… felt love in this capacity before, not once. I don't know how to control myself. You… It feels better than feeding. I'm so sorry Vera."

I shushed him, "Maybe we should take this a little slower. You need like practice or something." I said as I pulled on his neck to make him lay down next to me. "Who knows, it might be more fun this way," I said in all seriousness. "It's so much better when you wait!"

He wasn't amused, he felt too guilty. I pulled on his chin to bring his face to mine. "Nick," I kissed him gently, "We can do this, together."

He sighed sadly and started getting out of bed. I pulled on him, and he let me win.

"I'm so sorry!"

"Nick, stay. Things will be better in the morning- they always are. I'm in now, for life if you'll have me."

He huffed a chuckle and hid his face in his hands. "You still want me after that?!"

"Yes. I don't need sex to know I love you."

He breathed loudly and pulled me into his chest and kissed the top of my head. "You are my soulmate, and I'm so thankful to you."

And there we laid… A picture of imperfect, growing love, with perfect happiness and a willingness to love each other, flaws and all. With an unspoken promise to help smooth one another's imperfections and to be patient in the process-- we will be destined for a legendary love.

Vera Bianchi

Stefan

Chapter Ten: Here Comes War

Stefan had spent the better part of the last half year figuring out how I was snatched away so quickly and so easily. He had come back to Arcata several times to observe, he had noticed I always had a tail on me- either the King's or the Butlers. Through listening devices he learned we were all friends, and that they were not hired to help.

He saw some odd things about them as well, like how they were supernaturally fast, strong, and had other abilities that weren't normal.

After extensive research, he discovered the reality that vampires were real. He furthermore learned that the King and Canali family had had a feud for centuries, he wasn't sure why, but he knew the Canali's would do anything to know the location of one Nicholas King.

This worked out to his advantage, he could gain an ally and get rid of competition in one fail swoop, he had an offer they couldn't refuse.

Little did he know how Peter was also set out to capture Vera and how Nicholas's death would set in motion a full out war the vampire world had never known.

Stefan called a meeting with the Canali's set for the day after Christmas at the Bianchi villa in Italy.

The Canali's and Mr. Bianchi were in the study together.

"What is the meaning of this?! We were told to come here to meet for important business." Yelled Marcus.

"I didn't call a meeting." Mr. Bianchi said calmly.

"What a waste of time, come, we're leaving," Marcus snarled. They all waltzed out of the villa and into their car.

Stefan had paid their chauffeur off to switch him spots. Stefan pulled off into a quiet part of the Bianchi property far away from the house and any other ears.

"What are you doing?!" Peter yelled expecting to go home-- after all, he had Vera to pick up from the wolves in Louisiana soon.

"My name is Stefan, I called the meeting. If you join me on these tables, I have something irresistible to offer you." Stefan walked to a picnic sized table at the edge of the property by a frozen stream.

Marcus was getting ready to release his full fury on Stefan when Peter held his hand out to shush his Papa, something he never did. Peter reasoned this probably had something to do with Vera Bianchi and wanted to hear whatever proposal Stefan had.

"I want to hear, Stefan," Peter said deviously.

All the Canali family left the car in curiosity. After seating Stefan began, "I know what you are, you are all vampires."

The Canali's stiffened, though not visibly.

"I know the location of your greatest enemy, I will reveal it if you do something for me in exchange."

"What do you want," Peter asked.

"I want you to turn me into a vampire," Stefan said boldly.

Peter laughed and asked, "This so-called enemy had better be good, and accurate for you to ask such a thing of us." Peter was indignant now because Vera wasn't part of this deal.

Marcus interrupted, "I will turn you myself, and promise you safety from my family if you are indeed speaking of whom I desire."

Stefan smiled and nodded, "I know where Nicholas King is hiding."

The Canali's gasped wide-eyed. "That is better than I was expecting," Marcus said, "We have a deal."

The End.

For more from this author in the Vera Bianchi series read: 'The Book of Stefan,' coming soon.

Big Al and I took two men each; I was assigned the back entrance while he took the front. Before we reached the back door, they had kicked the front door down and started firing. I increased the speed of our assault if they were in trouble, we were completely inaccessible. When I kicked the back door down I saw many people all dressed differently, and unarmed. They looked more like farmers and civilians than evil thieves. They all stopped in horror upon us opening the door.

"Hold your fire," I ordered my men holding one hand up.

These people were running out in fear of getting shot, once a moment passed and we moved past them they unfroze and took off towards the exit.

We finally got through the extensive line of people, I suspect the whole town was in here. I ordered Kibby and Paul to stay with the blood bags while I scouted the monastery out. Even though we had finished through the line of people I didn't see Big Al or the others. Old buildings like these had a lot of twists and turns and secret passageways.

I reached a large room lined with chairs and large archways. One side of the old brick room had an altar and on the other end was a vat of holy water. I walked in slowly, there were a lot of dead bodies, but even more blood and I can only assume Big Al opened fire on the 'thieves' with the blood bags stuffed in their shirts.

It was silent, deadly silent. All I could hear were the splashes of red blood beneath my every step. I stumbled on a body or two while I kept my gaze ever searching for my comrades. Looking down to behold the mass destruction I happened to see Jeff, one of the two of Big Al's guys. He was dead. His eyes were open... staring at me almost warning me to leave.

I gasped in shock and nearly fell over a body behind me, but I caught my balance. I took cover on the floor crouching down. I slowly made my way back to Jeff to examine how it was that he died, I had to gain an understanding of what I was up against.

Nothing—I saw nothing that indicated what the cause of death was. There was no bullet hole, his neck wasn't snapped, and I didn't see a wound from a blunt object. But it was hard to tell because he was covered in blood like the rest of these bodies.

I looked around and saw Big Al's other guard dead as well, but not Big Al himself. I realized something was wrong, where was Big Al? How did these men die? Why didn't Big Al die with them? What happened?!

I ran to my men sloshing in blood and splashing it up on the walls. They were also dead, no signs of injury and the 1000's of blood bags were still sitting there. I started scoping up and down looking for possible sniper vantage points in these vaulted rooms. I ran back to the main room where the front entrance was, I scoped up and down and side to side until I was outside. After seeing our driver slumped over the steering wheel, I decided to walk in once more to see if I could find Big Al. It was too quiet in the church, and outside- no one was around. It was as though the universe was having a moment of silence for the sad state of its children that day.

I heard a slight noise behind me, I jumped forward and turned simultaneously. Right behind me was a man dressed in all black with some kind of needle in his hand. I have no idea how he had gotten so close to me, I didn't hear a sound. It was like he was the ghost of death coming to claim his souls.